THE BRIEF

Charles Holborne Legal Thrillers
Book One

Simon Michael

SAPERE
BOOKS

THE BRIEF

Published by Sapere Books.

20 Windermere Drive, Leeds, England, LS17 7UZ,
United Kingdom

saperebooks.com

ISBN: 978-1-913028-53-4

For RM and ADM

"The first thing we do, let's kill all the lawyers"
– HENRY VI, PART II

PART ONE: 1960

CHAPTER ONE

The clerks' room is its usual, frenetic, five o'clock worst. Stanley is holding conversations with two solicitors on different telephones, Sally is fending off questions from two members of Chambers while scanning the Daily Cause List and Robert, the junior, is optimistically trying to tie a brief with one hand while pouring a cup of coffee for the head of Chambers with the other. Sir Geoffrey Duchenne QC returned from the Court of Appeal ten minutes earlier, muttering that Lord Bloody-Justice Bloody-Birkett was to the law of marine insurance what Bambi was to quantum physics, ejected another barrister's conference already in progress from his room and slammed the door. He can still be heard giving a post-mortem of the day's defeat to the senior partner of the firm of solicitors that instructed him. Superimposed on all this is the clatter of the two typists generating an apparently endless stream of fee notes to go out in the last post.

Charles Holborne pokes his head into the clerks' room and wonders if he'll be able to make himself heard. Dark, curly-haired and described by his criminal clients as "built like a brick shithouse", Charles is the odd man out in these chambers. Indeed, he is the odd man out in the Temple and the Criminal Bar generally. The only barrister in Chambers to have been state-educated, he got into Cambridge by virtue of a scholarship and, perhaps, the DFC earned as a wartime Spitfire pilot. Charles had what they call a "good war" and it's been opening doors for him ever since.

He watches with a smile as Sally — pert, cheeky Sally from Romford — politely tells Mr Sebastian Campbell-Smythe, a senior barrister of fifteen years' call, to return to his room and not to disturb her. If he causes her to miss his case in the List, he'll not be best pleased, will he? Sally, thinks Charles, not for the first time, is ideally suited to life as a barristers' clerk. She's quick-witted and quick-tongued enough to keep in line twenty-six prima donna barristers all her senior in years, supposed social status and intelligence without actually crossing the line into rudeness. Stanley, the senior clerk, has high hopes of her.

She turns towards the door and sees Charles.

'Going to Mick's,' he mouths, making exaggerated saucer and cup-lifting motions with his hands.

She smiles. Notwithstanding Charles's education and carefully cultured accent, he's an East Ender like her, and there's something of an unspoken bond between them.

'Don't forget your buggery con…' she says, as nonchalantly as if the case had been a vicar summonsed for careless driving. She reaches for the diary and runs her finger down it until she finds his initials. 'Four-thirty.'

Charles nods. He's already read the case papers and there's time for a cup of tea and a bite to eat at the café on Fleet Street before his client and the solicitor arrive for the conference.

Pulling his coat around him, Charles steps out from Chancery Court into the rain. A gust of wind bows the bare branches of the plane trees towards him and threatens to dislodge his hat. He jams the hat more firmly on his head and walks swiftly across the shiny cobbles towards the sound of traffic. He still loves the sensation of dislocation he experiences every time he walks through the archway from the Dickensian Temple onto twentieth century Fleet Street. The Temple has barely changed in three hundred years, and the sense that it's caught in a fold in time is always strongest in the winter, when mist regularly drifts in off the Thames and the gas lamps are still lit at four o'clock each afternoon by a man with what resembles a six-foot matchstick. The Benchers responsible for running the Inn are debating the installation of electric lights and Charles knows it's only a matter of time, but he'll miss the hiss of the gas, the fluttering flames and the shifting shadows.

He turns onto Fleet Street and walks in the direction of St Paul's Cathedral, its dome barely visible in the murky light, past the Black Lubianka, the affectionate name of the *Daily Express's* art deco headquarters, and through a small steamy door. He's greeted by a hot exhalation of bacon fat and cigarette smoke.

"Mick's" offers cheap meals for fourteen hours a day and is second home to both Fleet Street hacks and Temple barristers. Its all-day breakfast, a heart-stopping pyramid of steaming cholesterol for only 1s 6d, is legendary. Charles loves the feel of the place, the easy conversations and ribald jokes about cases, clients and judges. The tension of a long court day, particularly the miseries of an unexpected conviction or swingeing sentence, can here be assuaged in a fog of smoke and chip fat. It also makes a welcome change from the rarefied atmosphere of 2 Chancery Court, where most of Charles's colleagues deal in the bills of lading, the judicial review, and the leasehold enfranchisement of civil work.

At this time of day, with courts adjourning for the night and Mick's being on the route to and from the Old Bailey, the clientele is more barristerial than journalistic, although Charles sees and waves to Percy Farrow, a hack friend who's covered several of his cases. Charles negotiates his way through the narrow gap between the tables towards the Formica counter and orders tea and toast. He looks for somewhere to sit, but Percy is deeply engrossed with a colleague, so Charles squeezes his way to a stool at the end of the counter, picking up a discarded *Daily Mirror* from an adjacent table. Then he recognises a tall man sitting two tables away from him, hunched over a cup of tea. Charles goes to the man's table.

'Thought it was you, Ozzie,' says Charles, joining him.

The man starts and looks up sharply. Charles hasn't seen Ozzie Sinclair, the tall lugubrious thief, for years. 'I thought you were away,' says Charles. 'Weren't you doing a stretch?'

'Fuck me,' says Ozzie, his eyes widening, making the puffy bags under them bulge like half-crescent satchels. 'Charlie Horowitz, as I live and breathe.'

'Charles Holborne now,' corrects Charles. 'For professional purposes.'

'Oh yeah, sorry. I 'eard you was doin' all right for yourself, Charlie.'

'Can't complain.'

'Good on yer.' Ozzie sighs. 'Yeah, I was away. That bastard Milford-Stevens gave me six for one measly lorry.'

Charles doesn't share the thief's outrage. Now in his late forties, Ozzie has been in and out of prison for offences of dishonesty since he was thirteen; with his record, six years for stealing a lorry full of condemned meat to sell to West End restaurants didn't seem excessive to him.

'Yes, I thought it was a bit steep,' he says diplomatically. 'But you're out now. On licence, I assume?' Ozzie nods. 'And what brings you to this neck of the woods? You're not in trouble already?' Charles hitches a thumb over his shoulder towards the Temple. 'Seeing a brief?'

Ozzie shakes his head. 'No, nuffin' like that. Harry Robeson's given us some temporary work as an outdoor clerk. It helped with me parole. I'm just dropping papers off at some chambers.'

'Harry Robeson, eh?'

There isn't a criminal lawyer in practice who doesn't know Harry Robeson, a villains' solicitor with a clientele that includes most of the serious criminals in south London.

'Interesting case?' asks Charles. Like every barrister in the Temple, he's always keen to know where the quality work is going.

'Can't tell you. All a bit 'ush-'ush.' Ozzie drops his voice and leans forward. 'It's not a proper case yet, but it's gonna be big.'

'What do you mean "not a proper case"?'

Ozzie taps his fleshy nose conspiratorially. 'Can't say no more. 'Cept it'll be a cutthroat.'

A cutthroat defence is one where the prosecution knows that one of the accused did the deed but can't prove which, and each defendant points the finger at the other. Charles likes them; they're usually as fun to prosecute as they are tricky to defend.

'Fair enough.'

They chat for a few minutes about old faces from the East End and how the remaining bombsites are only now being redeveloped, but Charles has little to contribute. After a few minutes he knocks back the dregs of his tea, pops the last bite of margarine-saturated toast into his mouth, and pushes back from the table. 'Best be off,' he says. 'Keep lucky, Ozzie.'

'An' you, mate.'

Returning to Chambers, Charles hears an argument in progress through the thick, centuries-old, oak door. A tall barrister in pin-striped trousers, in mid-rant at Stanley, whirls round as Charles enters.

'There you are! Now look here, Holborne,' he says, using the formality of Charles's surname to demonstrate his displeasure, 'this is positively the last time. I'm going to take it up at the next Chambers' meeting.'

Charles looks up at the man. Laurence Corbett is almost six inches taller than him, lean and fair. 'Is there a problem, Laurence?' asks Charles quietly, pointedly using Corbett's first name.

'Yes. That!' replies Corbett, jabbing his finger in the direction of the waiting room.

'Your con's arrived, sir,' explains Stanley patiently.

'And?' asks Charles.

'And my fiancée has been sitting waiting for me in there with that rapist of yours!'

'Yes?' enquires Charles.

'Don't act the fool, Holborne. I know for a fact you've been asked by several members to keep your smutty clientele out of Chambers during normal office hours.'

'Is my client with the instructing solicitor?' Charles asks Stanley.

'Yes, sir, he is sitting between Mr Cohen and his clerk. Mr Smith's conference is waiting in there too, sir.'

'Well,' continues Charles, turning to Corbett and quickly stepping backwards to allow Robert to scurry past with an armful of briefs, 'I'd have thought it unlikely that your betrothed would be ravished in front of five witnesses, even assuming my client was interested in her, which I doubt. You may find her irresistible, but Mr Petrovicj is charged with buggering another male. He's not, if you'll excuse the pun, into women.' Charles smiles.

'That makes no difference at all, as you well know.'

'I'd have thought it would make quite a big difference, particularly to Mr Petrovicj. However, if you'll let me go and start my con,' says Charles, turning his back on Corbett, 'I can remove the evil influence from the room.' Charles opens the door to leave, and pauses. 'By the way, Laurence, I know you don't do crime, but I'd've thought even you knew that a man's innocent until proven guilty. Mr Petrovicj isn't a rapist, or a bugger for that matter, till the jury says he is.'

An hour and a half later, Charles unlocks the main doors of Chambers, and directs Cohen's clerk and the client towards Temple tube station. He returns to his room where Cohen is still packing his briefcase.

'Thank you, Charles,' he says. 'That was very helpful.'

Cohen and Partners have instructed Charles loyally since his pupillage, and Charles doesn't mind Cohen using his first name. It's an informality that most of his colleagues wouldn't tolerate.

'My pleasure.'

'I don't want to hold you up,' says Cohen, 'but can we have a quick word about something new?'

Charles looks at his watch. He still has over an hour's journey to get home, where things are already difficult enough with Henrietta. Another late return is not what he and his wife need. He reluctantly resumes his seat.

'Fire away.'

'I was duty solicitor at Snow Hill police station last night. They had two men in custody for the Express Dairies robbery and murder. I didn't get a good look, but I think one's an old client, a chap called Derek Plumber. He's got a string of convictions for robbery, always as a getaway driver.'

Charles's ears prick up. 'Did you sign them up?' he asks. He's too junior to have been instructed on a murder case, but if Ralph Cohen has managed to get the two men to sign legal aid forms, a very tasty brief might be coming his way.

'No,' replies Cohen. 'They were about to be interviewed, and I would've sat in, but the officer in the case was called away and they were left in the cells. Eventually I went home but, as I

14

was leaving, I overheard that they're going to be produced at Bow Street tomorrow. I don't suppose you happen to be free, do you?'

'I'm not in court,' replies Charles tentatively, 'so I suppose it might be possible.'

Cohen shrugs. 'It might be a complete waste of time,' he says, 'and I can't promise you'll be paid. But if you happened to be there and they're not represented yet … we could *chap arein*.' The solicitor smiles and winks gently.

Charles is embarrassed at not knowing the Yiddish phrase and at the same time slightly irritated at the assumption that he would. Ralph Cohen, a greying man in his early sixties, has been in practice since just after the Great War. His offices, two rooms above a laundry in the East End of London where having a Jewish surname is a positive advantage, are emblazoned across three windows with "Cohen and Partners". Different rules apply at the Bar, the much more elitist, Establishment branch of the profession, where class and religious prejudice are endemic.

Anti-Semitism has been a daily nuisance throughout Charles's life. He and his brother David frequently returned home with bloodied noses, missing stolen schoolbooks and once, in David's case, without his shoes. As a result their father, Harry, took the boys to the gym where he and his brothers had boxed since they were young. There, Charles discovered a talent for violence. By fifteen he was London Schoolboy Champion; during the war he represented the RAF and, when he picked up his education again at Cambridge, he got a Blue.

From then on Charles's size and skill meant that he was rarely physically challenged. In any event, the anti-Semitism at Cambridge was more subtle; his peers and tutors traded not in fisticuffs but in snubs and closed doors. Still, by the time he was called to the Bar in 1950, Charlie Horowitz had metamorphosed into "Charles Holborne" and no longer considered himself part of the Jewish community.

Charles never refers to his Jewish background and prefers not to be reminded by others. Nonetheless, despite the camouflage of the false surname, shortly after he finished pupillage, a drunk driving brief from Cohen and Partners landed on his desk — the first brief in his own name, not a "return" from another barrister. Its delivery prompted glances and overheard comments about a "Jewish mafia", but that was unfair; had Charles been no good, he'd never have received another. On the other hand, if he was as good as the next man (or better) what was wrong, as old Mr Cohen used to say, with instructing a nice Jewish boy, even if he pretended he wasn't? A man's got to live, right?

'Sorry?' says Charles.

'*Chap arein;* to take advantage,' explains Cohen.

'Oh, I see.'

Charles considers the offer. His desk is loaded with paperwork in arrears and he's keen to have time out of court to clear some of it. He can't really afford to waste half a day, unpaid, hanging around a Magistrate's Court in the hope that two potential clients might be brought up without legal representation. On the other hand, it's a murder, and Cohen has been loyal to him…

'All right,' he says. 'I'll go and see what I can do.'

'Good man,' says Cohen. 'Take legal aid forms and sign them up if you get the opportunity.'

The two men shake hands and Charles shows the solicitor out.

Charles wrestles with the key in the lock of his front door, unable to get it to turn. His grip on the cloth bag containing his robes and the huge briefcase, both in his left hand, begins to slip and the set of papers clamped between his head and shoulder slides to the floor. He throws everything to the porch floor in exasperation and reaches again for the keyhole just as the door opens. A pretty blonde woman of about twenty stands on the threshold, her hair tied in a ponytail. She has some sheets over her arm, as if she'd been in the middle of making up a bed.

'Yes?' she asks. 'Oh, it's you, Charles,' she says, opening the door to him.

Her pretence of not knowing Charles raises his ire one degree further. Fiona, the au pair, joined the household against Charles's wishes three months previously. Her older sister had been at school with Henrietta, and Henrietta was prevailed upon to give her a temporary job while she looked around London for something more permanent. Within a fortnight of Fiona's arrival, Henrietta had warmed to the arrangement and Charles had cooled to it. They had no children and Henrietta worked only two half-days in the village; they also had a cleaner; so why on earth, protested Charles, were they paying Fiona to sit around drinking their coffee all day? Now, however, she's Henrietta's best friend and her stay has become indefinite. Charles is sure that her insolence, to which Henrietta seems oblivious and which grows more offensive daily, is learned at her mistress's shoulder.

Charles scoops up his papers and other burdens and brushes past her. 'Where's —' he starts, but Fiona has closed the door and disappeared towards the rear of the house.

Charles drops his things onto the Italian tiled floor and climbs the stairs to Henrietta's dressing room — another innovation he doesn't like. When they moved in, to a house he thought too large and ostentatious for the two of them, it at least had the advantage of two spare bedrooms. Then Henrietta decided that she required a "dressing room", which had metamorphosed into "her" bedroom, now with an en suite bathroom, where she sleeps half the week on account of her "bad heads" and the demands of his late-night working.

'Oh, there you are. You're late.' Henrietta stands at her dressing table, trying to fasten a necklace. 'Here, do this for me, will you?' she says.

She's in evening dress, her long chestnut hair piled in a complicated style on top of her head. The dress is cut very low at the back and Charles sees that she's not wearing a bra. As she approaches Charles and hands him the necklace, he smells the perfume he bought her for Christmas with the proceeds of the indecency plea at Bedford Assizes. Almost everything they own, with the exception of gifts from her family, are the indirect proceeds of crime, and it amuses him, and irritates Henrietta, to identify their belongings by reference to the crime that paid for them. Thus, last year's holiday was courtesy of the fraud at the Old Bailey; Henrietta's dress, the one she is wearing, came from the armed robbery at Canterbury. Who said crime didn't pay?

'You smell good,' he says.

'Thank you.'

He finishes fastening the necklace and kisses the nape of her neck. She moves away without response.

'You, on the other hand, look dreadful,' she comments, looking at him through the mirror of her dressing table while inserting her earrings. 'Late con?'

'Yes. That buggery I told you about.'

Henrietta shakes her head. 'I bet half the Temple covets your practice, Charles.' She disappears into the bathroom.

'Look,' he replies, calling after her and flopping onto her bed. 'I've had a hard day. Can we save the shabbiness of my practice for the next row? We've the whole weekend free, if it's important to you.'

'I still don't understand why you won't move completely into civil,' she replies from the bathroom. 'You'd earn more and keep up with the paperwork without working every night. Daddy says you've the mind for it.'

'How nice of Daddy,' says Charles, under his breath. Then, more audibly, 'I've explained this hundreds of times. Criminal work is important. Everyone's entitled to a proper defence, especially those at the bottom of the pile who can't afford to pay for it. You forget: I was there once.'

He stands and follows her into the bathroom. She's straightening her stocking seams before a full-length mirror.

'Fine words,' she says, 'but I'm not convinced you really believe them. I think if you really examined your motives, you'd find you just love the grubby excitement of it.'

Charles slides his arms round her from behind and cups her breasts. '"Grubby excitement"? But you used to like a bit of rough.'

She sighs. 'Once, maybe; not now. Take your hands away please. You'll mark the silk.'

'"Had a hard day, dear? Have a drink and I'll massage your shoulders. Dinner'll only be a few minutes",' says Charles with heavy irony, but he removes his hands as requested.

'Fuck off, Charles,' she says, walking past him out of the bathroom and beginning to search through her wardrobe. The words somehow carry added venom when spoken so beautifully, and by such a beautiful woman. Charles trails after her and sits on the bed again, watching her bare back and slim hips, hating her and wanting her. She finds what she's looking for: a fur coat, a gift from her father for her last birthday.

'Etta,' he says more softly, using what had once been his pet name for her. 'Please can we stop fighting long enough for you to tell me where we're supposed to be going?'

She turns to him, her face a picture of scorn. '*We* aren't going anywhere. *I'm* going to Peter Ripley's do with Daddy. It's been in the diary for weeks.'

'What?'

'Charles, for God's sake, don't pretend you didn't know about it. I asked you over a month ago if you wanted to come, and you made it plain in your usual charming way that you wouldn't — and I quote — "voluntarily spend an evening with that bunch of pompous farts". Close quote. So I made an excuse to Daddy as usual and agreed to go with him. Mummy's away till next week. Ring any bells?'

Charles nods. He doesn't remember the exact words he used to decline the invitation, but he'd have to plead guilty to the gist. This particular "do" is the dinner to mark the end of Mr Justice Ripley's last tour on the Western Circuit before retirement. All the judges and barristers practising on the circuit are invited and, of course, Charles's father-in-law, the erstwhile head of his Chambers and now also a judge on the same circuit, will be present. In the absence of Martha, Henrietta's mother, who is visiting her sick sister in Derbyshire, Charles and Henrietta rather unexpectedly received an invitation.

Charles often attempts to explain to Henrietta why he hates these dinners. It's not that he doesn't know which fork to use or how to address a waiter. It's just that the Judges, the

Benchers, their wives, the High Sheriff and so on all share a common background; they went to the same schools and the same universities; they play cricket in the same teams, attend the same balls, know the same people. Charles can "busk it", be convivial, pretend to show interest in what, or who, they are talking about, but it's an act. The sons of Jewish furriers from Minsk by way of Mile End just don't mix well with the sons and grandsons of the British Empire. Charles may have cast off his Jewishness while at university but he knows he'll never be one of them. And when he *is* persuaded to attend, he often returns home from the event hating everyone there and, for some reason he can't explain, himself as well.

Henrietta has read his mind. 'Tell me something, Charles: what made you choose a profession where you'd feel such an outsider? And why, if you wanted to do criminal work, did you accept Daddy's invitation to join a mainly civil set of chambers? You talk about "tribes", which you know I think is complete rubbish, but then you deliberately join those which are guaranteed to make you uncomfortable. And then you complain!'

'You don't understand. If you'd grown up —'

'Oh, for heaven's sake!' she interrupts. 'If you mention the Jewish thing once more, I'll puke. Your father may have grown up in Bow or wherever it was, but it's hardly the Warsaw ghetto. And not everybody's an anti-Semite. I'm not Jewish, remember, and I *married* you. The only person who's conscious of your religion is you.'

'You can't possibly be serious. Do you suppose for one minute I'd have got into Chambers had you not committed the dreadful *faux pas* of marrying me? Half the members of Chambers can't stand me.'

'I doubt that, but if it's true, it's nothing to do with your religion. Every time you upset someone, it's never your fault; it's theirs because they're anti-Semitic. It's the perfect self-defence mechanism.'

Charles stands wearily, pulling off his tie. 'Can we please leave this one for now, Henrietta? I've had a particularly difficult day.'

'Yes, we can leave it for now, Charles, because I'm off. I believe Fiona has made something for you to eat but, if not, I suggest you walk to the pub in the village.'

She sweeps past him, checks, and returns to plant a kiss on his cheek. She's about to move off again, but Charles grabs her forearms. He looks hard at her, shaking his head slightly, a puzzled and pained expression on his face. Henrietta looks reluctantly up into his eyes and holds his gaze for a second. Then the armour of her anger cracks; she bites her lip and looks away, no longer resisting his hold on her.

'I don't know, Charlie,' she says softly, in answer to his unspoken question. 'I wish I did.' He pulls her gently towards him, wanting to put his arms round her, but she pushes him away and runs from the room. Charles listens to the rustle of her dress and the sound of her feet flying down the stairs, and then the slam of the front door. He doesn't hear her crying as she drives away.

CHAPTER TWO

Bow Street Magistrates Court is a beautiful Victorian building, almost directly opposite the Royal Opera House and a stone's throw from Covent Garden, but it's shabby and it smells. The corners of the entrance hall are littered with rubbish and cigarette ends, and it stinks of stale cigarette smoke and unwashed bodies. It's been raining hard since dawn and the lobby is packed with defendants, witnesses, lawyers, policemen and reporters sheltering from the rain, and, as Charles enters the lobby, he is suddenly struck by a smell reminiscent of a damp sheep pen — wet wool.

The lobby heaves with people, far more than is usual for even a busy Friday. Charles recognises a colleague from chambers in Kings Bench Walk and pushes his way through to him.

'Morning, Matt. What's this circus all about?'

'Oh, hello, Charles. I've no idea, but I'm trying to get my plea on before it kicks off. What're you here for?'

'Nothing much,' replies Charles vaguely, but his colleague is not listening.

'Oh, there's my instructing solicitor! See you.'

Charles elbows his way to the door leading down to the cells, presses the bell, once only, as the grubby notice pinned to the door requires, and waits. There's a long pause. In the distance, from the other side of the door, he hears the jangling of heavy keys. The wicket in the door slides open and a face appears.

'Yes?'

'Do you have a couple of prisoners named...' Charles pauses and scans his notebook for his potential new clients' names, 'Plumber and Sands?'

The officer checks a list of names on a clipboard in his hand. 'Yes. They arrived a few minutes ago. And you are?'

'Counsel.'

The wicket closes and Charles hears fumbling with keys. The door swings inwards.

'Come in, sir,' says the officer. He closes the door behind Charles, and leads him to another constructed of heavy steel vertical bars. 'I'm afraid both interview rooms are occupied, so you'll have to speak to them in the cell.'

'That's all right, I shan't be long.'

'Down on the left,' points the officer, 'last door.'

Charles leads the way down the narrow corridor. As he passes the penultimate cell he looks through the open wicket. Sitting on the wooden bench facing the door is a good-looking well-built man of around thirty wearing prison uniform and the cropped haircut of a convicted prisoner. As Charles goes past, the man leaps to his feet.

'Charlie!' he shouts. 'Charlie Horowitz!'

Charles stops in his tracks and backs up a couple of paces. 'Reggie? What are you doing here?'

Reginald Kray had been convicted nine months earlier of involvement in what the newspapers called a "Chicago-style protection racket". It was ironic; he and his twin ran the most violent and successful protection racket in London, but on this particular occasion Reggie was almost certainly innocent, a fact which hadn't prevented his conviction. He is now halfway through an eighteen-month prison sentence.

Reggie Kray approaches the door and leans towards the wicket to speak confidentially. Charles can only see the bottom half of his face. 'Applying for bail, pending appeal,' he says in a fast, low voice. 'Look, Charlie, do us a favour, would you? It looks as though they're taking me up first, but my brief's not arrived. Can you do the application on my behalf? It's all settled; Old Bill ain't objecting.'

Charles has known the Kray twins for almost twenty years. He was a teenager when he first laid eyes on the two identical boys, all knobbly knees and grubby defiance, when they were first brought to the Rupert Browning Institute, the boxing gym at Elephant and Castle where Charles and his brother David had been training and fighting in junior championships for a couple of years. The twins matured into good boxers — Reggie could have had a professional career had he wanted — and for a while he and Charles shared the same trainer, an ex-pro named Charlie Simms. Charles hasn't seen either of the Krays in person for over a decade. The break with his family was the last straw, and he closed the door on his former life in the East End. He has no wish for that door to be re-opened.

Charles leans into the wicket to reply. 'I'm sorry, Reggie, but I've got my own clients here today. And I'm not allowed to take over the case when you've already got a barrister instructed. But —'

'Fucking hell, Charlie —'

'But ... but, I'm happy to see what's happened to him, maybe even get the case put back till he arrives.'

Reggie pauses, swallows, and nods. 'Thanks. But it ain't a "him"; it's a her.'

'Really?' says Charles, surprised. There are only a handful of women at the Bar and very few indeed who practise in crime.

'Look, Ronnie's upstairs somewhere. He's got her details. Go have a word with him, would you? For old times' sake? I'd really appreciate it.'

Charles doesn't want Reginald Kray's appreciation. Like many in the East End, the Krays have a strong sense of obligation. If you do them a disservice — or "take a liberty", as Ronnie Kray preferred to express it — they won't rest until they've exacted revenge. On the other hand, if you do them a favour they'll feel equally obligated to repay it. Favours from the Kray twins are the last thing Charles needs. He has enough trouble facing down the daily snobbery and prejudice evinced by most of his colleagues without creating the impression he's friends with major-league criminals. So he hesitates. On the other hand, he tells himself, what harm can be done by having a word with the court clerk about the listing? Every barrister does it, jockeying to get their cases on first, or last, depending on whether they're in a hurry or need more time with their client.

'OK. No promises, but I'll see what I can do after I spoken to my clients.'

'You're a diamond, Charlie.'

'No promises, Reggie,' repeats Charles.

The officer, waiting patiently by Charles's side, continues down the corridor and opens the next cell door.

'Counsel to see you,' he says to the occupants.

One, a short, stocky man with short hair and a long pink scar slanting from his eye to the corner of his mouth, looks up from the bench opposite the door. The second paces back and forth nervously. He's taller than the first and might once have been powerful, but what muscle he possesses has turned to slack, grey flab.

'I'm afraid I'll have to lock you in, sir,' says the officer. 'You know where the bell is, if you need me?'

'Yes,' replies Charles.

The door clangs shut behind Charles and the key turns in the lock. Charles draws a deep breath to introduce himself and immediately wishes he hadn't. As his practice becomes more established, he finds himself less frequently in the Magistrates' Court and he's forgotten the appalling stench of these cells. There's nothing like it on earth. There are the usual odours of sweat, stale food and faeces, but here there's another component, something bitter, sharp and completely unmistakable: fear. By the time a prisoner reaches trial at the Assizes, he's seen the Crown's case, met his barrister and worked out his defence; he's calm, ready for battle. On the other hand, arrested men in the Magistrates' Courts often come directly from being interrogated; sometimes they've been lifted straight off the streets after a fight or a chase. They're often drunk or high, their adrenaline's pumping and they're frightened and angry, sometimes raging. They still smell of the chase, and they're the animals at bay. Charles's theory is that, over the centuries, that smell of fear has saturated the pink porous bricks of these Victorian cells.

Charles peers into the lavatory bowl set into the floor next to the bench. It's full.

'We've asked them twice tae flush it,' says the seated man in a strong Glaswegian accent, seeing Charles's expression. 'They're too busy.'

Inmates are provided with no method of emptying the bowl for fear they may hang themselves with the lavatory chain. It's evident that this one's not been emptied for some time.

Charles presses the button on the wall and shouts through the door. 'Gaoler!'

There's a pause and a voice calls: 'Are you finished, sir?'

'No, but would you please flush this toilet?' There's no reply, but a few seconds later the toilet flushes.

'Thank you,' calls Charles.

He turns to the two men. 'OK. My name's Charles Holborne of counsel. Mr Ralph Cohen was at the police station last night, and was lined up to hold your hands while you were interviewed.'

'We ain't been interviewed yet,' says the taller man in a deep Cockney rumble.

'And yet you've already been charged, and here you are,' comments Charles. 'Doesn't that strike you as unusual?'

'Not if they've already made up the interviews,' says the Scotsman simply.

'The officer in the case is a bloke called DI Wheatley,' explains the other. 'He's a verbals specialist.'

Charles nods. The willingness of Detective Inspector Wheatley of the Metropolitan Police to fabricate false confessions, "verbals", has made him notorious within the criminal fraternity. A cunning and arrogant policeman with an upright bearing and a military manner, he is marked out for promotion due to a sparkling clear-up rate, courtesy of his preparedness to make up shortcomings in the prosecution case by concocting or planting evidence. His suspects have a tendency to suffer accidental falls down the cells steps before they reach the safety of the Magistrates' Court; one actually died while "assisting the police with their enquiries".

'I know Wheatley well,' says Charles. 'We've crossed swords before. Well, it's entirely up to you. Shall I sign you up or do you want to take your chances with the duty solicitor?'

'You gotta be joking!' says the smaller man scornfully. 'Have you met him?'

'Er … yes, I have. Mr Baker's a very pleasant gentleman —'

'He was just down here. The man's a fucking eejit!' says the Scotsman. 'I'd rather do it mesel'.'

The Cockney intervenes. 'Who did you say sent you?'

'Ralph Cohen, of Cohen and Partners.'

The tall man turns to his companion, who has still not moved from his place on the bench. 'I know 'im. He's a clever little Jewish geezer and 'e's represented me a couple of times before. Me dad used him on a long firm fraud, years back. Got 'im off, too. I'd be happy with 'im.'

'So, you *are* presently unrepresented?'

'That's right,' says the taller man, extending his hand. 'I'm Derek Plumber,' he says, 'and that's Robbie Sands.'

Charles shakes the hand of the tall Cockney and offers his to the Scotsman. Sands remains where he is, staring at him dispassionately.

Charles shrugs good-naturedly. 'Mr Sands, I'm perfectly happy to represent Mr Plumber alone. As you say, you could do it yourself, although I wouldn't recommend it on charges of robbery and murder.'

'How do I know you're any better than that duty solicitor?' he asks.

Charles smiles. 'You don't. But I've been a barrister for a decade, and I've dealt with serious cases at the Old Bailey and other criminal courts.'

'Murder?'

'No, not murder. But we're not talking about the trial. It's a capital charge, so you're entitled to a silk.'

'I'll wait for a silk then.'

'You'll be pushed to find one at Bow Street Magistrate's Court on a wet Thursday morning,' says Charles. 'It's a little downmarket for Queen's Counsel.'

Plumber turns to the Scotsman. 'I think we should go with 'im. We can always change our minds later.'

'Is there any conflict between the two of you which would prevent me acting for you both today?' asks Charles.

Sands looks up sharply and there's a pause before he answers. 'No,' he says. 'There were three men on the robbery, and we were supposed to be using imitation shooters. That's what Derek and I did, isn't it, Del?' Plumber nods. 'But the bastard took a real one. And used it.'

'I see. And the police haven't caught the third man?' asks Charles. The others shake their heads. 'Well, if your stories are the same, there's no reason why the same barrister can't represent you both. In fact, it's tactically better that way. But, as I say, today's not the trial. So, gentlemen, shall I leave you to it or would either of you like to instruct Cohen and Partners so I can represent you today?'

Charles brandishes the legal aid forms he needs completed.

'Ach, it's no skin off my nose,' says Sands nonchalantly. 'Show us where tae sign.'

'Just a few questions first,' says Charles, opening the document. 'Is there room for me to sit down for a moment?' Sands swings his legs down, and Charles sits. 'OK. You first, Mr Sands. From the top: full name of applicant.'

Another difficult discussion is also in progress at 2 Chancery Court.

It was sometimes said of Simon Ellison by his masters at school that he had been rather too conspicuously blessed. Tall and fair, with a "Boy's Own" hero's rugged good looks, he was a brilliant sportsman — cricket, rugby, athletics — it didn't matter what sport, he led the school team. He was, however, rather less clever than he thought he was, and he was certainly not as bright as his two older brothers. Nonetheless, he went to Buckingham where he scraped a third in English Literature, again excelling on the sports field rather than in the examination hall. He'd hoped that one of his father's friends might be able to get him something in the City, but somehow that had never materialised. Instead, he resurrected the former family tradition and joined the Guards, where he spent four happy years. Then he was injured in a riding accident, his left knee damaged so badly that even six operations couldn't restore it. His excellence in sports and his army career were both ended. He was changed too. The one thing at which he had always known he was good was taken from him.

He decided to go to the Bar. Two years of cramming for exams, and he was called by the Inner Temple at the relatively late age of twenty-nine. Once in Chambers his family connections, relaxed style and abundance of charm combined to ensure a satisfactory practice, but he was still not the man he'd been. 'The one thing about Scruffy,' his mother would say of him, 'is his temper. Ever since he left the Guards, he's had a deuce of a temper.' And as Stanley, the senior clerk at 2 Chancery Court, is now appreciating, "Scruffy" Ellison is at that moment in a deuce of a temper.

'Just look at that!' commands Ellison, throwing the court diary onto the desk before Stanley with a thump.

'What about it, sir?' asks Stanley.

He'd been summoned to Ellison's room and told to sit down, and is anxious not to prolong the interview. The telephones are ringing constantly in the clerks' room and, although Sally and Robert are very competent, he has to be there to fix fees and sort out the diary.

'What am I doing tomorrow?' demands Ellison.

'Well, nothing at the moment, sir. It's been a bit quiet the last few —'

'But what *was* I doing?' Ellison points to an entry against his initials which has been scored through. It is still possible to read "*R. v. Mousof*".

'That was a case for Richters —' starts the clerk.

'Not "was" a case, Stanley. It *is* a case. It's just that I'm not doing it anymore. What's that?'

He now points to the initials "C.H." further down the page. His finger traces a line across the page. The words "*R. v. Mousof*" have been inserted against Charles's name. 'That suggests that Mr Holborne's now doing the case.'

'Yes, that's right.'

'And I want to know why.'

'When the brief came in, I assumed it was for you, as Richters are your clients. So it went in the diary with your initials against it. But then they telephoned and asked to speak to Mr Holborne about it, and I checked. They intended it for him. So I altered the entry in the diary.'

'Do you realise what this case is? It'll be the best-paid case Mr Holborne does all year! Mousof is stinking rich. He'll pay £750 on the brief, and the case'll last a week. It's worth a fortune!'

'I'm sorry, sir. I did check with the solicitors to make sure there hadn't been a mistake, but Mr Holborne acted for them on the double-hander two weeks back while you were in Wales and they were very happy with him. He does have more experience than you at crime,' Stanley suggests gently, but rather unwisely.

'Of course he fucking does! He does all mine!'

'I'd appreciate it if you didn't swear at me, sir, please. And as for the brief, I don't know what I can do about it when the solicitors actually ask for someone else by name.'

'I'm going to tell you exactly what you can do about it, Stanley. You're bloody well going to ring Richters again and see if you can switch the brief back to me.'

Disputes of this nature over work are not uncommon in any set of chambers, and it's the clerk's job to ensure that ill-feeling is kept to a minimum. On one hand, all the members are part of a team, able to offer solicitors a range of experience and expertise on a particular subject, from the head of chambers to the junior tenant. On the other, each set of chambers is a microcosm of the Bar at large: every member is in competition with every other, and the rules of the marketplace apply. Touting for work is absolutely prohibited, but there's no preventing solicitors from expressing a preference for a particular barrister if he does a better job than his room-mate. Ellison's practice is mainly licensing work, which increasingly throws up criminal cases. Accordingly, if he's not available, the clerks consider Mr Holborne to be the obvious replacement.

Stanley knows that Simon Ellison is rather more sensitive about his "returns" than most and requires gentle handling, so he ignores Ellison's aggressive tone and replies as reasonably as he can.

'I can't do that sir, and you know it. If you think Mr Holborne's done anything improper to obtain the brief, you'd better speak to Sir Geoffrey about it,' he offers, referring to the Head of Chambers. 'But, honestly, sir, as far as I know, Mr Holborne had no hand at all in obtaining the instructions.'

Stanley has never before found himself having to defend Mr Holborne. Holborne's practice doesn't fit well with those of the rest of Stanley's "guvnors" and, frankly, Stanley is happier clerking civil work, where he knows what he's doing. He has nothing against Holborne personally but he wishes he'd go to some set where they did nothing but crime, and they'd both feel easier. But, on this occasion, Holborne just did a good job, and was rewarded for it by the delivery of this brief.

'Now, I really must get back,' Stanley says to Ellison as he stands to leave. He holds out his hand for the diary but Ellison doesn't move. Stanley picks the book up from the desk, and leaves the room.

The cell doors clang close behind Charles and he returns to the bustle of the entrance hall. He has sufficient instructions from his new clients to deal with the day's hearing, and he'll await service of the prosecution statements to understand precisely what evidence the Crown has to offer. The signed legal aid forms at least mean he'll be paid for the morning's work and, while he waits for the case of Plumber and Sands to be called on for hearing, he has time to do his good deed for the day.

He pushes his way around the bustling foyer and finally spots the other Kray twin on the court steps, deep in conversation with two men.

Most people still can't tell the brothers apart, not least because they persist in deliberately impersonating one other, usually to confuse the police, but sometimes merely because they find it funny. But Charles has watched them grow up and, since Ronald Kray's first breakdown and incarceration at Long Grove Lunatic Asylum where his reliance on antidepressants and alcohol began, he can reliably identify them. Ronnie's face is fleshier and less expressive than that of his brother, and his eyelids droop, as if he's constantly fighting sleep. Charles approaches the men.

'Ronnie?'

Ronnie Kray turns. It takes him a while for recognition to dawn. He looks Charles up and down, evaluating him.

'Yeah, I heard you was a brief now. What do you want, Horowitz?'

Ronnie has always been the more belligerent of the brothers, particularly since his mental illness, and Charles knows he needs careful handling, so he smiles and ignores Ronnie's tone.

'I spoke to Reggie in the cells. Something about his barrister being delayed?'

'Yeah. You gonna step in then?'

'No, I can't. I explained that to him. My professional rules —'

'What? Why can't you? It'll only take ten minutes. It's all fixed.'

'I explained to Reggie. I'm not allowed —'

'Not allowed?' says Ronnie, his voice rising and his temper slipping dangerously. 'Not allowed to help someone you've known since you were a kid? Too good for us now, are ya?' he spits.

'It's nothing like that Ronnie, if you'll let me explain.'

Charles raises his hands in a defensive gesture, seeking only to calm Ronnie, but Ronnie steps back swiftly as if he'd been attacked.

'Don't you fucking raise your hands to me!'

'I'm not, you bloody idiot! I'm trying to help,' protests Charles.

'Now, now boys,' says a new voice, 'let's calm down, shall we?'

The four men turn towards the voice. On the pavement, a step below them, is a strikingly pretty dark-haired woman getting out of a taxi. She carries an elegant umbrella under one arm and a brief under the other.

'Are you representing Reggie Kray this morning?' asks Charles.

'I am indeed. I've just been having a word with prosecution counsel,' and she indicates the man following her out of the cab. 'We shared a cab from the Temple.'

'Excellent,' says Charles, stepping back. 'Then I can leave this to you. Your client spoke to me in the cells while I was visiting my clients, and asked me to step in if you weren't here.'

The woman barrister smiles at Charles. 'Thank you. Shall we go inside, Mr Kray?'

She expertly turns Ronnie away from Charles, but Kray sweeps his arm out over her shoulder and points threateningly at Charles. 'We're going to have words, you and me, Horowitz.'

'Now, now, Ronnie,' says the woman sweetly. 'I'm sure it's just a misunderstanding. Let's leave Mr Horowitz to get on with his job.'

'It's Holborne,' corrects Charles, turning to walk away from the court.

'Like fuck it is,' are the last words Charles hears from Ronnie, as he disappears into the court building.

Charles's case is the last to be called on before the short adjournment at lunchtime, and by then the court building is almost deserted. He has not been instructed to make an application for bail, and the hearing is a formality. His two new clients are remanded in custody for a fortnight as expected.

He walks to the corner of Bow Street and the nearest public telephone booth, and opens the door. The wall in front of him is plastered with pictures of scantily-clad women offering massage and escort services. Most are in Soho, less than a two-minute walk from where he stands. He smiles, fishes in his pocket for some pennies, and dials Cohen and Partners. He waits for the receptionist to say "Hello?" and presses button A. He listens for the coins to drop and then speaks.

'Hello, this is Mr Holborne at the Magistrates' Court for Mr Cohen senior please.'

'Please hold, Mr Holborne, and I'll connect you.'

The solicitor comes on the line almost immediately.

'Hello, Charles. How did you get on?'

'You were right. One of them *is* Derek Plumber. I signed them up.'

'Both of them?'

'Yes.'

'Well done. That's very good news. What did you learn?'

'Not much, but I'll have a note typed as soon as I get back to Chambers.'

'Who's Plumber's co-defendant?'

'A chap called Robbie Sands, a Glaswegian. I had the impression that this is well out of Plumber's league…'

'But not Sands's?'

'No. He presents as a hard bastard.'

'Is he?'

'Probably. Can you get his CRB record and we'll check his previous? Anyway, they both admit the robbery and deny the shooting. They claim they were supposed to take imitations, but there was an unnamed third man with them and *he* carried the real gun, a sawn-off shotgun, without telling them.'

'What's the police view of that?'

'I'm sure they don't buy it, but I'm not sure they can prove otherwise.'

'Where does that leave our clients then?'

'If the jury are sure one of them did it, but can't make up their minds which, they'll both have to be acquitted. To convict, they must be satisfied so they're sure beyond reasonable doubt. If it could have been either, how can they be sure beyond reasonable doubt which one is guilty? You know: "It's better to let ten guilty men go free than to convict one innocent man", and all that stuff.'

'Yes,' says Cohen. 'But what about conspiracy to murder?'

'Ah, that'd be different. If the Crown can prove both men agreed to real weapons being carried *and used if necessary*, they might establish a joint enterprise in relation to the shooting. But that doesn't look likely in these circumstances. There were, after all, two imitation guns, and from what I can remember of the statements I was shown, our clients were both seen inside the depot with one each. It does tend to support their story of a third man with the real gun.'

'OK. It looks as if this could be quite an interesting case. Have they been interviewed?'

'Well, they say not, but the Crown says differently. Supposedly after you left Snow Hill.'

'Why am I not surprised? Did you get a look at the interviews?'

'No, they're still being typed. They'll be ready for the next remand, in two weeks. But I was told they both admitted the robbery and denied carrying or knowing about the gun. Which is what they told me, so the interviews seem kosher.'

There's silence on the line while Cohen considers this information. 'That's … surprising. What's that bastard Wheatley up to?'

'No idea. Maybe he's playing this one straight.'

'Ha!' laughs Cohen sarcastically. 'Anyway, got any ideas for a leader?'

'A leader? I thought I was doing this one solo,' jokes Charles.

'Sorry Charles; next time perhaps,' laughs Cohen. 'It's a murder, so we'll be using a silk. Get your clerks to put the return date in the diary. I don't expect you to do it, but do you think a pupil would be available?'

'I should think so. If there's a problem, I'll give you a call.'

Charles ends the conversation and dials Chambers.

'Stanley? It's Charles Holborne.'

'Yes, sir?'

'We've collected a murder brief, for the defence.'

'That's very good news, sir.'

'I'm on my way back, but could you get me the number of Mr Michael Rhodes Thomas? He's somewhere on King's Bench Walk. Number 5, I think, or maybe 7.'

Charles hangs up, pulls up his collar and steps out of the phone box. The heavy rain is giving way to drizzle. He splashes his way through the puddles and broken paving stones towards the Aldwych. Twenty minutes later, he's back in the Temple, hanging his saturated coat on the back of his door, when it opens slightly and Sally puts her head in.

'Afternoon sir,' she says. 'The clerk to Mr Rhodes Thomas is on the line for you. And I thought you might like this.' She offers him a mug of steaming tea.

'You're an angel, Sally,' says Charles gratefully. 'Can you put it on my desk?'

Sally enters, and Charles sees that she's wearing a new dress, tight in the bodice and flared. It reveals much more of Sally's chest and calves than he's seen before.

'My God, Sally, you're going to give half of Chancery Court apoplexy dressed like that!'

Sally's face flushes. 'Don't you like it, sir?'

'You look great. I just wonder what some of the more … conservative members of Chambers will say.'

'Stanley's already had two complaints,' she admits. 'He says it's too modern for the Temple.'

'There you are then. But you'll get no complaints from me.' Charles grins at her, and she smiles back. 'Put Rhodes Thomas through, will you?'

'Right away, sir,' says Sally, leaving the room.

The telephone rings again a minute later, and Sally announces the QC.

'Hello, Michael?'

'Yes, Charles, how are you?'

'Not bad, thank you. How's the family?' asks Charles.

'Growing more expensive by the day, thank you for asking.'

Charles worked with Michael Rhodes Thomas QC on a case some eighteen months before. He practises from a different set of chambers, where they deal with a wide mixture of common law, including quite a lot of crime. The members of the set are by and large friendly, and Charles had co-defended with a number of them over the years. Rhodes Thomas himself is very able, with an affable personality and a common touch that juries appreciate.

'I know you're extremely busy,' begins Charles.

'Overloaded, as always,' interrupts Rhodes Thomas.

'But I wondered if I might interest you in a little murder.'

'Yes?' asks Rhodes, now interested.

'It won't be up for a while — it's not been committed from the Magistrates' Court yet — but it's a goodie. The Express Dairies robbery.'

'I didn't know they'd charged anyone with that.'

'This morning. I've just seen them — it's a two-hander — called Plumber and Sands.'

'That's not Robbie Sands, is it?'

'It is,' replies Charles, surprised. 'Do you know him?'

'I represented him on the Shell Mex Payroll job, about six years ago. Got him off, too. Small world, eh?'

'Indeed it is. What do you think?'

'Subject to availability, I'd be delighted, assuming the solicitors are happy.'

'They're alright. They've asked me to suggest someone.'

'Fair enough. I assume you don't want me before committal?'

'I don't know yet, but I doubt it. I'll get the solicitors to have a word with your clerk if necessary. Otherwise, perhaps we can organise a conference at the prison after committal.'

'Fine. How are you keeping?'

'Me? I'm OK.'

There's a pause before Rhodes Thomas speaks again. 'How's Henrietta?'

Charles casts his mind back and remembers that he introduced Henrietta to Rhodes Thomas one day when they met him in the Temple. 'Fine, thank you.'

'Saw her a few weeks ago,' says Rhodes Thomas. There's something about the way the comment is left hanging that rings an odd note to Charles.

'At Peter Ripley's retirement dinner?' he asks.

'Well, yes, but after that too. At the Ellisons'.' There's another pause. 'I expect you were burning the midnight oil again.'

'Yes. I expect so,' says Charles, somewhat distracted. 'You do mean Simon and Jenny Ellison?'

'Yes. He's in your Chambers, isn't he?'

'He is. I just didn't know Henrietta saw them socially.'

'Oh, I think it's something to do with Jenny's charity work. I got the impression that Henrietta was involved too.'

'That must be it then.' There's another pause.

'Let me know if you fancy a drink after court one day, Charles. For a chat, you know?' said the QC sympathetically.

'Will do, Michael. Thanks.'

Charles replaces the receiver thoughtfully. What's Henrietta been up to this time?

CHAPTER THREE

Ralph Cohen leads the way up the narrow stairs and knocks on the door at the top. The door is unlocked and opened by a prison officer. Charles and Rhodes Thomas follow Cohen inside, the door is locked behind them and the lawyers turn to face three prison officers.

'You've all been here before haven't you, sirs?' asks one, evidently in charge. The lawyers nod their assent. Charles frequently visits clients in prisons, especially this one, HM Pentonville, where one section houses prisoners on remand awaiting trial, but he still experiences a thrill when "on the inside". It's like entering a secret country with its own language, customs, sounds and smells.

'If you'll just empty your pockets in the bowls, and your briefcases on the table? Then take off your jackets, please, and hand them to my colleague.'

Charles has already taken out his loose change and keys. He places two packets of cigarettes on the desk. He doesn't smoke, but prisoners on remand are allowed cigarettes and Charles has learned that to visit a remand client in prison without cigarettes is a cardinal offence. Even if the client doesn't smoke, a pack of cigarettes provides him with ready currency on the cellblock to buy soap, shampoo, phone calls and favours.

Charles has also learned not to bother taking a briefcase. He carries the bundle of case papers tied with pink ribbon, and he undoes the ribbon and fans the papers on the table. The year before, the press was full of the prosecution of the bent solicitor who smuggled a hypodermic in a hollowed-out part of his prosecution depositions. Since then Charles has anticipated the prison officers' wish to leaf through his instructions. He slips off his jacket and hands it to one of the other prison officers, who checks it thoroughly as Charles is frisked expertly from head to toe.

It takes ten minutes for the three lawyers to be searched thoroughly, after which they are allowed to dress and gather their possessions. Cohen leads them to the far end of the room where a fourth officer sits behind reinforced glass windows.

'Solicitor and counsel to see Mr Plumber,' he says, speaking into a microphone mounted on the wall. The officer records their details and they are eventually shown into a small room. A few moments later, Plumber enters.

'Hello Mr Cohen, Mr Holborne,' he says amiably.

'Hello Derek,' replies Cohen. 'May I introduce you to Mr Rhodes Thomas? He's the QC who will lead for the Defence.'

Plumber puts out his hand. 'Pleased to meet you, sir.'

'Take a seat, Mr Plumber,' says Rhodes Thomas. 'Am I mistaken, or do we get offered tea at Pentonville?'

'You're dead right, sir. He'll be along in a sec,' answers Plumber.

Tea having arrived, Rhodes Thomas slips the ribbon off his brief, spreads his papers on the table, and begins.

'Now, I've got a great deal to ask you, but what I want to know first is, what's happened to Mr Sands?'

'Beg pardon?'

'He's instructed new solicitors, hasn't he?'

'That's right, yeah.'

'You two haven't fallen out, have you?'

'No, not at all. He's used Robesons a couple of times before, that's all. Why?'

'Did you say "Robesons"?' intervenes Charles. 'Harry Robeson?'

'Why?' asks Rhodes Thomas.

Charles turns to him. 'I bumped into someone the day before the first remand, one of Harry Robeson's outdoor clerks. He dropped a hint that Robeson was about to acquire a big case that was going to turn into a cutthroat.'

Rhodes Thomas turns to Plumber. 'As far as you know, is Sands sticking to the "third man" story?'

'He ain't said differently.'

'You do realise that if you're both going to get off the murder charge, you've got to stick to your guns. Sorry about the pun. What I mean is, your stories are the same and there's no conflict between you. Normally, you'd be represented by the same team. So we wondered why he'd want to change solicitors.'

'I don't think there's nothing suspicious about it.'

Rhodes Thomas turns to Charles. 'No suggestion of it being a cutthroat then.'

'Just a coincidence?'

The QC shrugs. 'We'll see.'

'Do you mind if I ask a question?' asks Plumber.

'Not at all,' replies Rhodes Thomas.

'Do I have to plead guilty to the robbery?'

'Well, Mr Plumber, you've told us that you did take part in the robbery. Is that the case?'

Plumber looks embarrassed. He glances at Cohen but receives no assistance.

Charles intervenes. 'I'm sure you understand, Derek, once you've told Mr Cohen that you did the robbery, neither he, nor myself, nor Mr Rhodes Thomas can represent you if you want to plead not guilty. We're not able to lie to the Court on your behalf. You'd have to find other representatives, and if you tell them you're guilty but want to fight it, you'll lose them too.'

'Oh,' says Plumber, clearly disappointed.

'There is, however, one exception to that rule,' continues Charles. 'You're entitled to plead not guilty, despite what you've told us, and we are allowed to test the prosecution evidence. We're still prevented from actively suggesting to the Court that you're not guilty, and we certainly can't call any positive evidence on your behalf. But if the prosecution evidence doesn't come up to scratch, you'd be acquitted. On the other hand, if at the end of the prosecution's evidence, there's enough evidence to go before the jury, you'd have to plead guilty at that stage. Probably sounds rather artificial to you, but we are bound by rules of conduct.'

'Do you understand all that?' asks Rhodes Thomas.

'I think so. The thing is, see, I was wondering: if I plead not guilty to the robbery, at least at the outset, the prosecution might drop the murder if I offered to change me mind, and put me hands up to the robbery.'

Rhodes Thomas smiles. 'They might indeed.'

'Do you reckon?'

'Put it this way, Mr Plumber: if the evidence comes out exactly as it appears in the prosecution statements, and you both hold your nerves, I don't think a jury could properly find either you or Sands guilty of the murder. I think further that the prosecution will be well aware of that. That *may* make them amenable to an offer. On the other hand, you've made a full confession to robbery, and it'll be hard to persuade the Crown that there's any risk of your getting off that charge in any event. They may, therefore, decide to take their chances, and see if they can get you for both.'

'I'd like to have a bash anyway.'

'Very well. I'm sure Mr Cohen here will inform the Court that both charges are to be contested, and I will certainly have an informal word with the prosecution leader to sound him out. But just in case they do proceed with the murder charge, I suggest we have a look at some of the evidence.'

CHAPTER FOUR

Although his practice takes him there with increasing frequency, Charles still experiences a particular thrill, a special lightness of step, as he enters the Old Bailey. This is the "sharp end" of criminal practice, the Court where the seasoned practitioners work, meet and discuss cases, judges and trials. It is the heart of the web of English criminal justice.

Charles climbs the wide stairs and enters the Great Hall. The building work to repair the Blitz bomb damage was completed a couple of years after he started work at the court, and for several months the barristers mingled with stonemasons and plasterers. Many at the Bar were irritated, but Charles loved it. Instead of using the Bar Mess, he queued for lunch in the public canteen with the workmen, doffed his wig and sat with them, picking through the weekend's football or complaining about the price of a pint. He explained to Henrietta that it was essential for a jury advocate to have a sense of what the man on the Clapham omnibus was thinking, but in truth he felt more at home with these tradesmen than he did with his fellow barristers.

The Great Hall still holds a collection of paintings depicting the state of the building on 11th May 1941, the morning after the air raid, and Charles likes to look at them as he passes. His father was one of the many fire wardens who helped dowse the flames and carry out the injured and dead.

Charles goes up to the robing room. The place buzzes with barristers in various states of undress as they change into tunic shirts and wing collars, a couple of the younger men jostling for the mirror as they struggle to tie their court bands.

Charles's circuit tin containing his wig joins the shoal of identical black oval tins on the robing room table and he lifts the lid. He removes the wig and, as always, sniffs it cautiously. After a hot summer of sweat-inducing high-stress cases, horsehair wigs can smell dreadful. Cleaning them is a delicate, not to mention expensive, operation.

'Deceased?' asks a voice behind him.

Charles turns to see Philip Jewell, a barrister with fair, almost white, hair, pale blue eyes and a shy grin. Jewell is a couple of years older than Charles. His soft voice and diffident manner conceal a sharp mind and great courage. He was a Hurricane pilot in the Battle of Britain, downing eleven enemy planes, despite twice being shot down himself.

'I'd say not in the best of health, but not quite moribund.'

'Mine's dreadful. I forgot to get it cleaned during the summer vacation. The first time I opened the tin this term, it tried to crawl out on its own.'

Charles laughs. He likes Jewell. They went up to Cambridge the same year after the war and when they came down to London for their Bar Finals they often sat in the same tutorial groups. Their paths had crossed socially, too.

'What brings you here?' asks Charles.

'Oh, murder and mayhem, as usual,' replies Jewell.

'Same here. You're not in Plumber and Sands are you?'

'Certainly am. I'm your co-defendant. You're for Plumber, yes?'

'Yes. Are you being led?' asks Charles.

'Robin Lowe is leading me, but he won't be here today.'

'Why not?' asks Charles, puzzled.

Jewell doesn't answer, but instead grins mysteriously. 'Court Two, isn't it?'

'Yes.'

Jewell picks up his case papers and winks. 'See you down there, then,' he says, and disappears into the crowd of black-robed barristers heading down the stairs.

Charles walks right to the end of the line of lockers where there are a handful allocated to visiting barristers from other circuits. He is, in fact, a member of the South Eastern circuit, but as the only dedicated criminal practitioner at Chancery Court, Chambers declined to pay for a locker to be reserved for him. He's been meaning to get around to renting one for himself but for the moment, purely from habit, he uses the locker his pupil master let him use years before, while he was still a pupil barrister.

He turns over Jewell's words. If the case is effective today, it would be very odd for one of the accused men not to be represented by his silk. On the other hand, if Sands plans to apply for an adjournment, something Jewell could have done alone, why the mystery? Puzzled, Charles changes his everyday stiff collar for a wing collar, ties his bands, dons his wig and gown, and collects his papers. He glances at his watch; only 9:45, and plenty of time for a quick cup of tea.

He pushes his way against the flow of barristers and hurries to the Bar Mess where he finds an empty table and sits.

'Hello there. It's Charles Holborne, isn't it?'

Charles looks up to see another barrister. It's Marcus Stafford, the junior for the Crown. Stafford is enormously fat, with piggy eyes lost in great red cheeks, and he has the reputation of having one of the best minds at the Criminal Bar. He and Charles spoke on the telephone a few days before about the evidence in the case.

'Yes. Stafford?'

'Yah. Haven't seen my illustrious leader by any chance?'

'Sir Richard Hogg QC? No, not yet. And I don't suppose you've seen Mike Rhodes Thomas?'

'No, sorry. Do you mind?' Stafford indicates the seat next to Charles.

'Not at all.'

Stafford sits with a wheeze. 'Is this still to be a fight?' he enquires.

'That's up to you,' replies Charles. 'As we've already discussed, he'll plead to the robbery if you drop the murder. We both know you can't make it stick against either of them.'

Stafford smiles. 'We'll see.'

This sort of friendly sparring is nothing unusual, but there's a confidence about Stafford which makes Charles wonder again what's going on, and he is reminded again of his conversation with Ozzie. He doesn't have long to wait before discovering what it is, as a short middle-aged man bustles up to them.

'Morning Marcus,' he says, and sits next to them.

'Hello Richard. This is Charles Holborne. Charles, Richard Hogg QC.'

'Ah,' says Hogg, rifling through his papers, 'got something for you.' He hands Charles a document. It's a statement headed "Robert Reginald Sands". 'I expect you'll want some time to consider that with Michael, and your client, of course. I don't suppose the Crown could object to an application for an adjournment if you decide to make one. In any event, I've spoken to the clerk and told her we'll need some time before arraignment.'

Charles scans the document. It is a statement dated that day. In it, Sands retracts his earlier statement and alleges that only two men took part in the robbery, himself and Plumber. He claims that Plumber took and used the shotgun without his

51

knowledge. The reason for his earlier statement, he claims, was that Plumber threatened the lives of his family.

'May I take it that Sands is prepared to give evidence to this effect for the prosecution?' asks Charles, trying to appear unconcerned.

'You may.'

'May I also take it that the Crown is proposing to call him as a witness of truth?'

'You may,' repeats Hogg. 'We shall offer no evidence against him on the murder, and I shall apply to the Judge to sentence him for the robbery before he gives evidence against your client.'

'I'd better get some instructions,' says Charles. 'If you'll excuse me...'

Charles goes to the public canteen where he finds Ralph Cohen and his son, Marcus, at a table.

'Good morning —' starts Cohen senior. Charles silently places the new statement on the table before him. Marcus cranes his neck to read over his father's shoulder.

'Fucking hell!' he breathes.

'Language,' chides Ralph quietly, as he continues reading. 'So,' he continues, when finished.

'Yes. It's what I suspected. This has been Robeson and Sands's plan all along. They've just waited till the last possible moment to spring the trap. As long as the two defendants stuck to their stories the Crown was always likely to fail on the murder charge. No jury could be sure which one of them did it and would have to acquit both. This way the prosecution at least has a shot at getting one of them.'

'But probably the wrong one,' suggests Marcus.

Charles nods, but then shrugs. 'But that's not for us to say, is it? That's for the jury. Have you seen Mr Rhodes Thomas?'

'We agreed to meet him outside the cells,' Marcus glances at his watch, 'right now.'

'Let's go then,' says Charles.

The three men descend to the basement. Michael Rhodes Thomas is already waiting for them outside the main door.

'Well met,' he says, as the others arrive.

'Wait till you've seen this,' says Charles heavily, indicating that Ralph should hand the QC the new statement.

Rhodes Thomas reads it while they wait for the door to be opened. 'Well, you were right, Charles.' He returns the document to Ralph Cohen.

'Yes. Poor Derek Plumber is now facing the gallows on his own.'

'Indeed. He's going to need rather gentle handling. And we may have to reconsider our tactics.'

The door opens and they are greeted by the prison officer. 'Good morning gentlemen.'

The door is locked behind them and they follow the officer up a short corridor to another locked door. The air is redolent of frying bacon.

'I swear, the food down here's better than in the Bar Mess upstairs,' says Rhodes Thomas.

'Oh, yes, sir. We're the first Michelin starred restaurant in HM Prison Service,' says the man with a grin.

Five minutes later, Plumber is shown into the tiny cell already cramped with the three lawyers. Without speaking, Rhodes Thomas hands him Sands's statement. Plumber reads, his face growing ashen, his slack jaw dropping.

'Jesus Christ,' he whispers, 'I'm done for.'

'Sit down, Mr Plumber,' instructs Rhodes Thomas. 'Take a few deep breaths, and start telling us the truth.'

Plumber sits, but his hands holding Sands's statement shake violently and he gasps for air. 'I'm getting dizzy,' he says, and indeed he is swaying like a plant blowing in a breeze. 'I think I'm having an 'eart attack!'

Charles scans the cell quickly and his eyes land on Marcus's open briefcase. He reaches in and pulls out a large crumpled manila envelope. He tips out the contents — colour photographs of the Express Dairy building — and hands them swiftly to Marcus.

'May I?' he asks, holding up the envelope.

'Sure.'

Charles compresses the opening of the envelope and blows into it, forming a bag. He holds it out to Plumber.

'Put that in front of your mouth and breathe in and out of the envelope. Go on!' Plumber puts up a trembling hand, takes the envelope and applies his mouth to it. 'Either cover your nose or just breathe through your mouth,' orders Charles.

Plumber does as instructed and within a few seconds his breathing begins to return to normal.

'Better?' asks Charles. Plumber nods. 'He was hyperventilating, that's all,' explains Charles.

The other lawyers are staring at Charles in surprise. 'I didn't know you had any medical experience,' comments Rhodes Thomas.

'I don't. I grew up with an hysterical mother.'

It takes Plumber a further couple of minutes to calm down sufficiently to talk.

'There was only the two of us on the job. God, I never wanted to go, I swear it. I'd gone straight for four years. I had a job and everything. But he called me, straight after he got out, and threatened to grass me on the last job. It was cast iron, he said, this would be the last job ever, and it would set us up for life.'

'That's exactly what it has done,' says Marcus wryly. Rhodes Thomas gives him a sharp look.

'He persuaded me to take an imitation shooter. You can look up my record: I've never touched a gun, real or fake, in thirty years of being a villain till this job. I never knew he had a sawn-off in his jacket, on my baby's life, I swear it.'

'Very well,' says Rhodes Thomas. 'Now, tell us why you made up the third man.'

'That was his idea. He reckoned if we both stuck to the story we'd neither of us be convicted.'

'He was right. But he hasn't stuck to the story, and I don't think he ever intended to. And for some reason the prosecution believes him rather than you. They're proposing to drop the murder charge against him. Why should they believe him, and not you, Mr Plumber?'

'No idea. What're we gonna do?'

'That's up to you,' replies Rhodes Thomas. 'They're obviously not going to take an offer on the robbery alone now, and on your instructions, you can't plead guilty to the murder. The case will depend on which of the two of you the jury believes.'

'A cutthroat,' says Charles.

'Yes,' agrees Rhodes Thomas. 'A cutthroat defence: each defendant blaming the other.'

'What does that mean?' asks Plumber.

'In practical terms,' answers Charles, 'a dirty trial. No holds barred. Your credibility with the jury becomes all-important; they know one of you must be lying and have to decide which. Subject to what Mr Rhodes Thomas thinks, you'd be advised to plead guilty to the robbery and tell the jury the whole story. It'll look dreadful if he admits it, and you don't.'

'I agree,' says Rhodes Thomas. 'The question I need answered now is this: do we require an adjournment? The Crown won't oppose us asking for one, if there's any point. But I have your instructions on this new statement, and I personally cannot see what purpose would be served by delaying the trial.'

'But what about forensics, or whatever they're called? Can't they do tests on the shotgun to prove it was him what fired it and not me?' Plumber asks.

'Such tests do exist, but they'll have been done by now. No evidence has been served on us, and we can assume they revealed nothing, or we'd have been told about it.'

'What do you think, Mr Cohen?' asks Plumber, turning to the man he's known the longest.

'I think counsel are right. I can't see any benefit in delaying. It'll only give Sands the chance to make up more convincing detail.'

'If that's your advice, fair enough,' says Plumber. 'Let's go for it.'

The lawyers leave the cells and go directly to Court 2. The prosecution team and Philip Jewell await them.

'Well?' asks Hogg.

'Very, thank you,' answers Rhodes Thomas with a smile.

'Still fighting?' persists Hogg.

'My dear fellow,' replies Rhodes Thomas, 'I should hate to deprive us all of a few days' work. We're still fighting.'

'Very well. I've told the clerk we need to see the Judge in chambers to explain the position.'

'Why?' ask Charles.

'There are other matters I can't mention now. But they have to be aired in chambers.'

A grim-faced, grey-haired woman of about fifty wearing court robes approaches the barristers. 'His Lordship will see you now gentlemen, if you're ready.'

'Are we ready?' asks Hogg, turning to Rhodes Thomas.

'We are.'

The five barristers follow the clerk to a door behind the Judge's bench and out onto a carpeted corridor, the walls of which are hung with paintings. They file down the corridor for some distance until they come to a panelled door. The clerk motions for them to wait, and knocks.

'Come,' says a voice from behind the door.

The clerk enters, half closing the door behind her, and then opens it wide to usher the barristers in.

'Good morning, Judge,' says Hogg.

'Good morning gentlemen. Do sit down if you can.'

His Honour Judge Galbraith QC is a recent, and popular, appointment to the bench. He's of the new generation of judges; not quite as prosecution-minded as the old school. He is non-interventionist, too; he lets the barristers get on with their jobs in their own way with a minimum of judicial interference. On his appointment as a full-time judge he commissioned a small polished triangle of wood to sit on the desk in front of him with the words "Be Quiet" embossed in large gold letters. Since then, every morning, he has carried the little sign into court with his case papers, to place it carefully on the bench, facing himself.

Sir Richard introduces the other barristers, and explains who they each represent.

'There are a number of matters I'd like to explain with your permission, Judge,' he continues. 'The indictment contains two counts, robbery and murder. As I expect you'll have read, the prosecution case on the first is strong, whereas I concede we'd have difficulty on the murder. The position has now changed, in that Sands has offered to give evidence for the Crown.' He hands to the Judge a copy of the new statement. 'That is a Notice of Additional Evidence served on the Defence this morning.'

He pauses to allow the Judge to read it. The Judge turns to Rhodes Thomas. 'Are you asking for an adjournment?'

'No, Judge.'

'That presumably means that you'll no longer proceed against Sands,' says the Judge to Hogg. Charles now understands why Sands no longer needs a QC; he no longer faces a murder charge. 'If you accept this evidence as the truth,' continues the Judge, 'it follows that you accept that Sands didn't know of the shotgun.'

'Yes,' replies Hogg.

'What gives this statement credence in your view?' asks the Judge. 'It might just as easily have been Plumber who approached you. It's still a cutthroat.'

Charles smiles; this Judge is no fool.

'That brings me on to the other matter that I wanted to raise, Judge, and it's a matter that would be best not raised in open court. Sands has been of great assistance to the police in relation to other matters. He's provided information that's led to a number of arrests, and I am instructed that charges will follow. He appears to have been entirely frank in relation to those matters, some of which may result in charges against him personally.'

Of course! thinks Charles. They've left it to the last minute to allow Sands's "information" to bear fruit with arrests, so as to make him even more credible in the eyes of the Crown and the jury.

'And of course, you, Mr Jewell, want me to take into account the "information" given by your client, in his favour, when sentencing him,' says the Judge.

'Yes, Judge, I do.'

'And I expect you both want him sentenced for the robbery before we start the trial of Mr Plumber, so there can be no suggestion that he's trying to buy a light sentence with false evidence?'

'Yes,' reply Jewell and Hogg in unison.

The Judge leans back in his chair and stares at the ceiling as he thinks. 'If the only evidence against Plumber is that of a potential co-defendant, the jury will have to be warned against convicting him on Sands's word alone. There would have to be corroboration, won't there, Mr Hogg?'

'That's right, Judge. But the prosecution say that there *is* evidence capable of being corroboration, subject, of course, to your ruling.'

'I see. What do you have to say about this?' asks the Judge, turning to Rhodes Thomas.

'There's nothing I can say, Judge. The Crown has taken a view of the evidence. I can't change that. However, we're entitled to know exactly what information Mr Sands has given to the police, so we can consider if we want to cross-examine on it, and what other charges may follow.'

'Yes,' says the Judge. 'I think that must be right. I shall need a note signed from a responsible police officer setting out what Sands has told the police, so that it may be put in the file. I shall make no express reference to it in Court. I must say that I am not entirely happy with the turn of events, Mr Hogg, but I can't prevent you deciding to offer no evidence against one of two defendants.' Hogg doesn't answer. The Judge turns again to Rhodes Thomas. 'Is Plumber proposing to plead guilty to the robbery?'

'Yes, Judge, he is.'

'Well, thank you gentlemen. How long will you need before we can swear in a jury?'

'An hour?' answers Hogg, looking to Rhodes Thomas for confirmation. 'Once we've taken Sands's plea and dealt with sentencing. I suppose the jury in waiting could be asked to stand by for midday.'

'Very well,' says the Judge.

Outside the Judge's chambers, Rhodes Thomas winks at Charles. 'I'm beginning to think we might have some fun with this, Charles,' he whispers. 'I wonder if Hogg's backed the wrong horse.'

They return to the cells to see Plumber.

'He's turned grass,' announces Rhodes Thomas.

'What?' exclaims Plumber.

'He's given the police information regarding other crimes, and they've been busy making arrests. That's why they want to believe him on the murder issue.'

'Where does that leave me?' asks Plumber, his eyes darting from one of his advisers to the next in turn.

'Mr Holborne and I have been chatting about it on the way down. We're not optimistic, but we don't think all is lost. What I'd like to do, Mr Plumber, is keep a very low profile for almost the whole of the case. You admit that you took part in the robbery, and you don't deny the witnesses' accounts of the shooting. You simply say that it wasn't you with the gun. The dead man can't say which of you it was, and the other two members of Team 3, Gilsenan and...'

'Barrett,' offers Charles.

'Yes, well, they were both unsighted by their van and by Wright himself. In my view it's simply a question of which of the two of you the jury believe. Do you agree, Charles?'

'Yes, I do.'

'Very well,' continues Rhodes Thomas. 'I propose to ask no questions at all of the other prosecution witnesses. We shall save the whole attack for Sands himself.'

CHAPTER FIVE

Sands is sentenced to nine years for the robbery. It would have been less but for his bad record, and it would have been more but for the assistance he had given, and promised still to give, to the police. With remission, discounting parole, he would probably serve between four and five years. By the time his sentencing hearing is over it's almost one o'clock and the Judge adjourns for lunch.

At two o'clock the jury is sworn in. Plumber pleads guilty to robbery and not guilty to murder. The trial starts. By the end of the afternoon, the Crown's case is almost complete and the Defence haven't asked a single question. The jury are looking decidedly puzzled. Charles looks across at them every now and then, and can see them staring at the bench where the Defence team sit, wondering what's going on. There's no doubt: by the time Mike Rhodes Thomas stands to cross-examine Sands, he'll have the full attention of the jury.

The Judge adjourns at 4.15 p.m. and Charles heads back to Chambers. He arrives back at 2 Chancery Court at 6.30 p.m. suitably warmed with several cups of tea and rounds of toast. He goes first into the clerks' room. Unusually, Sally is still there and, Charles notes, she has bowed to the pressure; she wears her regular dark blue suit and cream blouse.

'Hello there,' he says, as he peers into the pigeon-hole reserved for his briefs, and, more importantly, cheques, as they come in. 'What are you doing here so late? We haven't started paying overtime, have we?' he jokes.

'You're kidding, right? No, I'm going out tonight and me boyfriend's picking me up. So, as I had to wait anyway, Stanley asked me to hang on for Mr Clarke's brief. It's being sent over by hand. Are you staying, sir?' she asks.

Charles doesn't answer. A large brief is awaiting him in his pigeon-hole, and he unties the ribbon on it to skim-read the instructions. 'Damn!' he says softly as he reads. 'Sorry, Sally, did you say something?'

'Are you going to be staying, as I've locked up on the other side?'

2 Chancery Court is split into two sets of rooms divided by a central landing, and each "side" requires its own keys.

'Well,' answers Charles, 'I *was* going straight home, but they want an indictment drafted by tomorrow *and* an Advice on Evidence,' he says, tapping the papers in his hand. 'Why do they always leave it to the last minute? The sooner we get a central prosecution service, the happier I shall be.'

He gathers the papers together and strides out of the clerks' room. He opens the door to the corridor, still reading as he walks, and bumps straight into someone coming in the other way. He knows instantly by the smell, without even looking up, who it is.

Ivor Kellett-Brown is the oldest, and the oddest, member of Chambers. He came to the Bar in the late 1930s, having failed at a number of other careers and promptly failed in the Law, too. However, incredible as the members of 2 Chancery Court find it, he seems to have friends in high places. Mr Justice Bricklow, head of Chambers until 1936, brought Kellett-Brown in and he's been there ever since. As far as Charles can tell, Kellett-Brown has no actual practice but, unlike in most other professions, every now and then a complete duffer manages to survive at the Bar by living off the crumbs from other barristers' tables. Thus, as long as he continues to pay his Chambers rent — and no one understands how he manages even that, as his earnings from the Law are certainly insufficient — and he causes no one any trouble, he will presumably be permitted to continue to occupy the corner of the pupils' room indefinitely.

Kellett-Brown lives in a single room in Lincoln's Inn with a dozen budgerigars whom he permits to fly free within its walls. Droppings and feathers cover every surface, and the floor crunches underfoot with decades of dried filth. Kellett-Brown himself invariably wears the same threadbare striped trousers, the seat of which is so shiny that the pupils in his room once all wore dark glasses to protect their eyes from the supposed glare. The joke was utterly lost on the wearer of the trousers. He appears to own only one jacket, the cuffs of which he trims regularly, and over that he wears, like an overcoat, the evidence, visual and odiferous, of his domestic companions.

To add to this prepossessing appearance, Kellett-Brown has an "unfortunate manner" as some of the more charitable members of Chambers term it. As far as Stanley, the senior clerk, is concerned, he's an argumentative old fool who should've been kicked out years ago. He frequently appears in Chambers in the late afternoon, plainly the worse for the subsidised sherry served in Hall at luncheon, when Stanley is trying to sort out the diary for the next day. He makes a nuisance of himself by looking over the clerk's shoulder, a tipsy, disgruntled vulture, repeatedly reminding Stanley that he's available for anything that might be going spare.

Charles wrinkles his nose with distaste. Kellett-Brown bears his usual pungent air of sherry and decrepitude.

'Sorry, Ivor,' he says, attempting to circumvent Kellett-Brown and get to his room.

'I beg your pardon?' replies the other with very great dignity, turning slowly to face Charles after he has spoken, and peering at Charles from under heavy lids.

'I said sorry, Ivor. For bumping into you,' explains Charles. He watches as Kellett-Brown sways slightly. 'Forget it,' he says impatiently, and brushes past.

Charles unlocks the far door and walks down to his room. He throws the new papers onto his desk, reaches across to the desk lamp and settles down to read.

He is unaware of the passing of time but, about a hundred pages in, he hears a faint tap on his door. It's so quiet that at first he ignores it but then it's repeated, slightly harder.

'Come in,' he calls. The door opens very slowly and Sally's head appears timidly round the door. 'Sally? What're you doing still here?' He looks at his watch. It's almost eight o'clock. 'You've not been stood up, have you?'

Sally looks down at the mass of papers spread about Charles's desk and the pile of law books on the floor.

'Oh ... no ... it really doesn't matter if you're busy, sir...' she says in a strange voice.

She steps back into the corridor and begins to close the door behind her. Charles pushes his chair back and follows her. She looks back at him like a frightened rabbit. Charles leads her gently by the arm back to the circle of light around his desk and turns her round. Her eyes are red and puffy, her eyeliner, which is usually applied — albeit in large quantities — very carefully, is smeared, and her hair is awry.

'What on earth's the matter?' asks Charles gently.

Sally is usually so competent and brisk that he's quite startled to see her upset. She takes a deep breath as if to start speaking but her voice breaks and all that emerges is a deep sob. Charles leads her to the one comfortable chair in his room, an old leather armchair in the corner, and sits her down. He returns to his desk, searches his drawer, comes up with some battered but clean tissues and hands her one.

'Now. Take a deep breath and tell me what's happened. Is it your boyfriend?'

'He didn't come —' she starts.

'Oh, I'm so sorry. Well, more fool —'

She waves her hand to stop him. 'That ain't it.' Charles waits for her to take another deep breath and lets her start again. 'I was waiting for him over there,' she says between gulps of air, pointing to the clerks' room, 'when Mr K ... K ... Kellett-Brown came in...'

'And?' asks Charles, crouching beside her.

'Oh, Mr Holborne sir, I don't know ... what's best... I'd better not...' Her voice rises sharply with each phrase. She's on the verge of hysteria.

'Just take it slowly. One word at a time.'

'I ... can't... I'll get into trouble, Mr Holborne.'

'No, you won't, I promise you.' He lifts her chin with his hand and looks into her smudged eyes. 'If something's happened, you must tell me.'

She stares straight at him, and nods. 'Mr K-B came in. I was waiting for Johnny. He ... Mr K-B ... he asks me if I didn't think it would be better if I shut the outer door, so no one could come wandering in.' Her voice is now calmer but she speaks very quickly, as if worried that pausing would render her unable to continue. 'Stanley told me about downstairs being burgled, so I thought perhaps I should. Johnny'd always knock anyway. So I did, I shut it, and went back to my desk. I was typing a letter, for Mr Smith, when Mr Kellett-Brown called on the phone. Wanted me to bring him in some paper. So I went in, and he weren't at his desk. I turns round, and he

66

was behind the door...' She laughs, a peculiar high-pitched giggle that turns into a cry. 'He had his ... thing ... you know? Sticking out his trousers. He kept saying he wouldn't hurt me ... just wanted me to ... to...' She stops again.

Charles stands and moves swiftly towards the door. Sally grabs his arm. 'Please don't go! Don't go, sir!' she cries.

'I'm not going. I just want to see if he's still there.'

'He ain't. He left after ... after...'

'After what?' asks Charles, pausing. 'Are you saying he ... did something to you?'

She shakes her head violently. 'No, he never, but he grabbed at me...' She opens her jacket, to show Charles her blouse. Two of the buttons in the middle of her chest are torn off. Charles averts his eyes from her breasts.

'I pushed him away, and he fell over. I ran to the loo and locked meself in. I've been there nearly 'alf an hour. I heard the door go, but I was too scared to come out till now.'

'My God, you poor thing,' says Charles gently. 'Let me get you a drink. I keep a bottle in the desk for —'

'No,' she replies firmly. 'I don't want nothing. I just want to go home.'

'Stay here,' he orders. 'I'll be a minute at most. Lock the door after me if you're worried.' He crosses swiftly to the other side of the building and pushes open the door to the clerks' room. The place is empty. He sees Sally's coat hanging on the back of the door and her handbag by her desk, and takes them with him.

'He's gone,' he reports. Sally's where he left her, looking forlorn. Charles draws up another chair facing hers. 'Now, what do you want to do?'

'Like I said: I want to go home.'

'No, I mean so far as Kellett-Brown is concerned. You're quite entitled to call the police and have him charged with indecent assault. Or maybe even attempted rape.'

'No!' she replies very firmly. 'No, I couldn't do that.'

'I'd come with you,' offers Charles. 'Or maybe you'd like your mum to be there. Shall we give her a call?'

'It's not that,' she replies. She takes several deep breaths to calm herself. 'He's a horrible old man ... a dirty old — no —' she says, half-smiling. 'I mean he don't wash and he smells. But ... I know what you're going to say, Mr Holborne ... but I feel sorry for him. He's lonely.'

'Doesn't matter how lonely he is! That doesn't give him the right to go flashing or grabbing at you!'

'I know. But I couldn't get him sent to prison —'

'It might not be prison.'

'I don't care,' she says, adamantly.

'Think about it, Sally. Don't make any snap decisions. You could easily have been raped.'

'No, I couldn't. I could punch his lights out any time, if it came to it,' she says vehemently, again half-laughing. Charles regards her with surprise and some admiration; he believes her, too. 'I was just a bit frightened,' she continues. 'That's all.'

'So, you're happy just to forget it? Smile and say "Good morning" to him tomorrow? Pretend it never happened?'

Sally looks at him with wide eyes; she hasn't thought about that.

'I ... now I don't know! I think I do need to talk to me mum.' She pauses, her brow contracting in thought. 'Ooh, I'm gonna have to give up the job, ain't I?' And now the tears begin to fall in earnest, thick and fast. 'I could never face him again. And they're never gonna throw *him* out are they?' She lifts her eyes to Charles's face, eyes streaming rivulets of black mascara down her cheeks.

'I don't know about that. My guess is, if Sir Geoffrey finds out about this, even if you don't report it to the police, it'll be the final straw. But if you're absolutely sure you don't want me to call the police or anyone else, I agree you should go home. I'll walk you up to Fleet Street, and you can get a cab.'

'I ain't got enough for a cab from here to Romford.'

'Don't worry about that; it can come out of petty cash. It's the least Chambers can do.'

Charles helps her into her coat, hands her bag to her and, leaving his papers where they lie, escorts her out of Chambers.

'It might be a good idea not to come in tomorrow, eh?' he adds. She nods in reply. 'I'll tell Stanley you weren't well tonight, and I sent you home. OK?'

She nods again and sniffs. 'Tell him it's me throat. I've been coughing all day anyway.'

'Fine.'

Charles locks the doors behind them and they set off. He feels Sally's hand reaching for his as they walk down the stairs.

'Thanks, Charlie,' she says, her voice now calm, looking up at him with a smile. She squeezes his great big paw in her delicate hand. This is the first time she's ever used Charles's first name and it is, according to the protocol of the Bar, quite improper. She could never have done it with any other member of Chambers, and they both know it. Charles is flattered and he smiles back at her. 'I don't know what I'd have done, if you wasn't in,' she continues. He squeezes her hand in reply.

CHAPTER SIX

Charles leaves home the next morning at 6.30 a.m. Relations with Henrietta over the past few days have been less tense, but she has spent the last three nights in her own bedroom and Charles decided not to wake her before leaving.

From Paddington he takes the Tube to Chancery Lane, rather than Temple, and walks down towards the Thames. It's a bright, clear morning, and at 7:45 a.m. the streets are deserted and seem fresh and clean. The leaves on the plane trees are beginning to emerge. Charles can smell spring around the corner.

The part of Lincoln's Inn where Kellett-Brown lives was built in the 16th century, and has barely changed since. The building containing his room is occupied on the ground floor by barristers' chambers, and Charles pauses by the board listing the names of the barristers practising inside, noting that he doesn't recognise a single one. He has little to do with Chancery practitioners; their working lives are so different from his that they might have been in different professions altogether.

He climbs the staircase to the upper floors. The staircase is oak, blackened with time and hundreds of years of footfalls, unchanged except for a lick of paint since the time of Dickens. The second floor houses a book-binding business and the third a firm of solicitors of whom Charles has never heard. The staircase leading to Kellett-Brown's room on the top floor is particularly ill-lit and Charles has to feel his way up step by step. He finally arrives at a door at the head of the staircase. There appears to be no bell or knocker, so Charles raps on the oak door with his knuckles. There's no sound from within. He repeats his knock, much harder this time and, after a few seconds, he hears movement.

'What do you want? Do you know what time it is?' comes Kellett-Brown's querulous voice.

'It's Charles Holborne, from Chambers.'

There's a pause. Then: 'What the bloody hell do you want?'

'Will you open the door, Ivor? This is very important.'

'For God's sake, Holborne, go away. I'll be in Chambers this afternoon if you want me.'

Charles hears Kellett-Brown's footsteps retreating from the front door.

'I suggest you open up now, Ivor. I doubt you want me to shout through the door, but if you give me no alternative, I shall. It's about Sally.'

The footfalls cease. Charles imagines the old man, motionless, only a few feet away from him on the other side of the door, debating whether to open up or not. Eventually, curiosity — or perhaps fear — gets the better of him, and the footsteps approach again. Charles hears a chain being withdrawn and a bolt sliding out of its place. The door opens. Kellett-Brown faces him wearing an old blue dressing gown, skinny pyjamaed legs sticking out of the bottom.

'You'd better come in.'

Charles walks past him into a smelly darkened lounge, overcrowded with heavy furniture. There are a number of small birds on perches dotted about the room, apparently asleep. Kellett-Brown closes the door and turns to Charles.

'Well?' he whispers, apparently so as not to disturb his pets.

'I'll come straight to the point,' replies Charles. 'I was in Chambers last night when you assaulted Sally.'

'Assaulted Sally? What on earth are you talking about?'

'You can pretend not to know if you like, Ivor, but if you take that line, you'll have to continue it with the police. I'm not here to mess about. I know what sort of state Sally was in last night after you finished with her and, if necessary, I'll give evidence of exactly what I saw.'

'The girl's raving!'

Charles shakes his head. 'Very well,' he replies. 'You may expect a call from the police.' He takes a step towards the door but Kellett-Brown doesn't move. 'Do you want to reconsider? I've told no one about this as yet and, if you choose, that's the way it can remain.'

'How do you mean?'

'I mean that I'm sure Sally won't press charges, and last night's events will be forgotten.'

'And what am I supposed to do to prevent these false charges being brought against me? You do realise this is blackmail? You could be prosecuted yourself for this!'

'I am trying, Ivor, to save your reputation, such as it is, and prevent this whole thing being dragged through the courts. I am also trying to save a young girl's job.'

'I repeat: what's the price?'

'Your resignation from Chambers, effective as from today.'

'Preposterous!' replies Kellett-Brown.

Charles pushes past him and opens the door. 'It's entirely up to you. If, by the time I return to Chambers this afternoon, I've heard nothing, I shall report the matter to Sir Geoffrey. What he does then is up to him. Likewise, it'll be up to Sally to decide whether or not she wishes to prosecute. In my view, there's absolutely no doubt but that she should. Good morning.'

Charles leaves the stinking apartment, slams the front door behind him — causing considerable fluttering and squawking — and descends the staircase.

Once at 2 Chancery Court, he continues reading his new papers until 9 a.m., hastily jotting some notes for the typists to decipher. He leaves a note on Stanley's desk saying that Sally became ill the night before while in Chambers, and that she wouldn't be in that day. He then departs for the Old Bailey.

In the Bar Mess he orders an enormous fried breakfast and settles down with a cup of coffee to read the newspaper.

At 10.20 a.m. it is announced that His Honour Judge Galbraith is dealing with a bail application and that all parties in the case of *The Queen versus Plumber* are released until 11.00 a.m. That is in due course extended to 11.30 a.m., and then midday. The case finally resumes at 12.15 p.m. By 4.20 p.m. the evidence for the Crown is completed, apart from the evidence of Sands. His Honour adjourns until the morning. It has been a frustrating day for the Defence, and the team is on edge.

Charles returns directly to the Temple. As he enters the clerks' room, Stanley beams at him in a most unusual way.

'Have you been drinking, Stanley?' asks Charles with a smile.

'Not a drop, thank you, sir, although a celebratory glass would be a very good idea. Mr Kellett-Brown has resigned from Chambers. Came in at lunchtime, paid a quarter's rent, and departed. Ill-health, he said.'

'Well I never,' replies Charles. 'He always looked perfectly healthy to me.'

Charles goes to his room and closes the door. He consults his Rolodex, picks up the telephone and dials the phone number for Sally's home in Romford.

'You can come back tomorrow,' he tells her. 'Kellett-Brown has resigned, and he's not coming back.'

'Have you said anything, sir?' Sally answers, reverting to formality.

'Not a word,' he assures her. 'It's between you and me, and not another soul.'

'I'll see you tomorrow then, Mr Holborne. I'll phone Stanley now and tell him I'm feeling better.'

'Fine. Goodbye.'

'Bye, sir.'

Henrietta is in the garden when Charles arrives home that evening, wearing trousers and a sun hat, a pair of pruning shears in her gloved hands. She doesn't often wear trousers, considering them too American and too modern, but Charles approves when she does. He finds it difficult to take his eyes off her swaying hips as she moves, and on this occasion he watches from the kitchen door for some minutes before she senses his presence. She removes her hat as she turns towards the house, brushing the hair out of her eyes with her upper arm, and Charles's heart quickens. She is so beautiful.

'What are you doing here?' she calls, surprised.

'I live here,' he says cheerfully, crossing the lawn and approaching her. 'Might I be addressing the lady of the house?' Charles kisses her on the cheek. She absently kisses the air beside his face.

'Yes, but it's only six-thirty. You've not been home this early for years. May one enquire if you are ill?'

'One may enquire and no, thank you, I'm perfectly well. I just thought we might spend some time together, that's all.'

'Good God, Charles, this is all rather unexpected. After all this time, you want to play at being a husband for a night?'

Charles gazes at her, not entirely hiding the fact that the remark stung.

Henrietta is almost his height, slim, with an oval face framed with silky chestnut hair. She looks, if anything, more beautiful than she did the day he met her at Cambridge, eleven years before. On that occasion he'd been dressed as a penguin, part of some student rag, accosting passers-by, and she was late for a lecture. He had held her by her skinny arms demanding she either make a donation of at least half a crown or promise to meet him for a drink. Having no money with her, she was forced to accept the alternative.

That meeting was only two weeks after Charles decided to change his name, one week after the awful scene with his father. The full implications of his decision had yet to sink in, and he was still exploring this new identity, Charles Holborne, English gentleman. Perhaps that was why he had the courage to grab her wrists in his flippers and demand a date with her, because it wasn't Charlie Horowitz asking, but this new, dangerous, dashing, Charles Holborne.

Everyone knew Henrietta, of course. The Hon. Henrietta Lloyd-Williams, eldest daughter of Viscount Brandreth, one of the fastest of the "fast set", as Charles's father used to call them, and yet with an unpretentious, easy manner and, so it was said, a good brain, too. What persuaded her to go out with this dark-eyed persistent penguin she didn't know. His arrogance was quite unlike the self-assurance of the well-bred languid young men with whom she grew up. It was dangerous, almost bellicose; it invited challenge, so much so that, for the first few months of their relationship, part of the attraction was her anticipation that something, *anything*, might happen when she was with him. There were a couple of fights in Cambridge pubs in which Charles demonstrated a thrilling ability to look after himself. There was also a bitterness about him, but softened by a gentle self-deprecating humour that hinted at a profound vulnerability. It was certainly his ability to make her laugh that persuaded her to see him again, but it was the little lost boy she discovered that so endeared him to her. That so big a man, both in intellect and in size, could at times look so perplexed by the universe was oddly endearing.

For his part, Charles sensed something in Henrietta which he recognised in himself. Her relationship with her father, the Viscount, an exacting impatient man, was fraught and punctuated by long periods during which the two of them didn't speak. Charles was unaware of it at the time, but Henrietta's third year at Cambridge when they first met was one such period. That year was the most intense of their lives; romantic weekends away, shared books, music and ideas, and sex at all times of the day and night, and in increasingly dangerous places. They couldn't keep their hands off one another. They inhabited their own private, intoxicated, world. And barely ten months after they first met, post-coital on a desolate Northumbrian beach, Henrietta proposed to Charles, and he accepted. A week later, still during term, they were married in Cambridge without a word to either family. Two days before the ceremony, Charles told Henrietta that he was Jewish by birth, but not practising. Charles didn't think to mention that to be Jewish doesn't require practice. She couldn't actually say she'd met a Jew before, practising or otherwise, but it didn't matter to her, she said, as long as they could continue to eat bacon and oysters.

Her parents loathed him, of course, albeit politely. Her mother had been overheard saying that there was nothing wrong with Jewish furriers from the East End of London, of course, nor indeed with their clever sons. They were just so ... *unsuitable* as in-laws. The Viscount took the match as a personal insult by his daughter, the most successful means she had yet devised to demonstrate her contempt for him, which in many ways it was.

For Charles's parents it was simpler still. When they learned of the marriage, they said *Kaddish*, the prayer for the dead, mourned Charles for a week and never mentioned his name again. As far as they were concerned, their eldest son, the apple of their eye, had died. Henrietta's family were grateful for this attitude. One Jew connected to the family was quite enough; an entire brood would have been intolerable.

At the end of term, Charles took Henrietta to his parents' home in the East End to introduce her. His father refused to come to the door and David, Charles's younger brother, apologetically barred his way at the threshold. Charles, hurt beyond description, shouted some unforgivable words from the doorway before Henrietta managed to drag him away. He still remembers some of those words with shame, but he has had no further contact with his family in the intervening years. Once, a couple of years after that event, Harry Horowitz discovered David eating breakfast while reading a court report in the *Telegraph* about a case where Charles's name was mentioned. David was by then in his early twenties, but his father still beat him as efficiently as his sixty-six-year-old arms and heart condition would allow. Five years after that, when viewing a development plot in one of his rare property cases, Charles discovered by chance that his family had moved. British Street, where his childhood home had stood, had been demolished. Where his parents were, and whether they were both still alive, he neither knew nor, he told himself, cared.

'Are you still here, Charles?' asks Henrietta.

'Yes. Sorry. I thought perhaps we could go out for a meal.'

'I'm sorry,' Henrietta replies, with sincerity, 'but I can't. I've been invited to the Robertsons' for dinner; they have some friends over from the States, and they're holding a small reception for them.'

'I'm sure Helen wouldn't mind if I came, too.'

'She didn't invite you because you've never once kept a mid-week dinner arrangement since we've been married,' Henrietta says, continuing with her pruning.

'I've told you a million times: don't exaggerate.'

'All right; maybe not "never". But you *have* let them down more than once. It's a bit unfair to her to ask at this stage, don't you think? It's a small party, and it's starting in two hours. You'll throw her into a tizzy if you ask to come now. But if you really want me to phone, I will.'

Charles considers and decides against it. 'OK; forget it.'

Henrietta rests her forehead on his chest and Charles drinks in the smell of her hair: cut grass and sunshine. She looks up at him. 'It was a nice idea. If you do it more often, I'll get used to it.'

She takes his face in her muddy, gloved hands, pulls his head towards hers and kisses him on the mouth.

'You smell nice,' he says.

'You smell nice, too.'

'What of?' he asks.

'Just Charlie,' she answers, hugging him.

'I don't suppose...' he suggests.

'What don't you suppose?' She snuggles closer to him.

'I don't suppose you might develop a dreadful headache at about ten o'clock tonight, which might mysteriously clear up on your arrival home?'

'Charlie! Whatever has come over you?'

'Nothing's come over me.'

'I'll see what can be arranged.' She grins and takes his arm and they walk slowly back towards the house.

'Charlie?'

'Present.'

'Can we both make a special effort? I know I've been a real bitch the last few weeks. And you —'

'I've been working too hard,' he interrupts.

'You've been distant, cold and thoughtless,' she corrects.

'Hmm.'

'I was adding it up this morning. I haven't seen you for more than six hours this whole week. That's three breakfasts, one trip to the shops and an hour on Monday night — and that was only because the power cut prevented you from working.'

He sighs. 'It's this murder. And there's the fraud next month. They're both important...'

'I know they are, and I'm proud of you, even though I think you're wasted doing this stuff. What does Daddy call it?'

'"The Verbals".'

'Yes, that. But I sometimes wonder how high our marriage is on your list of priorities.'

'We've been through this before, Etta. If you got yourself a proper job, which actually stretched you, you wouldn't be waiting at home with nothing —'

'"Proper job"?' she exclaims. She takes a deep breath and looks up at him. 'Don't you see how such comments demean me?' she asks. 'Do you never wonder how someone might feel, on the receiving end? Anyway that's not the point. I don't want a different job. I want —'

'I know what you want. You want a child. I know, Etta, really I do. But we've been through this, and we agreed to wait a year or two —'

He's interrupted by Fiona calling from the French windows.

'Is Charles in yet? Oh, you *are*. There's a chap called Stanley on the phone. He says it's very urgent.'

Charles looks at Henrietta. 'I'd better take it. I'll be right back.'

He runs up the lawn and into the house where Fiona hands him the telephone. Henrietta returns to her gardening, shaking her head.

'Stanley?' Charles asks.

'Hello, sir. Sorry to trouble you at home, but I've just had a call from Tony, the clerk to Mr Rhodes Thomas. Mr Rhodes Thomas has had an accident. It's not too bad, but apparently he's broken his leg, and he'll be out of commission, in traction, for at least six weeks.'

'For fuck's sake! What was he doing? Now what? Will we be adjourned? How long am I going to have to stay on remand?' wails Plumber.

Charles, Ralph Cohen and their client sit in a conference room at HM Prison Brixton, to which Plumber was moved at the start of the trial.

Cohen replies. 'He slipped down the stairs at the Bailey. It must have been just after I left him last night. He's in Bart's, right opposite the court. He says he'll be in hospital for as much as six weeks. But we're pretty confident we can get the case adjourned.'

'What, for six weeks?'

'I don't know about that. It'll probably be more than six weeks before he's back at work, maybe three or four months. It's a very bad break. I'm not sure the Court will delay for as long as that. We need to get a new silk in.'

'You mean start the trial again?' protests Plumber.

'Derek, we're going to have to do that, whatever happens,' replies Cohen, sympathetically. 'I understand how you feel. But a jury can only be sent away for a couple of days, certainly not for weeks. They'll have to be discharged.'

'And how long will it take to find another silk?'

Cohen looks at Charles for an answer. 'I don't know,' he says. 'The case isn't difficult in terms of what's got to be assimilated; it's just a question of finding someone who's free at very short notice. Good silks get booked up early.'

'So it means I've to put up with someone who's second rate? With me life on the line? You gotta be fucking joking!'

'Please calm down, Mr Plumber,' answers Charles. 'There is no question of you being represented by anyone second rate. Mr Rhodes Thomas was my first choice, but there are plenty of excellent leaders.'

'Yeah, but I need one right away. I've been on remand for months. I can't go through this again, Mr 'Olborne; I can't sleep, I can't eat, I'm at me wits' end. I don't want to put the case off at all. Why can't you do it? Don't you feel up to it?'

'It's not that. You're charged with a capital offence, and you're entitled to leading counsel.'

'I'm entitled to counsel of my choice, right? Well, one of 'em's crocked but I've still got one left, and I've got confidence in 'im. I don't want the case put off or started again.'

Charles looks at Cohen, who shrugs. 'You are aware,' says Charles to Plumber, 'that I have less experience than a QC would have?'

'Yeah. But, like I said, I have faith in you. I know you'll do it as well as anyone.'

Charles pauses. 'Thanks for the vote of confidence. I appreciate what you've said. But I need a little time to think about this. I've a professional duty to do the best I can for you, and if that involves getting in another silk, that's what I have to do. Would it be OK if I give you my answer tomorrow?'

Plumber nods.

'Well?' asks Charles of Cohen as they step out of the prison gates onto the forecourt.

'You've had express instructions from the client, Charles. He wants you to carry on. It's a murder, yes, but this is about as straightforward a case of murder as you can get. All you have to do is discredit one witness, and I've seen you do that hundreds of times. I think you'd cope.'

'But if I mess it up, our client's going to hang.'

'True. But that doesn't make me any less confident that you can do it. To be honest, Charles, you're better than half the silks I see every day. And I think the jury'll warm to you. You can talk like them, you come from the same part of London, and there's no front on you. It's your decision, of course, and if you decide it's a bit too early, I'll accept that and we'll find someone else.'

CHAPTER SEVEN

R. v. Plumber: Transcript of Evidence: Friday, 18 November 1960

Sands: *Examination in chief*

Mr Hogg: *Would you please give the court your full name?*

Witness: *Robbie — er, that's Robert — Reginald Sands.*

Mr Hogg: *Yesterday, you pleaded guilty to robbing the Express Dairies, London North Depot of £138,530.16 on 5th. February this year.*

Witness: *Aye, I did.*

Mr Hogg: *Did you commit that robbery alone or with others?*

Witness: *I did it wi' him.*

Judge: *Let the record show that the witness pointed to the Defendant, Plumber.*

Mr Hogg: *Were any others involved?*

Witness: *No.*

Mr Hogg: *Were any firearms used in the robbery?*

Witness: *Aye. We each took an imitation, at least that's what I thought.*

Mr Hogg: *Would you please show the witness Exhibits 4 and 5?*

Witness: *They're the ones. I cannae say which was mine or Plumbers, 'cos they're identical.*

Mr Hogg: *Who obtained these replicas?*

Witness: *I did.*

Mr Hogg: *When you obtained them, were you anxious to obtain real or imitation firearms?*

Witness: *I wouldnae have gone on the job at all had I known that real shooters were to be used.*

Mr Hogg: *What was your part in the robbery?*

Witness: *We both went in. I stood by the door and collared the employees as they came through; Plumber handcuffed them to the pipes. We took two cars, well, a van and a car. Plumber was the getaway driver. The van was used to block the alley after us.*

Mr Hogg: *There came a time when a member of one of the crews returning to the Depot was reluctant to enter, did there not?*

Witness: *There did.*

Mr Hogg: *Will you tell the jury what happened then?*

Witness: *The wee laddie on the door opened up, but the fella wouldnae come in. He must have been suspicious, 'cos he ran off, shouting something.*

Mr Hogg: *What happened then?*

Witness: *I rushed out to grab him. He was about ten yards ahead of me, running to his van.*

Mr Hogg: *Where was Plumber at this stage?*

Witness: *I thought he was still inside, 'cos that was his job, right? Guarding the employees. But then I heard something behind me, and the next second there was this bang. The guard caught it right in the middle of the back. Blew him off the ground and down by the van.*

Mr Hogg: *Did you see what had caused the noise?*

Witness: *Not till I turned. There was Plumber wi' that sawn off in his hand and smoke coming from it.*

Judge: *Let the record show that the witness indicated Exhibit 2. Have a look at it, Mr Sands, please.*

Witness: *That's the one.*

Mr Hogg: *Show us how Plumber was holding it, please. [Witness takes exhibit.] You are holding it at waist level with your right hand on the butt and the left supporting the barrels. Where was it pointing?*

Witness: *Straight at the dead man, or at least, where he had been when he was upright.*

Mr Hogg: *What happened then?*

Witness: *I ran up tae Plumber. He was, eh, stunned, like. I had tae grab him, turn him round. We ran back inside, grabbed the money, and left. I'm sure he didnae mean tae do it. It was just the panic.*

Judge: *It's for the jury to decide if he meant to do it or not, Mr Sands, not for you. Please refrain from comments like that. You are here to answer questions.*

Mr Hogg: *Wait there please, Mr Sands.*

[End of examination in chief]

Sands: *Cross-examination*

Judge: *Mr Holborne?*

Mr Holborne: *Thank you, my Lord. Mr Sands: who planned this robbery? [Pause.] Mr Sands?*

Witness: *We did it together, Plumber and me.*

Mr Holborne: *Mr Plumber was the driver of the getaway car, wasn't he?*

Witness: *Aye.*

Mr Holborne: *And he planned the getaway, isn't that right?*

Witness: *Aye.*

Mr Holborne: *But he didn't plan anything else did he?*

Witness: *Eh … not as such, no.*

Mr Holborne: *It was you who had the idea, and you took the proposal to Mr Plumber. You recruited him, rather than he recruited you.*

Witness: *Aye, that's right.*

Mr Holborne: *And as far as you were concerned, two imitation guns were to be taken on this robbery?*

Witness: *That's right.*

Mr Holborne: *You've told us that you were responsible for obtaining them?*

Witness: *Aye.*

Mr Holborne: *So, you know where one can obtain such things?*

Witness: *Aye, I do. Lots of shops sell them.*

Mr Holborne: *What shop did you buy them from?*

Witness: *Er, I didnae buy them from a shop.*

Mr Holborne: *You got them from a man in a laundrette. That's not likely to be a lawful source is it Mr Sands?*

Witness: *No.*

Mr Holborne: *That "unorthodox channel" is the sort of channel that could have provided you with a real gun, had you wanted one.*

Witness: *I don't know. I didnae ask him.*

Mr Holborne: *If you were only after imitation guns, which you have told us can be bought legitimately from "lots of shops", why did you get one from a man you met in a laundrette?*

Witness: *[pause] I don't know.*

Mr Holborne: *It was not because you wanted a real gun, too, and that had to be obtained illegally?*

Witness: *No. I suppose I didnae want the police asking at shops an' that.*

Mr Holborne: *Let's move on. How did you feel about Mr Plumber's having taken a real gun with him?*

Witness: *I've already said. I wouldnae have gone had I known.*

Mr Holborne: *You must have been furious with Plumber then, for taking the shotgun and for using it?*

Judge: *That's two questions Mr Holborne. First, Mr Sands, were you furious that he had taken the shotgun?*

Witness: *If I'd known before we went, I wouldnae have been exactly furious, but not happy. I woulda told him to leave it behind.*

86

Judge: *Were you furious when he used it?*

Witness: *I couldnae believe what he'd done. He had no need to. Once the guy had seen the imitation, he woulda stopped. They're no' armed, those men. Aye, I was furious.*

Mr Holborne: *Why?*

Witness: *You ask me why? Jesus, the guy had been shot in the back. Robbery's one thing. Murder, that's something else altogether.*

Mr Holborne: *Your concern then was that you might be implicated in a murder that you had no part in?*

Witness: *Exactly.*

Mr Holborne: *Did you express that concern to Mr Plumber?*

Witness: *Well, I gave him a right bollocking in the car, but what could I do? He'd already shot the guy by the time I knew what was going on.*

Mr Holborne: *Where did you go immediately after the robbery?*

Witness: *To my flat.*

Mr Holborne: *What did you go there for?*

Witness: *To divvy up.*

Mr Holborne: *Did you go there directly?*

Witness: *We did. Well, we changed cars once on the way, and dumped the guns and balaclavas and that.*

Mr Holborne: *Where did you do that?*

Witness: *We left them locked in the car, and scrapped the car.*

Mr Holborne: *When you say "locked in the car", it's true is it not, that they were left hidden under the rear seat?*

Witness: *Aye.*

Mr Holborne: *And when you say "scrapped", what do you mean?*

Witness: *A compacter. We sold the car tae a scrap metal dealer I know, and he agreed to squash it. He didnae do it, though. He got greedy.*

Mr Holborne: *I'm sorry?*

Witness: *Well, we paid him over the odds to squash it, but he obviously took a fancy to it, 'cos it was still in the yard when the police went there.*

Mr Holborne: *I see. And how did you get back to your flat from the scrap dealer?*

Witness: *In ma own car.*

Mr Holborne: *You scrapped the Rover before you went back to your flat?*

Witness: *Yes. I've already said.*

Mr Holborne: *Within minutes of the robbery?*

Witness: *Within half an hour.*

Mr Holborne: *And the reason you did that, I assume, was because you didn't want to risk being found in possession of incriminating evidence one moment longer than necessary.*

Witness: *You could say.*

Mr Holborne: *I do say, Mr Sands. What do you say?*

Witness: *Well, if you like. It's just common sense. I didnae want tae be connected to any of it.*

Mr Holborne: *Indeed. The one item of evidence that you would have been most concerned to get away from would have been the shotgun. Everything else ties you to a robbery. The shotgun ties you to a murder.*

Witness: *Well?*

Mr Holborne: *So the item you'd want to get rid of most, is the shotgun. [Pause.] Isn't that right, Mr Sands?*

Witness: *I suppose so.*

Mr Holborne: *We know from the police evidence that they recovered the car, as you say, before it was compacted.*

Witness: *So?*

Mr Holborne: *They found the two imitation handguns, two masks, and some pairs of handcuffs, but no shotgun. What did you do with it?*

Witness: *I didnae do anything wi' it. Plumber had it. I never touched the thing.*

Mr Holborne: *So you placed the other items under the seat?*

Witness: *Aye.*

Mr Holborne: *And locked up?*

Witness: *Aye.*

Mr Holborne: *But you did not put the shotgun there, too?*

Witness: *No.*

Mr Holborne: *Why not, Mr Sands?*

Witness: *It wasnae mine.*

Mr Holborne: *But you have just told the jury that the thing you most wanted to distance yourself from was that shotgun. There you are getting rid of all the other evidence, but you keep the most incriminating item, the shotgun. Why?*

Witness: *I told you, I didnae keep the shotgun. Plumber had it.*

Mr Holborne: *And you let him bring it into your car, driving with it to your flat, when you wanted it nowhere near you? You couldn't have wanted to distance yourself that much from it: you let him hang onto it and travel around with it in your car!*

Judge: *I think counsel's asking you a question, Mr Sands, although he's not phrased it as such. Why did you permit Plumber to bring the shotgun with him in your car?*

Witness: *I don't know. I just did.*

Mr Holborne: *What happened when you arrived at your flat?*

Witness: *We divvied up the money.*

Mr Holborne: *That must have taken some time, counting out and dividing £138,000.*

Witness: *Maybe.*

Mr Holborne: *How long?*

Witness: *I don't know; a coupla hours maybe.*

Mr Holborne: *And you let Plumber leave the shotgun in your car all that time?*

Witness: *No.*

Mr Holborne: *In your flat then?*

Witness: *[pause] I cannae remember what happened to it.*

Mr Holborne: *From when do you not remember?*

Witness: *I don't know. I'm not even sure I saw it in the car at all. Maybe he did leave it at the scrapyard, but someone found it.*

Judge: *Mr Sands, in answer to a question from me, not two minutes ago, you said you didn't know why you let Plumber bring the shotgun in your own car. So you must remember seeing it at that stage.*

Witness: *I must remember it then, yes.*

Mr Holborne: *So you remember it in your car. Why did you not tell Mr Plumber to get rid of it at the scrapyard?*

Witness: *I didnae think to. I must have been in too much of a panic.*

Mr Holborne: *Yes, but your panic was because of the shotgun. Are you really telling this jury that although you wanted nothing to do with the shotgun, and having had the opportunity to get rid of it with all the other incriminating evidence, you allowed Mr Plumber to bring it into your car and your flat?*

Witness: *I don't know. I suppose so.*

Mr Holborne: *Thank you. Now, Mr Sands, when you were first arrested for the offence of robbery, you were interviewed under caution, were you not?*

Witness: *Aye, I was.*

Mr Holborne: *During the course of that interview, you are recorded as having said there was a third man on the robbery, and that it was he who took and used the shotgun.*

Witness: *I said that, aye.*

Mr Holborne: *That was a lie, wasn't it?*

Witness: *It was, but I only said it because he threatened me if I didnae.*

Judge: *You pointed at the defendant. Are you saying that Plumber threatened you?*

Witness: *I am. Well, ma family.*

Mr Holborne: *When did he make this threat?*

Witness: *On the telephone, the day after the robbery.*

Mr Holborne: *And what, exactly, did he say?*

Witness: *He said that he reckoned we might be caught, and that if we were, we should both give the same story, about the third man.*

Mr Holborne: *Did you agree to this plan?*

Witness: *No' at first. Only after he made the threats. He said that if I didnae agree, he would see to ma family.*

Mr Holborne: *He wasn't going to see to you personally?*

Witness: *You gotta be joking. Him?*

Mr Holborne: *I take it that you are not personally afraid of Mr Plumber?*

Witness: *Correct.*

Mr Holborne: *Exactly what members of your family did he refer to?*

Witness: *He didnae say.*

Mr Holborne: *Does he know your family?*

Witness: *I don't know.*

Mr Holborne: *Well, what family do you have?*

Witness: *I've got a mother.*

Mr Holborne: *Is that all?*

Witness: *Eh ... I got an uncle, too.*

Mr Holborne: *Where does your mother live?*

Witness: *I don't know. I have nae kept in touch. She remarried a while back.*

Mr Holborne: *To whom?*

Witness: *Some chap. I cannae remember his name.*

Mr Holborne: *Where does your uncle live?*

Witness: *He used to live in a place called Helmsdale.*

Mr Holborne: *Where's that?*

Witness: *The north-east coast of Scotland, about 100 miles north of Inverness.*

Mr Holborne: *Have you ever introduced Mr Plumber to your mother?*

Witness: *No.*

Mr Holborne: *To your uncle?*

Witness: *No.*

Mr Holborne: *So, to summarise: you neither know your mother's married name nor her address, and your uncle used to live in the wilds of north eastern Scotland, but you don't know where he lives now. Correct so far?*

Witness: *Aye.*

Mr Holborne: *Mr Plumber has met neither of them, and probably didn't know that they existed?*

Witness: *Maybe.*

Mr Holborne: *And the threats were being made by a man of whom who you are not in the least frightened?*

Witness: *So?*

Mr Holborne: *You must've been quaking in your boots, Mr Sands. [Laughter.] I suggest that your evidence that Mr Plumber threatened your family is completely untrue. You have made it up.*

Witness: *No. It's true.*

Mr Holborne: *I suggest that your evidence that he bullied you into saying there was a third man is also untrue. I suggest the bullying was the other way around. You threatened him.*

Witness: *No.*

Mr Holborne: *Mr Sands, you have, I think, six convictions for robbery, do you not?*

Witness: *Maybe. I have nae counted.*

Mr Holborne: *Well, I have. In 1948 you robbed a Post Office in Croydon of six pounds, five shillings and four pence.*

Witness: *So?*

Mr Holborne: *The way you got the postmistress to hand the money over was to threaten her with a knife. After you came out of prison you were convicted in 1951 of three offences in which you robbed rent collectors in*

Sheffield. Is that right?

Witness: Yes. But I served my time. It's got nothing to do with this.

Mr Holborne: I say it has everything to do with this. How did you get the rent collectors to hand over their money?

Witness: I dinnae know what you mean.

Mr Holborne: Oh, yes, you do, Mr Sands. You understand me full well. You made the rent collectors hand over their money by threatening them with physical violence. One with a knife and two with an unloaded ex-army revolver. Isn't that right?

Witness: If you say so.

Mr Holborne: And during the last of those three offences, the rent collector, a Mr Thompson, gave evidence that you threatened to hurt his wife and baby if he didn't comply.

Witness: I never said that! That's a lie.

Mr Holborne: I have the sentencing remarks of the judge in front of me. He referred specifically to that as an aggravating feature when he sentenced you to prison. Lastly, in 1957 you were convicted of another robbery, were you not?

Witness: Aye.

Mr Holborne: On that occasion you didn't threaten violence. Instead you bashed a security guard over the head and put him in hospital for three weeks. So, I suggest, Mr Sands, that you have no compunction whatsoever in threatening or using serious physical violence to get what you want.

Witness: And what about him?

Mr Holborne: Yes, I was about to come to Mr Plumber. It is quite true that Mr Plumber also has a long criminal record. A full list of his convictions has been agreed with the Crown, my Lord. It is agreed by the Crown that Mr Plumber has never been charged with any offence in which he personally used or threatened violence. His involvement in robberies has always been as a getaway driver.

Judge: *Is that agreed, Mr Hogg?*

Mr Hogg: *It is, my Lord.*

Mr Holborne: *Now, Mr Sands, let's change subject. In August this year, you had a visit in Brixton from Detective Inspector Wheatley, is that correct?*

Witness: *Yes.*

Mr Holborne: *You asked your solicitors to get in touch with him, and, as a result, he paid you a visit?*

Witness: *I don't remember.*

Mr Holborne: *That's his evidence. Do you disagree?*

Witness: *I suppose not.*

Mr Holborne: *And, at that visit, you told Inspector Wheatley that you had lied before about the third man, and that Plumber had carried the shotgun?*

Witness: *Aye.*

Mr Holborne: *You obviously felt by then that your dear lost mother was no longer in danger from Mr Plumber. [Laughter.]*

Judge: *That's a comment, Mr Holborne, not a question.*

Mr Holborne: *I apologise, my Lord. Let me put it this way, Mr Sands: you tell us that you were forced into agreeing to making up the existence of a third man by Mr Plumber's threats to your mother, but at some point you decided, despite that threat, to request a visit from DI Wheatley so you could tell him your present story. Correct so far?*

Witness: *Maybe.*

Mr Holborne: *Well, what part of what I have just said is wrong?*

Witness: *Nothing.*

Mr Holborne: *So the answer isn't "Maybe"; the answer is "Yes". So, what changed?*

Witness: *I thought about it some more and realised that that pansy would never actually do it.*

Mr Holborne: *I see. So, on reflection, you decided that Mr Plumber was not really the sort of man to carry out a violent attack on your family. Right?*

Witness: *Aye. I changed my mind.*

Mr Holborne: *Now, I want to ask you this: when you changed your story, did the Inspector believe you at first?*

Mr Hogg: *My Lord, I object to that question. It is of no relevance to the jury whether the inspector believed this witness or not; the question is, do the jury believe him?*

Judge: *That's right, isn't it, Mr Holborne?*

Mr Holborne: *Put thus, my Lord, yes. But the purpose of the question is not to usurp the function of the jury. I wish to ask about the witness's motives for discussing other matters at the same time.*

Judge: *You may certainly ask about other things spoken about, and Mr Sands's motives, but not about how they affected the officer's mind.*

Mr Holborne: *Very well. Mr Sands: in addition to telling Inspector Wheatley about what you say was Plumber's role, you gave the officer other information, did you not?*

Witness: *I ... er ... I really don't remember now. It was a couple of months ago.*

Mr Holborne: *Do try and assist the jury, Mr Sands. I'm sure you'll remember if you think hard about it.*

Witness: *I cannae recall what we spoke about.*

Mr Holborne: *Let me refresh your memory, Mr Sands. You gave the police information about other crimes, didn't you?*

Witness: *I don't know.*

Mr Holborne: *You informed on a number of your friends.*

[Disturbance in the gallery. Shouting at the witness.]

Judge: *If this noise does not cease immediately, I shall clear the court!*

Mr Holborne: *You turned grass, didn't you, Mr Sands?*

Witness: *No, I never!*

Mr Holborne: *Do you wish me to call Inspector Wheatley to prove that that's a lie?*

Witness: *No.*

Mr Holborne: *Then the truth please, Mr Sands. You informed on a number of your criminal friends, did you not?*

Witness: *I ... I was helping the police with their enquiries.*

[Continued disturbance in gallery]

Judge: *Master at arms, take those men out! Any further person making noise from the gallery will be committed for contempt forthwith! Carry on, Mr Holborne.*

Mr Holborne: *The reason you informed on your colleagues was so the Inspector would believe you. You wanted him to believe that Plumber, and not you, used the shotgun, isn't that right? [Pause.] Do you intend answering that question? [Pause.] May I take it that you have no answer? [Pause.] Very well. As a result of the information you gave to the police, you hoped to receive a lighter sentence for the robbery, didn't you?*

Witness: *I don't know.*

Mr Holborne: *Of course you know! By giving information to the police did you hope to receive a lighter sentence or not?*

Witness: *Well, I thought if I scratched his back...*

Mr Holborne: *Exactly. And having been originally charged with murder, as was Mr Plumber, the charge was dropped against you.*

Witness: *Aye, it was.*

Mr Holborne: *I suggest to you, Mr Sands, that in giving evidence to this jury you are not in the slightest motivated to tell the truth.*

Witness: *I am telling the truth.*

Mr Holborne: *I suggest that your sole motive was to escape conviction for murder yourself, and if that meant dropping Plumber and all your other mates in it, then so be it.*

Witness: *No.*

Mr Holborne: *You were the one with the gun, Mr Sands.*

Witness: *No.*

Mr Holborne: *You threatened Mr Plumber into saying there was a third man who carried the gun.*

Witness: *No.*

Mr Holborne: *You then turned Queen's Evidence to avoid a murder charge, and falsely accused Mr Plumber of carrying the gun.*

Witness: *No.*

Mr Holborne: *You murdered William Wright.*

Witness: *No. Plumber did it, I tell you.*

[End of cross-examination]

'If you don't let go of my hand, Mr Plumber, it'll fall off!'

'I still don't know what to say, Mr Holborne, it was terrific! I'll never be able to thank you enough,' says Plumber, still pumping Charles's hand. 'You've saved my life!'

'Take it easy now; you do have six years to serve for the robbery.'

'Yeah, but even that's a result. I'd resigned meself to the same as Sands got, you know, nine. To get six, on top of getting off the murder, well...'

'You don't have anything like as bad a record as he does, don't forget,' says Cohen.

'Not only that,' adds Charles, grimly, 'but your six will be a doddle compared to his nine. He'll have to spend it all under rule 43 — solitary.'

'That's right,' says Cohen. 'Life inside as a grass will not be pleasant.'

When Charles returns to Chambers a new problem awaits him in the form of an envelope addressed to him in his pigeon-hole.

Holborne

You may think you have won, but I assure you, no filthy little Jew shall defeat me. The disgrace you have made me suffer will be as nothing to what I shall cause you. I shall repay you with interest. Isn't that what your race expects?

The note is unsigned and there's no clue from the envelope, which was delivered by hand, but Charles has a suspicion. He lifts the notepaper to his nose and sniffs. There's no doubt: it has the same musty bird smell as Kellett-Brown's clothing and budgerigar-infested flat. Charles reads it again, laughs, and throws it in the bin.

PART TWO: 1962

CHAPTER EIGHT

The rain stops almost as suddenly as it starts and the black clouds scud off towards the east, underlit by horizontal orange shafts of the setting sun.

'Look at that,' says Charles, nodding through the windscreen. 'Amazing. If you painted those colours, people would think you were making it up.'

Again, no reply. Henrietta hasn't spoken since they got into the car an hour earlier and she continues to stare, unseeing, out of the passenger window. Charles turns on the radio. Without a word Henrietta turns it off.

'Don't you like Cilla Black? You were humming that yesterday.'

Henrietta turns her head slowly and stares at Charles's profile. 'The music's fine, Charles,' she says, after a pause. 'I'm just not pretending anymore. Our situation isn't normal; we're not singing pop songs; we're not enjoying the sunset on the way to a party; we're not pretending there's nothing wrong.'

'Why can't we make an effort? Draw a line under the last few days, maybe have a nice evening?'

'I'm too angry.'

'Can't you put it aside for a few hours?'

'No. I'm not like you, Charles. If I'm unhappy, I'm unhappy. I can't fence it off and pretend otherwise.'

They remain silent for the rest of the journey. When they arrive in the Temple, Henrietta is out of the car before the engine stops, clip-clopping in her high-heeled boots across the cobblestones. Charles's eyes follow her lovely backside up the wooden staircase stairs, and he sighs. Yet again, he wonders what's happened to them. There was a time, until maybe a year before, when despite Henrietta's disdain for him, the cold fury of their rows and the nights spent apart, he was able to locate in himself the deep tenderness he felt for her from the first. It takes a lot to make Charles really angry and, once roused, the storm soon passes. Half an hour of pottering in the garden, working on some papers or watching television, and the substance of the row no longer seems important, and all he wants is to ambush her with a hug and watch the corners of her mouth crease reluctantly into a smile. And then they'd have make-up sex which, if only for half an hour, would bring oblivion and stillness.

Now, for the most part, he feels empty and exhausted. Keeping the peace has become such hard work. Once or twice, he has allowed himself to be goaded into responding to her distance and the drip-drip-drip of her bitching and, with a glorious and dangerous freedom, he has let the brakes off. Then Henrietta weeps silently and he feels mortified, as if he's kicked a puppy. By now, however, the brake lever is useless in his hands, and their marriage is a runaway train rattling downhill at an increasingly terrifying speed towards inevitable wreck. Whatever he says or doesn't say, whatever he does or doesn't do — it makes no difference.

Charles hauls himself out of the car and follows Henrietta into Chambers towards the sound of animated talking and music. The door is just closing after Henrietta and for one moment he toys with the idea of simply turning on his heel and leaving. Henrietta would barely notice his absence, and an hour or two of walking along the Thames embankment at dusk appeals to him. But, as he hesitates, the door opens again and Sebastian Campbell-Smyth is looking at him.

'I did wonder for a moment if Henrietta had come on her own,' he says. 'Has she?'

Charles shakes his head sadly and steps inside. 'No, although you did catch me wondering if I could bunk off.'

Sebastian smiles grimly. 'Still no better?' The state of the Holbornes' marriage is an open secret in Chambers. Charles shakes his head. The other barrister leans forward confidentially. 'I did wonder about the wisdom of buying that flat.'

Charles shakes his head again. 'No, that's nothing to do with it. It's convenient, and Henrietta agreed it makes sense. It takes me exactly three minutes from here to Fetter Lane.'

'Sure. But what message does it send? Might she not think that you've given up?'

Charles nods sadly. 'I know. If truth be told, I needed … a redoubt. Somewhere to regroup.'

Sebastian puts a friendly arm round Charles's shoulder. He's about to say something else when someone drops the heavy brass knocker on the outside of the door and he resumes his reception duties.

Charles walks towards the party noise. To his right the double doors into Sir Geoffrey's room, the largest in Chambers, are wide open. The room has been cleared of office furniture and now contains two large tables laden with food and drink. In a corner are the unattended instruments of a jazz trio. Two waitresses circulate among the guests with champagne and *hors d'oeuvres*. Most of the members of Chambers are already there with their wives. The only female member, Gwyneth Price-Hopkins, nearly eight months pregnant, clinks champagne glasses with her husband and flicks cigarette ash onto an empty plate. The guest of honour,

Sir Geoffrey Duchenne, soon to be Mr Justice Duchenne, has still to arrive.

Charles scans the room for Henrietta but can't locate her. He wanders over to the makeshift bar and waits to be served. He finds Sally next to him.

'Hello,' he says, looking down at the diminutive clerk. 'You look lovely.'

'Thank you, sir,' she replies, blushing slightly at the compliment. She wears a strapless, and almost backless, cocktail dress in crimson. Her hair is now much shorter and Charles finds the contrast between her full figure and tomboy haircut enticing. He waits for his drink to be poured, wondering idly how the strapless dress holds itself up, and that thought leads easily to another: what would she look like without it?

'Pardon?' he asks.

'I said, is Mrs Holborne here?'

'Yes ... somewhere.'

He glances over his shoulder and sees Henrietta in the far corner, engrossed in conversation with Laurence Corbett. Their heads are close together, as if sharing some confidence, and they both laugh. *She hasn't laughed like that with me for months*, thinks Charles bitterly, noting, but unable to suppress, his self-pity. As Charles watches, Henrietta pats Corbett on the cheek. The gesture is both affectionate and patronising, as if teasing a child who's said something daft but endearing, and Corbett flushes. Then, as if suddenly aware of being observed, Henrietta turns and catches Charles's eye. Her mouth hardens and the smile dies on her face. Charles wonders for a moment if the scene was staged for his benefit. At a dinner party earlier in the summer, Henrietta flirted outrageously with another of the guests and became progressively more drunk and furious as

Charles ignored it. That evening prompted an entire week of silence.

Corbett moves off, casting a glance in Charles's direction. Charles turns away, anxious to find something to distract him. He wanders through the guests, greeting and chatting to a few solicitors he knows. The music starts and a few of the younger members of Chambers begin to dance. Charles sits alone. After a while, his eye is caught by the tall and handsome Simon Ellison as he approaches Peter Finch, one of the senior members of Chambers. They share a brief whispered conversation, Finch nods, and the two men slip outside. More plotting, thinks Charles; the Bar will never change.

He wonders where Sally has got to, but can't see her anywhere. He reaches up to grab another drink from a passing tray and remains seated. Henrietta disappeared some time ago. He's not sure whether she's gone home or is just in one of the other rooms, but he doesn't care enough to go looking for her. He realises that he's beginning to feel drunk and decides that he's had enough.

He stands, drains his glass and makes for the door, slipping behind the substantial bulk of his head of chambers. Sir Geoffrey arrived an hour late, having been celebrating his elevation with some of the Benchers, and made an impromptu and largely unintelligible speech before drinking several more glasses of champagne. So far, Charles has managed to avoid him. Geoffrey Duchenne's bonhomie is all he needs to give the evening the *coup de grace*, but as that very thought enters Charles's head, a heavy hand lands on his shoulder.

'Ah, Charles!' booms Duchenne, 'I shall miss you, you and your tacky little clients.'

'Will you, Geoffrey?'

Duchenne's ruddy face is redder than usual and his eyes sparkle. He is now unequivocally drunk. 'I certainly shall. You know, I was against your coming in. But you came, and I don't mind admitting it: I was wrong.' Duchenne's hand, still on Charles's shoulder, grips with every other word as if to add emphasis or punctuation to his confession. 'Thoroughly nice chap ... and I can tell, you know, you're going places. I admire someone who doesn't let his background hold him back.'

'Thank you, Geoffrey,' says Charles, trying in vain to extricate himself. 'That will always be a great comfort to me.'

'You know, there's this Indian chappie. Bought the corner shop near me a few years back.' He frowns, trying to concentrate. 'Worked every hour God sent. Dammit if he doesn't own the whole bloody block now! Huge supermarket!'

'It's amazing, isn't it? Sorry Geoffrey, but I really ought to find Henrietta.' Charles wrenches himself out of the other's grip.

'Certainly, old chap. You really must bring her round some time soon. Ages since we saw you socially.'

'Never.'

'What?'

'We've never seen you socially, Geoffrey.'

'Oh, of course, no one's been to the new house, only been there a few months —'

'Not to the new house, nor the old house, nor any bloody house! For all I know, you live above your mate's supermarket.'

'You know, I could have sworn...'

Charles walks off. He opens the door, letting it slam behind him, and descends to the courtyard. The clouds have cleared completely and the sky is alight with stars. He pauses. He can't see the car and, for a second, can't remember where he left it. Then he realises: the parking space is empty.

'Oh, Henrietta!' he moans softly to the night air.

Charles looks into the corner of the cobbled courtyard to another vehicle, a battered orange sports car with cobwebs bridging the gap between the wing mirrors and the door, and peers at his watch. He doesn't fancy trying to start the damp and draughty sports car and driving all the way to Buckinghamshire. So, options? If he's lucky with a cab he might just make the last train, but it'll be tight, and what's the point? By the time he arrives home, Henrietta will be asleep or, worse, still up and so drunk they'd be bound to have another row. Resigned to another night on his own, Charles pulls his collar up and sets off on foot for Fetter Lane.

Laurence Corbett watches Charles's dejected back as he sets off up Middle Temple Lane. He sits with his feet on the desk in a panelled room on the opposite side of Chambers to the party. The lights are off. The door opens, allowing a gale of music and noise to enter briefly and Peter Finch enters, followed by Simon Ellison. Finch reaches for the light switch.

'Leave it off, there's a good chap,' comes Corbett's voice from the desk.

Finch starts as he realises that his desk is occupied. Corbett slouches in Finch's chair at an angle, smoke curling lazily from a cigarette between his index and middle fingers.

'Get your bloody feet off my papers!' protests Finch.

'Certainly Peter,' replies Corbett, but he doesn't move. After a few seconds he languorously folds his long legs like a crane fly and stands.

'Well? I was *summoned*,' says Finch sarcastically, 'so what do you want, Corbett?'

Finch is in his early sixties, and sports a long grey combover, partially concealing a bald patch. When it's windy the thin mat of hair sometimes falls forward over his face like a silver curtain, much to the merriment of his pupil. He has watery grey eyes, and he seems to blink more frequently than is normal.

Corbett perches on the edge of the older barrister's desk, making it difficult for Finch to reach his seat. Finch casts an eye over his shoulder. Ellison leans nonchalantly against the door, lighting a cigarette and though he is not quite blocking Finch's escape, Finch still feels trapped, and stands awkwardly in the middle of the room.

'A few of the chaps and I have been chatting about the succession,' explains Corbett, 'now that Geoffrey is moving up. I've been asked to canvass your views.'

'My views aren't important,' replies Finch irritably. 'We all know who's going to be head of Chambers.'

'That's not a safe assumption,' comments Ellison from behind him.

Finch turns. 'What do you mean?'

Corbett answers. 'Well … we wondered if *you* would like to stand?'

'Me?' says Finch, genuinely astonished. 'I have no ambitions in that direction.'

'Liar,' replies Corbett quietly, without malice.

'We're not all as ambitious as you, Corbett. And I couldn't afford the rent. The Inn wouldn't have me.'

'They might, if a number of us stood as joint guarantors.'

Finch considers this. 'You're saying that if I were to stand against Bob for the tenancy from the Inn, you and some others would support my application? Which others?'

'Enough.'

'No. I need to know exactly who. A contest would be divisive, and ... well, I may have had my differences with Bob over the years, but I'm not going to be responsible for splitting Chambers.'

'I can't tell you at the moment. Just believe me.'

Finch pauses. 'What would you want from me in return?' he asks shrewdly.

Corbett smiles in the darkness. 'Move Holborne on.'

Finch utters a half-laugh. 'What *have* you got against that poor man?'

'Do *you* like his child molesters sitting in the waiting room? How do your banker clients enjoy sitting next to unshaven derelicts, smoking roll-ups and stinking of cider?'

'Granted —'

'And have you noticed how long Stanley's out every afternoon checking the criminal lists? At the busiest time of the day? A hugely disproportionate time is given to one man's practice, at the expense of everyone else's. How many times do I have to say it? We're not set up to do crime here. He'd be far better off somewhere else.'

Finch listens patiently, a small smile on his face. 'All very good reasons, no doubt, but we all know the truth: you just can't stand him.'

'Well, can you? He's a common barrow boy, like most of his clients. And a Jew. But that's really not the point. There are plenty of perfectly valid grounds for sacking him if one needs them. The tenant of the Inn can give notice to any barrister in Chambers. Like everyone else, he'd be one of your licensees.'

'He'll appeal to the Inn. I would. He's done nothing to merit sacking. He pays his rent on time, which is more than many do, and he's never been caught with his hand in the till, or his trousers down.'

Ellison interjects from the other side of the room. 'Not yet maybe, but have you seen the way he looks at Sally?'

'This is all academic,' says Corbett. 'This isn't a *sacking*, but a case of Chambers specialising in civil work. Anyone wanting to continue doing crime has to find a more suitable home. It's the way the Bar's going. It's what they did at KBW and no one so much as turned a hair. Give him six months to find somewhere else, and he can't possibly complain.'

The door suddenly opens and Ellison finds himself propelled further into the room. A couple of the junior members of Chambers enter. 'Oh, sorry,' the first apologises, giggling.

'That's all right,' says Corbett. 'Why don't you both stay?'

'Have you...?' enquires the other, indicating Finch.

'Just doing it,' replies Corbett. 'Well?' he asks, returning to Finch. The door closes silently, and the two young men line up on the wall next to Ellison.

'There wouldn't be enough support. Bob's very popular. You'd need at least twelve to vote against him, and I can't see...' His voice falters as Corbett raises a hand.

'We have fourteen.'

'I don't believe it.'

Finch looks towards the others and receives nodded confirmation. He wavers. His pale eyes water at the prospect, but he nonetheless shakes his head. Corbett takes several steps towards him, leaning over the shorter man menacingly.

'Why don't you face facts, Peter? Your practice is going nowhere.' Finch splutters a half-protest but Corbett holds up a finger to silence him. 'I've looked in the diary: you've only had two decent court appearances in the last six weeks, and your desk's almost empty. Don't tell me you're doing paperwork, because I know you aren't. You're, what, sixty-two, sixty-three? Your practice is winding down and you know it. If you're going to keep the twins at university for the next two years, you need to get on the Bench. And the cachet of being head of Chambers ... well, that would certainly help, wouldn't it? Principles are fine, but not enough to support kids at university. You're going to be our next head of Chambers, in a purely civil set, and Holborne will be out. Congratulations.'

CHAPTER NINE

'Charles?' calls a voice across Essex Court. 'What on earth are you doing with that old jalopy?'

Charles withdraws his pounding head from under the rusty bonnet with some effort and squints into the bright morning sunshine. It's the morning after the party. Back at the flat on Fetter Lane he'd opened a bottle of Scotch, intending just to have a nightcap, but he'd put on the TV for company and by 2 a.m., and the end of a film he'd seen several times before, he'd finished half the bottle. It then seemed like a good plan to phone Henrietta at home to make sure she got in safely. There was no answer. With impeccable drunken logic, Charles concluded not that Henrietta was asleep, but that she was deliberately not answering his calls, so he continued ringing every ten minutes until, at last, he fell asleep in the armchair. Having failed to close the curtains he woke at daybreak and managed to stumble to the bed for another hour's fitful dozing. Now he is awash with coffee and aspirin, feeling awful.

The voice is that of Simon Ellison. He's on the far side of the courtyard, a large bundle of papers tied with ribbon under his arm.

'Oh, hello, Simon,' replies Charles. 'Frankly, I begin to wonder. It's been sitting here for a few weeks and now I can't get the bloody thing to start.'

Ellison saunters over. 'Yes, I spotted it last week,' he says, arriving at Charles's side, 'and wondered whose it was. I didn't know you tinkered with cars. They take a bit of looking after, these Austin Healeys. And it doesn't look as though this one's had much love and attention.'

'I know, I know,' confesses Charles. 'It was a bit of an impulse buy. You know, a run-around for when I'm in town? The Inn said I could leave it here for a while till I organised permanent parking.'

'Here, let me have a look.'

'Do you know anything about these things?' asks Charles hopefully.

'Well, not about Sprites in particular, but a bit about cars,' answers Ellison. He leans into the car, drops his papers onto the leather passenger seat and returns to look under the bonnet. 'Have fun last night?' he asks.

'Not much. Henrietta took the Jag and stranded me.'

'You poor sod,' replies Ellison sympathetically. ''Fraid I've no advice to offer there, old chap.'

'You and Jenny seem very happy. How do you manage it?'

'No idea. Probably just good luck. Let's have a look at this…'

Charles watches as Ellison inspects the rusting metal to which the distributor is fixed. Ellison grunts with effort and finally shifts the distributor cap. He emerges from under the bonnet and holds it up to Charles.

'I'm not surprised she won't start. This thing hasn't been serviced in years. The points are worn so badly they're almost useless. Look.' He shows them to Charles.

'Now I know why it was such a bargain.'

'If you want my advice, get yourself a nice new Mini. I'm not sure you're the sort of chap to be driving a neglected sports car.'

'Here, use this,' says Charles, handing Ellison a screwdriver. 'You'll never turn it with your fingernail.'

Ellison fiddles with the points for a minute. 'There,' he says, 'let's try again. It may not get you as far as Buckinghamshire, though.'

'I've only got to get it to the flat for the moment. 150 yards.'

'I heard about your little London pad. Very convenient,' says Ellison, nudging Charles in the ribs.

'Nothing like that,' replies Charles with a tired laugh. 'It's just for those nights when I finish too late to get back. Or can't get home for any reason. If I work till ten or later there's no point waiting half an hour for a train just to get home by midnight, by which time Henrietta's already asleep, just to get up again at six.'

'Why move out so far then?'

'*Force majeure.* Henrietta wanted to be nearer her pals, and her parents.'

'You're near Thame, aren't you? I ride near there quite often.'

'You must pop in some time, then. We'd like to see you and Jenny.'

'Just give us a date, tell us how to get there, and we'll come.'

Ellison replaces the points in the distributor and, without closing the cap, sits in the car to turn the engine over. Charles watches the distributor as he does so.

'It's opening,' calls Charles. 'Let's try starting her.'

Ellison gets out again and joins Charles at the front of the car.

'Been busy?' asks Charles.

'No. Far too quiet in fact. Keep it under your hat, but I may be leaving Chambers soon. I've applied for an appointment.'

'What, you too?'

'Yup.'

'Well, best of luck, your Honour.'

'I'm not counting my chickens, but it's looking promising. I got great support from McDowell J.'

'How long before you know?'

'Shortly. Right,' concludes Ellison, 'do you want to get in and turn over the engine?'

Charles climbs in and turns the key. The engine coughs into life. He revs a few times and leans out, the engine ragged, but running.

'Well done!' he shouts. 'I owe you a pint! I'll be off, before she stalls again,' he says, and closes the door. He hands Ellison his papers through the open window and moves off.

Five minutes later Charles drops the car keys on the shelf in the hall of his tiny apartment, reaches immediately for the telephone and dials.

'Hello?'

'Henrietta? It's me.'

'Yes, Charles.'

Charles pauses to see if she mentions her premature departure from the party. She doesn't.

'I'm just calling to see how you are.'

'That's very thoughtful of you, dear. I'm very well, thank you. Are you still in London? I half expected you to call from the station last night.'

'No. I … I had hoped we might spend the day together, here.'

'No, sorry, Charles, but I have plans. I'm not coming back to town.'

Charles peers down at the sparse traffic on Fetter Lane. The city is wonderfully quiet at weekends and he's disappointed. Before the events of the night before, he'd planned everything: a lazy morning in bed with coffee and newspapers; Brick Lane for fresh bagels; the National Portrait Gallery and, if the weather was good enough, a walk by the river and a romantic meal at a new restaurant in Soho.

'I did mention spending the day in London,' he reminds her gently.

'You did mention it, yes. But I didn't agree.'

'But if you didn't want to do it, why didn't you say? We could've done something else.'

Charles hears her sigh. 'I just didn't want another fight,' she says.

'Fine. So there's no point my coming back to Thame, as you won't be there anyway.'

'Well, on and off, but basically, no. I've a tennis match this morning, and I said I'd pop in to see Mummy afterwards. You go and do whatever it is you wanted to do, and I'll see you Monday night. Call and tell me which train you're on if you want collecting from the station.'

'If that's what you want.'

'And, by the way, I've been meaning to tell you: I'll be away next weekend. I've been invited to Shropshire.'

'With whom?'

'With friends, Charles. I have some, you know? I'm not cross-examining you about your plans for this weekend, am I?'

'How's that the same?' demands Charles, his voice rising in frustration. 'I want us to spend the weekend *together*, so why on earth would you cross-examine me about it? You, on the other hand, are proposing to go away on your own — or at least without me — and you won't tell me with whom.' He hears, and hates, the whine in his own voice.

'Please don't shout, Charles. I'm enjoying a tranquil Sunday morning, and I don't want any of that.'

Charles draws a deep breath, willing himself to remain calm. There's silence from the other end of the line. 'Are you still there, Henrietta?'

115

'I'm here.'

'Do you have nothing else to say?'

'Not really, no. If there's nothing else —'

'Oh, Etta —'

'Bye Charles.'

The line goes dead.

Charles replaces the receiver. He stares out of the window for a while and then looks round at the papers on the small dining table, a two-day fraud listed for the following week. He makes a decision, picks up his jacket and keys again, and leaves the flat.

The day is fresh and sparkling and a warm breeze off the river speaks of summer around the corner but, as Charles walks along Lower Thames Street towards the Tower of London, he is lost in contemplation and barely aware of his surroundings. For the first time he wonders if his marriage is unsalvageable. The thought appals him. There has never been a divorce in the Horowitz family; indeed, Charles can think of no Jewish family among his parents' circle which had ever suffered the shame of a divorce. He imagines his parents' reaction were they ever to hear that he and Henrietta had parted. Well, that'd certainly end any prospect of a family reconciliation, he thinks grimly; after all the pain their union had caused, he didn't think he could tolerate a lifetime of "I told you so"s.

He pauses at the railings in front of the Tower and watches for a few moments as a squabbling unkindness of ravens hops about the battlements. He is asked to take a photograph of an American tourist family and obliges distractedly before walking on towards Whitechapel.

Blooms, the kosher restaurant at Aldgate, is doing brisk trade. A group of black-hatted Hasidic men emerge onto the pavement as Charles passes, talking volubly in Yiddish and gesticulating, reminding Charles of the ravens, and he smiles sadly to himself. Blooms, an East End institution, used to be a special Sunday morning treat for the Horowitz family. Millie and Harry took the boys, usually with another family or two from their synagogue, and they'd push together three tables at the rear of the restaurant. The rudeness of the harassed waiters and the size of the enormous portions were legendary, and the group would dally for up to three hours over chicken soup ("with everything"), cholent or Vienna sausages and chips for the children, lokshen pudding and tall glasses of sweet lemon tea. No one cared if the group of children at the far end of the table made a noise or got in the way of the waiters. It was often dusk by the time they emerged, their throats sore from cigar smoke and shouting over the din.

Charles resists the impulse to go in and assuage his woes with nostalgia food. Instead, he continues past Aldgate East station and turns north up Osborn Street into Brick Lane. For a century this was the hub of East End Jewish life, as successive waves of immigrants arrived from the Levant and North Africa, Russia and Eastern Europe, but over the last couple of years Charles has noticed an increasing number of Pakistanis moving into the area, initially single men but now, three or four years later, entire families. The first curry house opened recently and both the clothing of the people on the street and the produce in the shop windows are now more multi-coloured and varied. Intriguing cooking smells assail Charles as he walks north and he is suddenly hungry. He quickens his pace.

Halfway up Brick Lane he enters a kosher bakery and joins the queue. The place, famous throughout London, serves fresh-baked bread and bagels twenty-four hours a day, seven days a week, to an ever-changing population that includes local residents, builders, taxi drivers, nurses and policemen coming off duty, students and, late at night, opera-loving refugees from Covent Garden in top hats and tails.

Charles orders two plain bagels and is about to leave the shop when someone speaks.

'Excuse me?'

Charles turns to see a slender dark-haired woman in her late twenties with pale skin and very large almond-shaped eyes. She carries a grey duffel coat over her left arm, a plastic cup of coffee in her left hand and a large bag of fresh bread clutched in the crook of her right arm. She wears a slightly embarrassed smile.

'Yes?' answers Charles.

The woman's smile broadens and she nods. 'Charlie Horowitz. I'll be dammed. I thought it was you. And you don't recognise me, do you?'

Charles frowns and studies her face more closely. It's a pretty face, and there is indeed something familiar about her wide mouth and her large eyes, but Charles cannot place her.

'I forgive you,' she says. 'I expect I've changed in the last sixteen years. I was eleven when we last met. You were eighteen, and just off to join the RAF.'

'I'm really sorry, but I can't remember...'

'Rachel,' she says, managing to extricate her right hand and offer it to Charles. 'Rachel Golding.'

Charles searches his memory. A very faint bell of recognition rings about the name — friends of his parents? — but not about its owner. She's very striking and he thinks he'd have remembered her had they met before.

'We went to the same school, and *chaider*,' she explains, referring to Jewish Sunday school.

'I'm sorry, Rachel, I remember the name but … how on earth did you recognise me after all this time?'

'Perhaps it's something to do with the dreadful crush I had on you,' she says with disarming candour. 'To you,' she continues, 'I was a plump little girl, if you noticed me at all, which you obviously didn't. But *you* were the success of the school — flying ace, and then Cambridge, yes? — and then a barrister. Everyone was very proud of you. And our parents still meet at *shul* so your name comes up every now and then. "Holborne" now, is that right?'

Charles smiles apologetically. 'It is.' They leave the shop together. 'Which way are you…?' asks Charles.

Rachel looks at her watch. 'I've only got another fifteen minutes. So, back towards Whitechapel. You?'

'I'm just wandering. Mind if I walk with you?'

'That'd be nice.'

They set off southwards, back the way Charles came. 'Only fifteen minutes?' asks Charles. 'Do you have an appointment?' He hopes not; Rachel intrigues him.

'I have to get back to work. This is my lunch hour.'

The bag of bread in Rachel's hand tips over suddenly but Charles catches it as it falls.

'Thank you! It'd be a lot easier if I put this on —' she indicates the coat on her other arm — 'but I didn't expect it to be this warm.'

119

'That's fine. I'll carry it. So, what do you do?'

'Well, I'm working in the Whitechapel Gallery for the moment.'

'Oh, I read about that,' replies Charles. 'Haven't you got that bloke…?'

'David Hockney? Yes, the exhibition opened last week. You should come.'

'Only if you explain it to me. What do they say? I don't know anything about art, but I know what I like. But I'm not even sure I know what I like.'

'You're asking the wrong girl, Charlie. I doubt I know more than you. It's not my day job. I'm just filling in for a friend.'

'Oh, OK. What is the day job?'

'I dance. Well, I danced. I went to the Royal Ballet School.'

Charles hears deep disappointment in her voice. 'But?'

'I was the corps at London Festival Ballet.'

'And…' prompts Charles.

'Sorry, I assume everyone knows. Well, basically, they're going bust, so most of us are out of a job. A friend offered me some hours at the gallery, but it's only part-time, and only temporary. Unless something comes up soon, I'll be back at my mum and dad's. I don't have next month's rent.'

They walk in silence for a while, Rachel taking careful sips of her coffee every few steps. 'Anyway,' she says, forcing a smile, 'now I have before me the famous Charles Holborne, DFC, Barrister at Law: so how are you? Rich? Famous? Happy? Rich? Did I mention rich?'

Charles laughs. 'You remind me of a joke my dad used to tell, about a Jewish tailor knocked down crossing the road. A policeman runs over and puts a jacket under his head and asks him "Are you comfortable?" The tailor replies: "Well… I make a living.'" Rachel laughs. 'And, well,' he shrugs, 'I make a living.'

'I like your dad,' comments Rachel.

Charles nods. 'Yes, most people do.'

They turn left onto the main road. 'But not you?'

'It's ... complicated.'

Rachel stops. 'I heard. In fact my parents went to the *shiva*. I'm so sorry, Charlie. That must have been really hard.'

Charles looks down at her thin, almost waif-like face and her enormous brown eyes full of concern. He's about to make a glib comment, but as he inhales to speak he feels a sob catch in his throat. 'God, sorry, I really...' he says, confused and embarrassed, 'that took me by surprise. It's been a difficult few weeks. Few months actually.'

Rachel puts a sympathetic hand on Charles's arm. 'I noted you didn't say anything about happy.'

'No. Maybe that's it. Things are ... like I said, difficult. At home.'

'I'm so sorry. Look ... I know this is a terrible way to leave things, but I've got to go.' She points and Charles realises they've arrived outside the gallery.

'No, of course...'

'I feel so rude. I haven't seen you in half a lifetime and I've managed to make you cry!'

'I'm not crying,' answers Charles, flushing.

'Now you're embarrassed too and I feel really terrible! Look ... I know this is going to sound very forward but I'd really like to carry on talking — only if you want to...?'

She darts over to a rubbish bin, throws her coffee cup in it, and returns to Charles's side. She reaches into her duffel coat pocket and pulls out a pen. 'I haven't got any paper...'

Charles puts out a hand. 'I'd like to. Put your number there.'

Rachel stares hard at Charles's face, takes his hand and scribbles a telephone number on his palm.

'I'll never wash again.'

'Then don't bother calling. On the other hand, if you *do* wash again you have my permission to call,' she said. 'If you'd like to.'

Charles returns her steady gaze. 'I would like to.'

'Good.'

Rachel grabs the bag of bread out of Charles's arm, waves, skips across the pavement and pushes open the door to the gallery. Charles turns to leave but feels a hand on his arm. Rachel spins him round and plants a kiss on his cheek. This time she blushes.

'Waited sixteen years to do that,' she confesses. 'Bye.'

CHAPTER TEN

The "Mafia", otherwise known as The Barristers' Clerks Association, doesn't need many formal meetings. There are several watering holes in and around the Temple where most nights (and quite a few lunchtimes) groups of criminal clerks congregate to share gossip, discuss lists and list officers and report on the rising young stars, the grand old men and the fading lights of the Bar. The "Guvnors". The operation of this bush telegraph is informal and extremely effective. Most clerks know long before any official announcement who is about to "be made up" — become a Judge — and who is having an affair with whom.

The term "Mafia" is not altogether inappropriate either. Barristers' clerks are powerful enough to dictate the course of the careers of their guvnors. Everyone knows at least one story in which the clerk ruins the practice of a good barrister on the grounds of offence taken at a chambers party, a perceived slight to the clerk's wife or simply a personality clash.

One of the most popular watering holes is the "City Squash and Tennis Club". Stanley has never played squash in his life and last held a tennis racket at the age of fifteen but then, despite its name, strenuous sports do not figure large in the Club's activities. Its principal attraction, at least as far as Stanley is concerned, is its selection of twenty-five whiskies.

On this particular evening, Stanley only popped into the Club for a quick one before catching his train home. Rita, his beloved, has extricated a promise from him that he will, finally, repaint the bathroom, and woe betide him if he returns late. He chats for a few minutes to a number of clerks he knows quite well, and downs the rest of his drink. As he's about to leave, he recognises a familiar face. Peter McPhee clerks a set of common law chambers in Essex Court. He and Stanley are old mates, having come into the Temple as juniors together thirty years before. McPhee waves at Stanley as he bustles up to the bar.

'Have another, Stan,' he suggests, somewhat out of breath. 'I've some interesting gossip.'

Stanley regards his watch. 'I can't stay, Peter. I've got to get the six-fifty.'

McPhee leans over and looks at Stanley's watch. 'Plenty of time,' he concludes. 'This won't take long. It involves one of your ex-guvnors,' he adds tantalisingly.

Stanley is hooked. 'OK,' he concedes. 'Just a single. Highland Park.'

Peter obtains the drinks and the two men move away from the bar to a side table.

McPhee lights a cigarette, exhales a lungful of smoke, and leans forward confidentially. 'I've just bumped into your favourite barrister,' he says. His words are almost lost in the chatter of the drinkers and the click of snooker balls from the tables behind them. Stanley looks puzzled.

'Ivor Kellett-Brown,' announces McPhee with a flourish.

'My God, I thought he was dead. Wasn't he dossing in Temple Gardens?'

'He was. I saw him myself only ... what? Eighteen months back? He was evicted by the Inn when he couldn't pay his rent. Nutty as a fruitcake, always talking to himself, shouting at thin air, you know. One of my juniors once saw him addressing one of the statues on the Embankment as "My Lord".'

Stanley grins and takes another a sip of whisky. He looks again at his watch.

'Anyway,' continues McPhee, 'the point is, he's come into some money. Quite a lot of money from what I could tell. He's driving a brand-new MG Princess — almost ran me over actually — and dressed up like Fred Astaire, tails, spats and all.'

'Good heavens,' replies Stanley. 'You sure it was him?'

'I spoke to him. He was parking in the Temple and I had to jump out the way. When he got out, I recognised him and said hello. He remembered I was your mate and asked how you were.'

'Is he back in practice?' enquires Stanley, suddenly fearful that Kellett-Brown might reapply to Chambers. 'I thought he'd packed up originally because of poor health.'

'That's what I'd heard, but he reckons he was never ill at all. I tell you, Stan,' and here McPhee leans over even further and drops his voice almost to a whisper, 'he's barmy. He said, straight out, that he was being blackmailed.' McPhee leans back in satisfaction, his punchline delivered.

'Blackmailed? Who by? And for what?'

McPhee shrugs and throws back his drink. 'He said it was someone in your chambers, and that they had a nasty shock coming to them. He was ranting on and on; it was like lighting a firework. I'd just asked if he was recovered enough to go back into practice, and he was off like a greyhound,' says McPhee excitedly, mixing his metaphors. '"There was never anything wrong with me!" he stormed. "I was forced out by that blackguard!"'

'"Blackguard?" Who says "blackguard" these days?'

'Ivor Kellett-Brown does. And he was shouting, weird stuff, like "Retribution shall be mine!" I was reminded of me old vicar. He had the same wicked look in his eyes, too. Then, without another word, he storms off, still ranting to himself.'

125

'And you've no idea who was supposed to have been behind all this?'

'Well, there's the thing. How many "Jew-boys" have you got in Chambers?'

Stanley stares at his colleague, mouth open. 'Holborne?'

McPhee shrugs, hands outstretched and open in a passable imitation of Fagin.

'That's enough of that, Peter,' says Stanley, sternly. 'Even in jest.'

'No, you're right. Sorry. I'm not, you know, anti-Semitic. And from what I hear, your Mr Holborne's a decent bloke.'

'He is, Peter. Which is what makes this so odd. I'd never have him down as a blackmailer. And what on earth could he possibly be blackmailing old K-B about?'

'No idea,' replies McPhee. 'I 'spect it's all in his head. Anyway, I thought you'd like to know. Gotta run.' McPhee replaces his glass on the counter and pats his friend on the back. 'See you,' he says, and he disappears into the crowd.

Stanley remains where he is for a moment, idly examining his empty glass. Then he remembers the time, picks up his briefcase and runs for the door.

A tall man with a hat pulled low over his eyes watches Stanley's departing back from a nearby table. He also knocks back the last of his drink, picks up a robes bag and slips out of the bar.

Henrietta weaves her way unsteadily through the hubbub and the guests to the far side of the room, oblivious to the contents of her champagne glass slopping over the edge and down her forearm. Her face is flushed and her eyes sparkle. She wears her hair up, accentuating her lovely neck and shoulders, but a few strands have escaped and fallen over her eyes. She reaches her destination but stops suddenly, unable to see the person she's been seeking. She frowns and squints around, sweeping her wayward hair back over her forehead with an impatient gesture of her free hand. She eyes a group of men standing in a tight circle to her left. Most of the male guests are in dinner suits and are difficult to distinguish from the rear, particularly to someone who's drunk almost two bottles of champagne. Henrietta appears to recognise a member of the group and turns rather unsteadily towards him. She giggles to herself. She creeps up behind a tall man with a broad back and fair hair, slips her hand up the back of his jacket and pinches his bottom.

The man whirls round, jogging Henrietta's arm in the process and causing her to lose the final drops of liquid in her glass.

'Henrietta!' he hisses severely, but with a smile on his lean face. 'Behave yourself!'

She shrugs and laughs. 'I want to dance,' she pouts, taking hold of his arm and tugging at him. 'Oh, come on, Laurence, you've been talking for ages.'

Henrietta beams an unfocused smile round the group of men she has interrupted. One or two of them smile back politely.

'For heaven's sake,' replies Laurence Corbett, turning away from the group slightly, 'can't you be even a little discreet?'

'No one minds,' she protests. 'Why do you think Polly invited us both?'

Corbett lowers his head to speak confidentially. 'That's no reason to make a spectacle of yourself! Some people here know Marjorie,' he hisses. 'We've still got to be careful.'

She's not listening. She watches his lips as he speaks, noting his even, white teeth, and the pinkness of his tongue, and is reminded of what they'd been doing to her nipples a few hours before while they changed for the party.

She leans towards him and whispers wetly in his ear. 'Take me upstairs and fuck me,' she says, just loudly enough to be heard by everyone in the group. One or two smirk; others pretend not to have heard.

'For God's sake, Henrietta, stop acting like a whore!' This time Corbett makes no attempt to keep his voice low and a number of people outside of the immediate group turn and stare. 'Just go away, and please: stop drinking!'

Corbett turns his back on her and resumes talking. Henrietta looks peeved for a moment, but then shrugs. She walks away, an aisle of silence opening for her.

'You're boring, Corbett, just boring,' she announces, with that curious distinctness that often characterises the speech of habitual drunks. 'Would someone *please* tell me where I can get a drink?' she asks plaintively as she makes her exit.

Simon Ellison moves from the far side of the room where he was talking to his wife, and joins the group of men.

'Hello, Simon,' says Corbett amiably. 'Do you know everyone?'

'Yes, I think so. Sorry, gents, but could I borrow Laurence for a moment?'

Ellison moves off and Corbett follows. They reach a quiet corner by the French windows.

'Chambers business?' enquires Corbett.

'In a manner of speaking,' replies Ellison. 'Look, Laurence, I know it's none of my business, but don't you think you should ditch Henrietta Holborne? She's pretty much out of control, and it's only a matter of time before she spills the beans to Charles.'

Corbett smiles. 'That's half the fun.'

'My God, you *really* hate him. But then … you don't actually care for her either, do you?'

'Not much. She's a bit of a shrew to be honest, 'specially when she's had a few. But my God, Simon, she's hot stuff in the sack.' He pauses. 'As I think you know,' he adds meaningfully.

Ellison's eyes narrow dangerously. 'Just exactly what do you mean by that?'

Corbett raises his eyebrows insouciantly. 'Sorry, Simon. Perhaps you misunderstood me. I thought Henrietta's reputation was well known.'

Ellison continues to glare at Corbett, although no longer sure he understood the other's meaning. His face relaxes slowly. 'The point I'm making,' he continues, 'is she's a loose cannon. You may not care if she tells Charles, but it won't stop there, will it? Your Marjorie's bound to hear of it. And she won't forgive you like she did with that nanny…'

'Gretchen,' says Corbett with a wide grin.

'Yes, Gretchen. She was a bit of fun; over for a few months and now safe back in Sweden.'

'Switzerland.'

'Wherever. But Henrietta Holborne's a different kettle of fish altogether. Like I said, none of my business, but wouldn't life be simpler if you just found yourself another nanny?'

'You're quite right, Simon, it *is* none of your business,' Corbett says with cold intensity. His tone softens. 'Look, I realise you're just trying to be a pal but, honestly, there's nothing to worry about. Now,' he continues, looking about the room, 'where's that lovely hostess of ours? Ah, there she is. Excuse me, but I'm owed a dance or two.'

Simon Ellison's brow furrows in thought as he watches his colleague's back threading its way through the guests.

Henrietta wraps her fur more tightly round her and paces slowly around the car again. The country road is pitch dark and little used. She waited in the car for twenty-five minutes listening to music on the radio but then her legs began to get stiff, so she got out and has since been standing outside. Shortly after her "thing" with Laurence Corbett started — she can't call it an "affair" as that implies romance, and while this might be dangerous and sexy, it's anything but romantic — she began to realise that the greatest part of it was not, as she'd expected, snatched hours of passion. It was waiting; waiting for him to call, waiting in hotels and waiting in restaurants. All too often he'd not turn up at all. Now she's waiting in a layby where they agreed to meet on the way back.

This is the first time she and Laurence have ever spent an entire weekend together, and it's been a complete disaster. She looked forward to it for weeks: two whole days without looking over their shoulders, giving false names or pretending to be strangers; *days* of planning and lying to provide credible cover should Charles ask questions which, of course, he hadn't. He never does, and she finds it infuriating. She can't work out if his determination to look the other way is because he doesn't care or because he's too squeamish. He once told her that there'd never been a divorce in his family, so perhaps that was it; they all just looked the other way.

And, of course, Laurence was two hours late, by which time other guests were arriving, so they managed only a snatched half-hour before going downstairs. And then, on top of everything else, it turned out that Simon and Jenny Ellison had been invited too. Of course, Simon would never say anything, but Jenny was an unknown quantity and could easily say something inconvenient to Marjorie, Laurence's wife. So, after all the planning and sneaking, once she and Laurence joined the others they had to pretend they weren't a couple after all; at least until she'd drunk so much she no longer cared. And throughout she was aware of Simon's eyes burning into her back, which at first made her uncomfortable, then angry and, finally, reckless.

And then there was Laurence's excuse; he'd been held up on a case! The very same excuse Charles had given her hundreds of times over the years. She vowed to herself that the next time she committed adultery it'd be with a bus conductor; at least *his* sex life wouldn't be governed by the vagaries of the administration of justice.

So they'd rowed, and then made up, which was lovely, but the atmosphere had remained. She'd drunk too much and he'd been rude, although quite how rude she can't now recall. She remembers being very upset, but the precise events before she left the party are a bit fuzzy in her head. What she does remember quite clearly, however, is that Laurence and some other chap, an ex-member of Chambers she thought, were planning to do something horrid to Charles, and Laurence took great delight in gloating over it with a number of the people there. So she'd had enough. She packed and departed, telling Laurence she'd wait an hour for him and then go home, but it's now well over an hour later and for some reason, here she is, still waiting in a deserted layby.

Not for the first time, Henrietta wonders if it's all worth it. So much effort for so little return. *If I put half as much effort into pleasing Charles as I do Laurence*, she thinks, *I'd probably have a successful marriage*. The thought amuses her at first. Then she considers it seriously and is no longer amused. She returns to the car, miserable. 'I'll give you five more minutes, Laurence Corbett,' she says out loud.

She turns on the heater, but by now the engine has cooled completely and it blows freezing air onto her bare legs. She'd taken off her stocking and panties in preparation. Henrietta hates hotel rooms — seedy and unspontaneous — and experiences a particular excitement making love only feet from complete strangers as they race past, the black interior of the car suddenly ablaze as headlights sweep across her, straddling Corbett's thighs on the back seat.

On top of the prolonged wait and an emerging headache, the blast of cold air is the final straw.

'Fuck you, Corbett!' she cries, and turns the key. She revs the engine and is in the process of moving off when she sees headlights in her mirror. She waits for them to pass, and then realises they're slowing. Corbett pulls alongside, still on the carriageway, his engine idling. He winds down his window.

'I was just leaving,' says Henrietta.

'Sorry. I got held up. Your place or mine?' he asks with a grin, referring to their two cars.

'Neither. I'm cold and tired, and getting a hangover. So I'm going home.'

'Just hang on a sec,' he says, engaging gear to pull in in front of her.

'No, really, don't bother,' she insists, 'I want to go home.'

'Can't we even talk?'

'I don't want to talk to you, Laurence. We can speak later in the week. I want to have a think first.'

'What about?'

'Everything.'

'What are you talking about, Henrietta?'

'I don't know. I just want time to think. This is all so...' she searches for the right word, 'unsatisfactory. I mean ... I don't know. Maybe I need a break for a while, just to think things through.'

'What's there to think about?'

'Everything ... you, me, us, Charlie, Marjorie.'

'What have Charles and Marjorie got to do with it?'

'For heaven's sake, Laurence, we're married to them! What's more, Marjorie's my friend, my best friend, for that matter.'

'Look, let me pull in and talk to you sensibly. This is ridiculous,' he says, indicating their two cars standing side by side with their engines running. 'I feel like we're about to start a race.' He applies his most winning smile but she's not to be budged.

'No! Stay there!'

She suddenly realises that, above all, she does not want Laurence Corbett in her car. She knows what will happen. He will start whispering in her ear and stroking her neck; his other hand will travel up her thigh under her skirt; he'll nibble her earlobes; his index finger will start making little circular motions, and she'll be lost. In separate cars, with the cold night air on her face from the open window, she can be resolute. He regards her with suspicion, trying to decipher her expression in the darkness. Then his face hardens.

'Are you telling me it's over?' he demands.

'No,' she says uncertainly, 'at least ... I don't know. Maybe I am, but I haven't realised it yet.'

'Well, you can get that out of your head immediately,' says Corbett aggressively. 'You're not dumping me!'

Henrietta stares at him, astounded. 'What the hell do you mean by that?' she demands. 'If I don't want to see you again, I bloody well won't!'

'You're being completely unreasonable! Everything was fine this morning, and suddenly you spring this on me.'

'I've nothing more to say, Laurence,' she says, closing her window.

'Well, I've got something to say to you,' he says, getting out of his car, 'you gin-soaked, spoilt little —'

But Henrietta doesn't hear the rest. She lets out the clutch and her car shoots forward, narrowly missing him, and swerves into the road. She puts her foot down hard, and races off. She looks back in her mirror and can see him standing in the road, staring after her. She catches sight of her face, white and frightened.

CHAPTER ELEVEN

Charles sits at the kitchen table, reading the Sunday papers. The first arrests have been made in what is now being called the Great Train Robbery. Charles isn't surprised. He knows Detective Chief Superintendent Butler, the officer heading the London end of the investigation. Butler is a strange man, but Charles has enormous respect for his policing skills.

He drains his coffee cup and looks at his watch. Rachel will arrive in ten minutes. He again scans the tiny apartment to ensure everything is tidy.

Charles phoned Rachel and they met for a drink during the week after work to swap outlines of their lives over the last sixteen years. It was comfortable, and the following evening they met for dinner. That was better still, but nothing overtly romantic; no kiss goodnight, no touching, not even accidentally during conversation. At the end of that evening, standing outside the restaurant, Charles asked if she would take him round her gallery on her next day off. She agreed, and there'd been a pause. Charles had wanted to kiss her and sensed that the moment might be right, but he'd hesitated and it was gone. Rachel said goodnight and walked away.

As Charles walked back to Fetter Lane he wondered if she'd have bolted anyway, and was relieved he'd not tried. He'd told her about his marriage and his suspicions concerning Henrietta's affairs and Rachel had been sympathetic, but the fact is, he's married and, until he has some clarity with Henrietta, it makes him uncomfortable even to consider another relationship, no matter how attracted he might be to Rachel. He senses ambivalence in her, too. He thinks she's interested in him, but not in an affair. So, he's not sure how to characterise this meeting, the fourth "date" in less than three weeks; *something* is happening, but what?

Charles hasn't been back to Thame during the week or spoken to Henrietta. He has filled his evenings with working late in the Temple, going for long runs on the embankment and sparring at the gym, and he's felt dislocated and out of sorts. However bad things have been previously, he has never before spent a week away from Henrietta unless away on a case, and even then he'd call every night from his hotel room. The fact that she has neither phoned nor made any comment about his remaining in London speaks volumes. Charles has started to wonder if divorce is inevitable and to imagine what life would be like without her. He's resolved to go to Thame and get things sorted out.

Charles stands and rinses his cup, leaving it on the draining board. There's a light tap on the door. Charles takes the two strides necessary to take him from the kitchen to the front door, and opens it.

'Hello,' says Rachel. Charles frowns, puzzled. 'One of your neighbours let me in downstairs,' she explains. She stands on tiptoe and kisses Charles on the cheek. She wears sandals and a summer dress printed with large pink roses on a white background. She carries a pink beret in her hand. For the first time since Charles met her, she is wearing make-up. She looks younger than her twenty-seven years.

'You look lovely,' says Charles. 'Come in.'

Rachel enters the tiny lobby and the two of them dance round each other while Charles shuts the door and takes her bag.

'Would you like a drink before we go?'

'No thanks.'

'OK. Take a seat. I'll just get my jacket and some money.'

Charles disappears and Rachel sits where he'd been reading the paper. She notes the article about the Great Train Robbery. 'Do you have any professional interest in this?' she calls.

'What, the train robbery? Not yet, but I have my fingers crossed. Every criminal barrister in the Temple wants one of those briefs. That's the sort of case on which careers are made.' He returns to the room, pulling on a jacket, and smiles at her. 'Shall we?'

The Holbornes' house at Putt Green, Buckinghamshire, was once a large farmhouse on the edge of the village. The last farmers of the land, brothers, were killed in action and their executors sold the herd of dairy cattle, the land and the house to different purchasers. By the time the Holbornes acquired the house in 1955 it was badly rundown, but a gift from Henrietta's parents helped restore it and now it's a stylish well-appointed family home, ideal for a couple with three or four children. It's too large and isolated for a young wife who spends much of her time there alone.

The garden, carved originally from one of the fields, is huge. Someone has clearly spent a great deal of time working on it, as the lawns are well manicured and the flowerbeds colourful and orderly. Outside the French windows, on a patio that runs the width of the house, stands an oak garden table and six chairs. A long, striped seat with its own awning swings back and forth in the gentle breeze. The far end of the garden is separated from the rest by a massive clipped beech hedge through which there is an archway. Beyond the archway the garden is semi-wild, the grass taller and dotted with wild flowers. There is the stump of a huge old oak, now long dead, and several apple trees, ideal for climbing. It would have been an exciting place had there been any children in the household. Through the fence at the wild end of the garden is a stile leading to open fields.

Vehicles pass the front of the house infrequently and the noise of their engines is only just audible at the back. Children's voices can be heard in the distance, and occasionally the sound of horses' hooves float over from the stables in the lane.

Beside the stile at the rear of the house, hidden from the house by the hedge, a man keeps watch, shuffling from one foot to the other. He wears an anorak, heavy comfortable boots and thick socks, for his work often requires waiting patiently in uncomfortable situations. He is short, with a round, jovial face and ruddy cheeks. He looks as if in another life he should have been an innkeeper. He's been standing there for over two hours and is getting tired. He takes a pad out of his jacket pocket and makes a note with a small stub of pencil. He replaces the pad and chews the pencil thoughtfully. It's been a dull shift. The subject sat reading in the garden until the wind picked up and it got a bit too cold, and then made herself a drink. Thereafter she spent most of the time in the kitchen. He looks at his watch; another two hours before he is relieved at 2 p.m., when he will return to his car where a hot flask of tea and a sandwich await him.

The telephone rings in the house, and the watcher leans out slightly to obtain a better view of the kitchen windows. The subject sits at the kitchen table. She picks up the receiver and speaks slowly, calmly at first. Then her voice starts rising until she is shrieking into the receiver. She stands and starts pacing back and forth as far as the telephone cable will allow. The call ends with her slamming the receiver down. There's a pause, then a further scream — frustration or anger, the man can't tell

— then a fast movement followed by the sound of an object smashing, a vase perhaps. The watcher grins. *Temper, temper,* he says quietly to himself, as he records the event in his notebook, in slow careful pencil strokes.

INTERIM REPORT No. 4 to BSI ON OBSERVATIONS AT 'The Old Farmhouse', Putt Green, BUCKS.

Surveillance continued. Subject apparently retired for the night and surveillance about to end when at 22.23 hours lights were seen in the master bedroom. At 22.41 hours the subject left the house and jogged to the junction of Church Road and the A428 bypass. Waited for ten minutes. Red Mercedes Saloon, index mark. LUC 800 approached travelling east on bypass, stopped, and subject got in. Vehicle drove into church car park without direction from subject, suggesting the car park had been used for venue in past. Due to lack of cover, an approach to vehicle deemed not safe, and observation continued from corner of church at distance of 150 yards. Driver: male Caucasian, late-thirties/early forties, light colouring, no facial hair. Driver attempted to kiss subject, was resisted, although parties clearly familiar with one another. Discussion in car for ten minutes. Driver continued to press himself on subject. Raised voices heard, but distance too great to decipher words. Impression: driver attempting to persuade subject. At 23.05 hours subject descended from car, slammed door, and began to run out of church car park. A few feet from car, subject turned and shouted to driver. Subject's back was turned to operative, but words appeared to be: "And don't phone anymore. I mean it. I'll tell —" and here subject used a name, possibly "Melanie" or "Marjorie". Subject ran back to house. Vehicle remained stationary until 23.10 hours, then rejoined the A428 and continued in an easterly direction.

INTERIM REPORT No. 5 TO BS1 ON OBSERVATIONS AT 'The Old Farmhouse', Putt Green, BUCKS.

Surveillance recommenced at 08.45 hrs. Subject seen to be up and about house. Visit from female neighbour 10.45 hrs. to 11.13 hrs. Subject left address driving Jaguar index mark CLH 7 at 11.54 hrs. Followed to local shops. Returned to address 12.48 hrs. Jaguar broke down outside address. Subject enlisted two male workers from adjoining farm to push it into garage. Subject returned to house. Worked in rear garden until operative relieved. No further incident.

CHAPTER TWELVE

The phone rings in the clerk's room and Stanley picks it up.
'May I speak to Mr Holborne, please?'

'Is that Mrs Holborne?'

'Yes, Stanley? How are you?'

'Not bad, thank you. A bit rushed this week as Sally's on holiday. Just putting you through. Mr Holborne? Your wife for you, sir. And your nine-thirty conference has arrived.'

Charles hears a click on the line.

'Charles?'

'I haven't time for another row, Henrietta. I have a conference starting right now.'

'The bloody car's broken down.'

'OK. Where?'

'Just outside the house, thank God. I'd been shopping, and it conked out as I was driving back into the garage. I got some of Jim's men to help push it back in, but I've tried it since and it won't start at all.'

'What do you want me to do about it?'

'It's your bloody car.'

'Then I'll bloody manage without it until the weekend, won't I?'

'What am I supposed to use in the meantime?'

'You just said it was my bloody car. What you mean is, it's my bloody car, but you want to drive it.'

'Charles, you know very well how isolated it is here. There's no way I can get around without transport. Particularly if

141

you're not proposing to come up again until Friday. I've got arrangements this week.'

Charles takes a deep breath and adopts as reasonable a tone as he can command. 'I'm really sorry, Henrietta, but I can't get there before Friday. If you need it urgently, book it into Breck and Co on the village green.'

'They're Volvo dealers.'

'They repair other cars, too. They're very good. You might even persuade them to lend you a car while the Jag's in for repair. But I'm afraid I really have to go; my conference is waiting to begin.'

'You're a real bastard sometimes, you know that, Charles?'

'That's a bit unfair, don't you think?' starts Charles, but Henrietta has hung up.

It is 3.30 a.m., a dark and damp night. No lights show from any of the houses in the deserted lane. A thin blanket of mist rises gently from the brook running parallel to the lane opposite the houses. The clear water usually gurgles over its rocky path under a line of willow trees, but tonight the mist seems to muffle the sound and the lane is unusually quiet. A man wearing overalls and a woolly hat pulled low over his ears stands patiently under one of the willow trees and observes the Holborne residence. He is completely still and almost invisible. Heavy drops of water drip from the leaves of the willow onto his head and face. The house is in darkness. Satisfied, the man steps lightly across the lane and walks up the drive of the Holbornes' house towards the garage. He tries the main doors but finds them locked. He skirts round the garage, keeping to the shadows, and enters by the rear door. A minute later the main doors swing silently open. Then, like the silver snout of a large animal, the nose of the Jaguar emerges silently from the shadows. The man pushes the motor car from the driver's door, steering it with one hand. It's slow going at first and takes an enormous amount of effort, but the drive slopes gently down towards the brook and after a couple of car's lengths the vehicle picks up speed and the man has to jog to keep up with it. Where the drive joins the lane he expertly steers to the left and allows the vehicle to roll to a stop. He walks on a few paces to the tow-truck in which he arrived, gets in the cab and lets off the handbrake so that it rolls silently backwards to within a few feet of the front of the Jaguar. Then he walks quickly back up the drive and closes the garage doors, returning to the tow truck.

Curled on the back of the truck is a steel hawser with a hook at its end. The man uncurls the hawser, crawls under the front of the Jaguar and attaches the hook to the front axle. He returns to the tow-truck and operates the electric winder for three or four seconds, tightening the hawser, and the front of the Jaguar rises smoothly off the ground. The noise makes this the riskiest part of the operation, but he keeps his eyes on the darkened upstairs windows for signs of movement or light, and is satisfied that all remains still. The man then climbs swiftly into the cab of the truck, starts up, and drives off, towing the Jaguar behind him. The operation has taken less than four minutes, and within seconds of the tail lights of the tow truck disappearing, the lane is again completely silent.

By mid-morning in the Temple the early rush of barristers dashing off to court has slowed, and the ancient courtyards have resumed their sedate pace. 2 Chancery Court is silent with concentration as members of Chambers settle down to draft documents and research the law in Chambers' library.

Charles tries to work for a while but throws down his pen, stands and paces about the room. He's been trying to draft what should have been a very simple Advice on a personal injury matter, but has written and crossed through the first paragraph four times. He can't concentrate and when he looks at the uncharacteristic chaos of papers and instructions lying on his desk, he realises that he's achieved little in the last few days.

He reaches for the telephone. 'Peter?' he says as he dials.

Peter Bateman, Charles's pupil, looks up from the papers on which he is working.

'Yes?'

'Make yourself scarce for a few minutes, eh?'

'Sure,' replies the young man, and he scurries off for a quick cigarette. Charles doesn't permit smoking in the room, and the chance for a coffee and a smoke with the other pupils in Chambers is always gratefully received.

The call is picked up at the other end.

'Henrietta?'

'Yes?' she says, recognising his voice, and truculent.

'Do you agree that it would be sensible for us to have a discussion about the future?'

There's a long pause at the end of the line but Henrietta's voice when it comes is sadder and gentler than Charles expects. 'What do you propose?'

'I can come up tomorrow night, if you've got no plans.'

Another pause. At first Charles can hear breathing but then the line falls silent. Just as he's about to check that she's still there, he hears a sob and realises she's crying.

'Etta, don't cry. I'm sure we can sort it out, whatever the outcome. But we can't carry on like this, can we? We're just making one another completely miserable.'

'Yes,' she agrees, gathering herself somewhat. 'I'll make something for dinner. You'll need to get a cab from the station.'

'Have you booked the car in?'

'Yes, but as it needs towing, they're too busy to come for a couple of days.'

'OK. I'll be there around seven.'

Henrietta replaces the receiver and allows herself to cry. She thinks of calling her mother, but can't stand another hour's worth of "I told you so"s. So she dries her eyes and goes into the garden. Gardening normally calms her, but even that's no good. After fifteen minutes she decides instead to cycle into the village and pick up something nice to cook. She puts her gardening gloves on the garden table and goes to the garage for her bike.

At first she doesn't appreciate the significance of the emptiness of the garage. Then, with a shock, she remembers. She does all the foolish and illogical things one does when refusing to believe the obvious: she checks the drive and the road and even looks over the road to the stable yard. The Jag isn't there. Eventually she acknowledges with surprise that someone really has stolen it.

'What idiot steals a car that doesn't run?' she says out loud in astonishment.

She catches part of herself enjoying in anticipation Charles's frustration when he finds out, but the nicer part of her decides to report the theft. There isn't a police station in the village but there's a police house with a blue lamp outside it where the local bobby lives. She rings the number but receives no reply, so she scribbles a note informing the policeman that her husband's broken-down car has been stolen from their locked garage. She reads the note over, wondering if it reads like a practical joke, but content that she's fulfilled her duties as the owner's wife. She locks the house and cycles into the village, dropping the note through the police house letterbox on the way.

She needn't have bothered. Late that night, while she sleeps, the man who took the car quietly drives it up to the house, now repaired, carefully opens the garage doors as he did before and backs the car into the garage. Had Henrietta looked in the garage the following day and seen the Jaguar there, she'd no doubt have thought she was going mad or, perhaps, that she'd drunk too much gin. In fact, she has no cause to go to the garage again, and so never realises that the car is back in its place.

CHAPTER THIRTEEN

Henrietta watches out of the window as Jo, the stable girl, closes the stable gates opposite the house. Jo waves goodbye to someone still in the stables and walks off down the lane, her riding boots crunching on the gravel at the side of the road.

It's 6:40 p.m. and Charles might arrive at any minute. The thought causes Henrietta to gulp down half a glass of gin and tonic. She knows what's on the agenda for the evening's discussion. She's been hoping for a frank but kind conversation between the two of them for months; years in fact. Now it's imminent, and she still hasn't decided what she's going to say or even what conclusion she wants. About the only two fixed points in her emotional reference frame are that, firstly, she was right to finish the thing with Laurence and, secondly, despite all, she still loves Charles. Maybe some counselling? She heard someone at the tennis club talking about the Marriage Guidance Counsel. The idea of discussing the details of their relationship with a total stranger fills her with shame, but maybe they just have to do it. She's sure they still love one another, but she can't fathom how matters have deteriorated to this degree, how they are now so far apart, so maybe a third party could help.

Despite her earlier resolve, she takes her empty glass back to the cocktail cabinet and replenishes it with another two inches of neat gin. She catches sight of herself in the mirror above the mantelpiece. She's made an effort with her makeup and wears a long, quite formal dress which shows off her slim figure. The smell of Basque lamb stew, one of Charles's favourites, drifts from the kitchen. If it's going to end, she wants Charles to see what he'll be missing.

She leans closer into her reflection, noting the puffy eyelids and bloodshot eyes. Too much gin and too many tears, she thinks, and for a second her nerve deserts her and she considers calling a taxi and disappearing.

She takes a deep breath to steady herself, smiles experimentally at herself in the mirror, and goes into the kitchen to poke at the stew and check that the pommes dauphinoise are browning nicely. Earlier she'd thought to calm herself by playing some music, but she was so distracted that, an hour later, Albinoni still revolves soundlessly under the raised stylus. She throws herself into an armchair and stares into the garden.

Charles puffs, pants and curses his way over the stile at the back of the garden. He's hot and sweaty and extremely cross. He arrived at the station to find himself in a losing battle for the one taxi waiting there and was forced to carry his briefcase and coat for a mile and a half over rutted and extremely muddy fields, made all the more treacherous by the recent rain. Having taken off his jacket, he then slipped, fell, and got it and his trousers covered in mud and grass stains.

His shoes heavy with adherent mud, he trudges across the garden, aware that he's leaving footprints on Henrietta's beautiful lawn, and clatters through the back door. Henrietta, startled by the noise, runs into the kitchen to find him swearing as he tries to hook off his shoes without touching either of them with his hands.

She stares at him, aware of the risk of laughing, but unable to suppress giggles.

'You look quite a sight,' she says, covering her mouth with her hand.

'Can you get some newspaper?'

'OK, hold on. Just stay there.'

Henrietta opens a cupboard and takes out an old newspaper which she spreads on the floor in front of him. He attempts to hook a shoe off the heel of one foot with the toe of the other, managing only to spray gobbets of mud onto the clean floor.

'Mind out, Charles!' shouts Henrietta. 'This is a decent dress. Be patient, and I'll do it!'

He obeys, and looks down at her shiny hair as she crouches in front of him. 'This isn't quite the civilized, dignified entrance I intended,' he says wryly.

'Right,' says Henrietta, standing up, having taken the second shoe off. 'I think the shoes have had it; they're saturated inside and out. You actually look as if you've been wading. And your socks and trousers are a complete mess. Why don't you go up and have a bath, get changed, and I'll put dinner on hold.'

'Won't it spoil?' he asks. 'I'm already late.'

'No, luckily, it's quite forgiving. Twenty minutes won't do any harm.'

Charles does as he's told. Five minutes later he's in the bath. There's a knock on the door and Henrietta enters with a glass of whisky.

'Thank you,' he says, smiling. 'That's kind.'

'Mind if I stay?'

'Of course not.'

Charles pats the side of the bath. Henrietta takes a hand towel to dry enough space for herself, and sits. She leans forward on impulse and kisses Charles on the lips. She means it to be a light gesture of affection but Charles's lips soften and he bites her lower lip gently. She responds with her tongue and leans into him, bracing herself with her hands on the tiles above Charles's head. Charles would have touched her — earlier in their marriage he'd have pulled her into the bath on top of him, clothed or not — but he keeps his hands to himself and after a moment Henrietta disengages and sits up.

'Hmm,' she says. 'I'd forgotten how nice that was.' She looks down at his hairy muscular body, the dark triangle of hair between his legs and his response to her kiss. 'I see you approve,' she says.

Charles follows her gaze and lies back in the warm water.

'You're not in the least shy, are you?' she says.

'Not with you, no. God knows what I'd be like with someone else.'

The comment, meant to be innocuous, touches a nerve in Henrietta. 'I'll see you downstairs, then,' she says abruptly, and leaves without making further eye contact with him.

Fifteen minutes later, cleaned and refreshed, Charles sits down opposite Henrietta to eat.

'Well,' she says brightly, as she takes a spoonful of soup, 'you called this meeting.'

Charles takes a deep breath and replaces his spoon on the table. 'OK. Before anything else I want you to believe that despite everything, despite the fact that I may be the worst husband on the planet, and despite the fact that I know we've torn huge chunks out of each other, I love you. That's never changed.'

'Thank you for saying that.'

'But —'

'There's a "but"?'

'You know there is; look what's become of us! And I've come to the conclusion that we can't live together. I don't know how to make you happy, Etta. And I don't think you really want me to try anymore.'

'But upstairs —'

'That's never been the problem, has it? The passion's always been there. But it's the rest. I can't live with this constant fighting. The ups are wonderful but the downs are too depressing, and too frequent. I'd trade half the passion for someone who wanted to share my life in peace and quiet.'

'So what are you saying?'

'I'm saying I think we should divorce.'

Charles looks up as he delivers his conclusion, the first time he's looked at Henrietta's face since he started speaking. She too has stopped eating. She stares silently into her soup, her arms resting on the table either side of her bowl. He stands and looks out into the darkening garden.

'I've known you've been having an affair for some time.' Henrietta doesn't reply. 'And it's so out of character for the girl I met at Cambridge. You were so repelled by your father's sordid entanglements over the years, so scathing of him, and yet here you are doing exactly the same. But I don't think that alone would make me give up on us. It's more that ... well... I think it just tells us how unhappy you are. And...' he pauses, 'I think it makes you hate yourself. And me.'

He turns back to her and sees a fat tear roll down her cheek and splash into her home-made tomato soup. She seems unaware of the spots of red accumulating on the tablecloth and her white dress.

'Oh, Etta!' he exclaims, from the heart, and rushes over to her.

'No, Charles! Don't touch me!'

She shoves her chair back from the table, scraping noisily on the tiles, and retreats from him to the kitchen door, her shoulders heaving. After a moment she controls her breathing enough to speak quietly, with deathly calm. 'I want you to go. Right now. Don't say another word, just leave.'

'But —'

'I mean it! Not another word. It's over. You said so. So, just leave.'

Charles hesitates, his mouth open to say something, but he then brushes past her into the hallway. He runs upstairs, packs a bag and collects a spare suit. His saturated shoes are by the front door on the mat and he forces his feet into them. For a few seconds he hesitates, his hand raised to the doorknob, wondering if he should say something more, but then he opens the door, closes it quietly behind him and sets off up the muddy lane, and away from his home.

Henrietta is still in the kitchen, crying as she empties the soup into the sink. She hears the back door and assumes that Charles has forgotten something. She doesn't turn when she hears footsteps behind her. She is unaware of the cosh as it descends onto the back of her head. She does, however, move at the last moment, and it ends its downward arc by striking her cheek and then her shoulder. She cries out in pain and surprise and turns for the first time. The man raises the cosh again, but before he can bring it down, she lashes out with the heavy ironware saucepan in her hand. It strikes her attacker in the eye and he grunts with pain. He nonetheless gets in his second blow, and this one lands directly on Henrietta's temple. She collapses the instant it lands.

The man bends over the sink and washes cold water into his eye. It's extremely painful and already closing, but it isn't bleeding much. He bends and retrieves the saucepan which rolled onto the floor. Holding it by his gloved hand, he rinses it thoroughly under the hot tap and places it neatly with the other utensils in the drying rack. Pressing a dishcloth to his face to prevent blood dripping onto the floor, with his free hand he drags Henrietta's unconscious form by an ankle into the lounge. He places her in the middle of the Persian rug, and takes out of his coat pocket a cut-throat razor. Bending over her from behind, and careful to stand away from the direction of his swing, he brings the blade down swiftly and efficiently across her throat. Blood spurts out in a great leap, arcing over the coffee table and splashing in bright red washes over the wall. It continues pumping for a few seconds, and then gradually stops, as Henrietta's life ebbs away.

The man stands, picks up a chair and throws it at the display case of vases given to Henrietta and Charles for their first wedding anniversary by her godparents. It smashes, sending shards of glass and porcelain over the room. He then turns over the other occasional table and flings the decanters at the wall. At the same time, he shouts; oaths, curses, meaningless words, a one-sided argument, concluding in a long, high-pitched shriek.

He hurries back to the kitchen. He picks up the briefcase and blue cloth bag he brought with him and leaves the house by the kitchen door. He enters the garage. He unlocks the main doors from the inside but doesn't push them open. He runs back to the house, sprinting through it to the front door, the cloth bag and briefcase sending an umbrella stand flying, and re-emerges onto the front drive. Now he pulls wide the garage doors, allowing them to swing against the walls with a loud double crash. He unlocks the Jaguar, throws the case and bag inside, gets in and starts the engine. He revs it loudly, and then, just to make sure, drives the car at an angle out of the garage, dragging the nearside coachwork along the concrete doorpost. The screech of protesting metal would have been heard a street away.

The Jaguar shoots out of the drive, sending dust and gravel into the air, and disappears down the lane.

CHAPTER FOURTEEN

It is nearly midnight by the time Charles reaches the flat in Fetter Lane. He throws his things on the couch and sits, staring out of the window. The streets are almost deserted. An occasional vehicle passes beneath his window, its true colours leached by the yellow sodium lights on the pavement. He's exhausted, having trudged from the station to the house and back again and then having to endure the last all-stations slow train back into London, but his mind is whirling and he knows that sleep will be an impossibility. After a while he stands, fixes himself a Scotch and returns to the fraud papers he left open on the kitchen table.

Half an hour later he realises that he's forgotten to bring Archbold, the criminal practitioner's Bible, from his desk in the Temple. With a heavy sigh he puts his muddy shoes back on, throws on a jacket and walks downstairs to Fetter Lane.

The streets of the City are empty. Not a single vehicle is in sight as Charles crosses Fleet Street. There's an unnatural stillness, as if the night is holding its breath. Charles walks through the arch into the Temple. The trees are utterly immobile, their branches, now in full leaf, fixed against the night sky. His footsteps echo around Chancery Court. He's about to climb the staircase to number 2 when he notes that one of the lights on the first floor had been left on. It takes him a moment in the dark to find the right key for the great studded outer door. It stands open during office hours and the barristers, although supplied with keys, rarely have to use them. Eventually he gets both doors open, and walks through the silent waiting room and up the stairs to the first floor. The place smells of old books and stale coffee. The light was shining from the room next to his but, having reached it, all the rooms on that side of the landing are now in darkness.

'Hello?' he calls.

There's no answer. He reaches forward to push open his own door when the hairs on the back of his neck suddenly rise and he knows he's not alone. He whirls round, and remembers nothing more.

'Sir! Mr Holborne sir!'

Charles opens his eyes. There's a woman's black court shoe in front of him and an ankle in stockings, and Charles can't fathom why a shoe or an ankle should be on his pillow. He then realises that he's extremely uncomfortable and not, after all, in his bed. He tries to sit up and a wave of nausea overwhelms him. He closes his eyes again to prevent the world spinning.

'Sir? Are you all right?'

Charles tries again, opening one eye just a fraction. 'Sally?'

'Yes, sir. Have you fainted, sir?'

'Do you want to try to sit up, sir?' says another voice, a young male's.

'Yes,' responds Charles, and he feels hands from each side under his armpits pulling him into a seated position. Charles realises that he's on the floor just outside his office in Chambers. He's still disorientated.

'Should I call a doctor?' asks the male voice, apparently of Sally.

'Sir, should we get an ambulance?'

'No … at least I don't think so. I don't understand… What's the time?'

156

'Just gone eight in the morning, sir,' says the male. 'Have you been here all night?'

Charles moans. His head is full of little men with big hammers. 'I'm not … yes, I must've been. The last thing I remember is coming up here late last night to get my Archbold. I remember … there was a light on … but then there wasn't…' Charles opens his eyes further and sees Sally and Robert, the office junior, both crouched in front of him, looking concerned. 'Christ, my head hurts.'

Charles reaches behind him and discovers a painful lump on the back of his head. He takes his fingers away and examines them, but there's no blood.

'Looks like you hit your head as you fell,' says Robert.

'Yeah … maybe… Robert, can you help me into my room?'

'Don't you want to go to the flat, sir? You're pretty muddy, if you don't mind me saying so, and maybe you need to change.'

Charles looks down at his clothes, shakes his head and wishes he hadn't. 'Jesus, remind me not to do that again. No, I'd just like to sit down for a few minutes. I'll make my own way over in a bit.'

'Would you like a cup of coffee?' asks Sally. 'I'm about to put the kettle on.'

Robert helps Charles back to his room where he collapses in his leather chair. He has barely sat down when there's a knock at his door. Coffee, he thinks.

'Come in.'

Sally enters, looking worried. 'Erm … sorry, sir … but there's a couple of men here to see you. They say they're policemen.'

Charles frowns. 'Better show them in,' he says, standing unsteadily.

Sally stand back and permits two large men to enter the room. The first of them speaks.

'Mr Charles Holborne?'

'Yes?'

'I am Detective Constable Sloane, and this is Detective Constable Redaway.' The officer shows Charles his warrant card. 'We're from Buckinghamshire Constabulary.'

'Yes, officer. Do you want to take a seat?'

'Er, yes, all right. You'd better sit down too, sir.'

'Yes, I know,' replies Charles, sitting back down cautiously. Standing suddenly had made his head swim again, and he thinks he might be sick. He feels the back of his head again.

'Something wrong, sir?' asks one of the policemen.

'Not sure,' replies Charles groggily. 'The clerks found me on the floor outside, with this on the back of my head. I must've been there since late last night.'

Charles turns his head gingerly and shows the lump to the two officers. He doesn't see the look passing between them.

'Mr Holborne?' says DC Sloane, the officer who introduced them. 'Mr Holborne, I need you to focus on what I'm saying.'

Even in his befuddled state Charles recognises the stress in the officer's voice. He looks at the two men's grave faces and knows he is about to receive very bad news. His heart is suddenly pounding. 'What is it?' he asks, aware of a slight tremor in his voice.

'Your wife, sir, Henrietta Holborne. I'm afraid there's been an incident at your home in Putt Green. I am very sorry to tell you that your wife is dead.'

'Dead? She can't be. I saw her yesterday evening.' Charles doesn't register his answer being quietly recorded by the second officer. 'What sort of incident? You mean a car crash?'

'No sir, I don't think it's that sort of incident. I've been asked to collect you sir, if that's convenient, and take you to Putt Green now to identify the ... your wife. I'm sure the situation will be made clearer when we get there.'

'Yes, but ... what happened? Please, tell me.'

'I'm sorry, sir, I would if I could. But we're just chauffeurs, so to speak. We've been asked to come here and drive you to your house. Do you have a coat?' he asks, as he stands.

'Jacket, yes, there,' replies Charles, pointing.

The second officer picks it up carefully by the collar, noting the mud stains. 'I'll carry it for you, shall I, sir? You won't need it in the car.'

'Yes ... sure. I just need to speak to the clerks, tell them what's happening.'

'We've already had a word with them, sir. Best we get a move on.'

During the journey that follows Charles tries several times to get the officers to divulge more detail about what's happened, but he soon realises that either they don't know or have orders to say nothing. By the time they come off the A40 the occupants of the police Ford Zephyr have been silent for forty minutes. Every now and then Charles is aware of being observed via the driver's mirror.

The car swings into the drive of The Old Farmhouse. There are already several cars there, two obvious police cars with their lights still flashing, two or three unmarked cars and, on the grass verge, an ambulance. A small crowd of onlookers has been confined to the opposite side of the road under the willows and Charles recognises a couple of the stable boys and Mrs O'Connell from the post office in the next village.

Standing on the doorstep is a man in a light grey raincoat and a shiny grey suit speaking to two other men, one with a dog on a lead. They depart, and skirt round the house to the back. The man in the raincoat approaches the car as it stops and opens the door.

'Mr Holborne?' he asks. He's Charles's height, with thinning grey hair cut in a military short back and sides, in his late fifties. He sports a thin pencil moustache perched on an unusually long top lip. The moustache, which is so dark in colour that Charles wonders if it's dyed, moves precariously when the man speaks, as if it might fall off. Charles recognises the policeman from somewhere, but at that moment he can't place him.

'Yes.'

'I'm Detective Superintendent Wheatley, in charge of this investigation.'

Recognition dawns. 'Yes, Mr Wheatley, I remember you now. Aren't you in the Met?'

'I was promoted on transfer to Buckinghamshire, sir.' Notwithstanding the circumstances, Charles hears pride in the policeman's voice.

Wheatley helps Charles out of the car, keeping a grip on his upper arm.

'Would you please tell me what's going on?' Charles pleads. 'All I know is that Henrietta's supposed to be dead.'

'That's right, sir. In a moment I shall show you inside —' Charles tries to walk straight into the house but finds his other arm grabbed from the side by DC Sloane.

'In a moment, sir,' insists the Superintendent. 'I must warn you that it is not a pretty sight. It appears that your wife's been murdered.' Wheatley studies Charles's face intently as he delivers this information.

'Murdered?' says Charles, shaking his head in disbelief. 'Who by?' he asks stupidly.

'Now, we don't know yet, sir, do we?' replies the other. He leads the way to the front door, but then pauses and turns back to Charles. 'All I'd like you to do at the moment, sir, is identify her. Please can I ask you to take off your shoes before we go in?'

Charles complies and finds DC Sloane holding out his hand for them. With an instant's hesitation, Charles hands them over to him.

Wheatley continues. 'And can you tell me where the keys for the garden doors are kept?'

'The French doors?'

'Yes.'

'They're usually on the bookcase to the left of the door, under the little window.'

'Thank you.' He nods to DC Sloane, who hurries off down the hallway towards the back of the house. 'Follow me.'

Wheatley leads the way through the front door. As he enters, Charles examines the door frame and door: no signs of forced entry, and judging by Wheatley's comments, none at the back either.

Two men crouch by the overturned umbrella stand, dusting it with silver powder. Wheatley guides Charles around it and into the lounge. Charles's heart is pounding so hard in his chest he's sure the police officers must be able to hear it. He rounds the door and stops suddenly. The walls are splattered with blood; there is overturned furniture everywhere; broken glass crunches under his feet. A blanket, the blanket he and Henrietta used to take on their country walks, is spread over a bundle in the centre of the room, as if it had been laid on a grass hillock for some obscene picnic. From under it there emerges a viscous pool of black glistening liquid which has saturated the thick pile of the rug.

'Just stay there please, sir. I'm sure you appreciate it's important not to touch her or to disturb the crime scene,' says Wheatley.

He takes a step towards the centre of the room and lifts a corner of the blanket. Henrietta's white face stares up at them. Her eyes are closed tightly, like those of a child waiting for a surprise. A wide black grin disfigures her neck.

'That's her,' confirms Charles, choking back tears.

'Thank you, sir.'

Wheatley replaces the blanket and takes Charles firmly by the arm, guiding him back through the carnage to the hallway.

'I shall ask an officer to take you to Aylesbury police station where we've set up an incident room. We need to take some details from you, and it would be better to do it there. He'll be able to arrange for some tea. Sergeant Bricker?' he calls.

A stocky broad man who was doing something on the stairs bends down so he can see them over the stair rail. 'Sir?'

'This is Mr Holborne.'

'Right, sir,' he says, coming down. He reaches the foot of the stairs. 'Are these yours, sir?' he asks Charles, holding up a pair of black brogues which Charles hasn't worn in years.

'Yes. Where did you…'

'From your wardrobe, sir. The ones you arrived in are a bit wet, so we thought…'

'Thank you,' says Charles. He takes the shoes and slips them on.

'If you're ready, sir?' he says.

'Bricker,' says Wheatley quietly. The other turns, and Wheatley leans in and whispers to him. 'By the book, Sergeant. *Everything* by the book.'

'Understood, sir.'

The sergeant walks Charles out through the open front door. Charles knows it's a cliché even as he thinks it, but he wonders if it's all a dream and in a moment he'll wake to find himself on the floor of Chambers' library. He has the detachment to wonder also if everyone in this sort of situation takes refuge in hoping it's a fantasy. Probably.

Charles sits in the interview room, nursing his second cup of tea, now cold. Brief details have indeed been taken from him but that took ten minutes, after which he was asked to await the return of the Superintendent. At that stage he felt no compulsion about his remaining, but he's now been alone with his thoughts for almost two hours, and he's started to wonder. The officers who have spoken to him have been scrupulously polite but certainly not as friendly or sympathetic as Charles would have expected when dealing with a recently bereaved widower. The last time he checked, he found the door unlocked, so in theory he could just leave, but somehow he doubts he'd be permitted to do so.

The scene that greeted him as he walked into the lounge keeps replaying in his head, over and over, the jagged glass, the horrible mound under the blanket and the metallic smell of blood. And Henrietta's face, most of all her beautiful face, so white, so frightened. It's a struggle to accept that it's real. *In some alternate reality I'm at my desk drafting an indictment*, Charles thinks, *and everyone in Chambers is getting on with their day as normal but, somehow, I'm in a police room at Aylesbury Police Station and Henrietta has been murdered.*

He's about to get up to complain when the door opens and Superintendent Wheatley enters, flanked by another officer.

'I am sorry to have kept you waiting so long, Mr Holborne, but there were a number of matters that I had to deal with before speaking to you. I must now officially arrest you on suspicion of the murder of your wife, Henrietta Holborne. You are not obliged to say anything unless you wish to do so, but anything you say will be taken down and given in evidence.'

CHAPTER FIFTEEN

The dream-like impression that Charles has exchanged roles with one of his clients grows ever stronger. He knows the script all too well, it's one he reads every day of his life, but he's acting the wrong part. He's been taken to the custody room, his possessions taken from him and his personal details recorded. A custody record sheet bearing his name at the top has been opened, and he's been locked in a cell. His request for a solicitor has been refused on the grounds that the presence of a solicitor would lead to harm to the evidence connected with the offence. Charles knows that the grounds for refusal are questionable at best, spurious at worst, but he's powerless to do anything about it. It's all very well scoring points in court, but he's now a long way from the armour of his wig and gown and the protection of a fair judge.

The temptation to do as he normally could — knock on the door, make some quip with the station sergeant, and be let out — is almost overwhelming. The question keeps returning: why would anyone want to murder Henrietta? Was it a burglary gone wrong? But if there was no damage to the doors and they were both locked, Henrietta must have let the burglar in; she usually keeps the doors locked when he's not there. No, Charles corrects himself; that would depend on the time of the attack. The garden doors had been open when he left, so it could have happened shortly afterwards.

He paces the cell, unwilling to sit on the filthy bunk and the even more disgusting blanket which bears questionable brown stains. Now his watch has been taken from him he finds it difficult to judge the time, but he guesses from the growling of his stomach that it's past lunchtime. He remembers his clients telling him that the best way of keeping track of time is the state of one's digestion.

Finally, he hears footsteps from the far end of the corridor and his door is unlocked. 'This way, sir,' says a young police officer, and he is led back to the interview room in which he had first sat.

Superintendent Wheatley and DC Sloane await him. Wheatley carefully cautions Charles again and the interview begins. Charles finds himself in such a familiar situation that he almost laughs. Time and time again throughout his career he's told his clients to say nothing. Even when you're innocent, say nothing! Words get twisted, displaced, muddled, only to be dissected in minute detail by experts, surgeons of syntax, in the harsh glare of a courtroom, until you don't remember what you said or what you were trying to say. And yet … and yet, the impulse to speak, to explain everything, persuade them you're innocent, so the nightmare can end! For the first time ever, Charles appreciates how experienced, clever criminals, those who ought to have known better, say too much and give themselves away. And yet, knowing all this, he still speaks.

Wheatley asks all the questions and DC Sloane makes notes. The Superintendent proceeds slowly, carefully, watching Sloane's pen to make sure that nothing remains unrecorded.

'How was your married life, Mr Holborne?'

'In what sense?'

'Were you and your wife happy?'

'Not very, no.'

'Did you live at home?'

'Er … yes. I have a flat in London which I use some week nights. But we live together.'

'Did you have arguments?'

'Yes, we argue. What couple doesn't?'

'Violent arguments?'

'I wouldn't say so, no.'

'So, you'd say it would be impossible for your neighbours to have overheard arguments on occasion?'

'No. It wouldn't have been impossible, but it would have been rare. I don't like to argue.'

The policeman looks at some papers in front of him, and changes tack.

'You come from London, do you not?'

'Yes.'

'East London?'

'Yes.'

'Your parents are ... what?'

'My father was a furrier when I was last in touch with the family.'

'Would you agree there's not much money in your family?'

'I can see you from a mile away, Superintendent.'

'I've no doubt, Mr Holborne. We're both experts at questioning, so let's not play games. Your wife is dead, and you're under suspicion of killing her. I'm trying to arrive at the truth, so just answer the questions if you will. She was the daughter of a Marquis?'

'A Viscount, but if you're asking if she was rich, the answer is, obviously, yes. If you're asking if I killed her for her money, the answer is, definitely, no.'

'You stand to gain a fortune from her death.' It was a statement, not a question.

'I have no idea, but I doubt it.'

'Really?' sneers Wheatley.

'You'll have to ask her family. They didn't approve of the marriage. She gets her money through a family trust. I doubt any of it'll fall into her estate; they'll have made sure I don't receive a penny.'

'Did she have a will?'

'Er … yes. We did our wills together some years ago, unless she changed hers, I suppose.'

'Might she have changed her will?' asks the Superintendent.

'It's possible.'

'Why?'

'Because, as I said before, we weren't very happy.'

'So divorce was a possibility?'

'Yes.'

'At whose instance?'

'I wanted to divorce her. I went there last night to talk about just that.'

'And what do you claim was her attitude?'

'I resent the implication that what I am about to say is a lie. That's hardly open-minded questioning.'

'I've already told you I suspect you murdered your wife. I am not open-minded. What was her attitude?'

'She was very upset. She cried and shouted, and told me to get out of the house.'

'So you say that she was not happy at the prospect of a divorce?'

'It appeared that way.'

'Did you not write to her only last week, threatening her that if she divorced you, I quote,' and here he picks up a document, *"it'll be something that you'll regret, I assure you"?'*

168

'May I see that?' asks Charles.

'No. I may show you a copy later. For the present I shall read it to you.'

He did. It purports to be a letter in which Charles tells Henrietta that his career depends on being perceived as a happily married man and that he'd never countenance divorce, threatening her in veiled terms were she to proceed with it.

'I suggest it was your wife who wanted the divorce. You, on the other hand, were opposed to it.'

'No.'

'Now, this,' says Wheatley, brandishing the letter, 'was written on a typewriter. Can you see how part of the "a" and the "e" are missing? It's caused by wear on those keys. Before they left your Chambers, my officers asked your clerk to type a short passage on the typewriter in the clerks' room. What would you say if I told you that the typing they produced demonstrated exactly the same defect with those two letters?'

'I would say, if I was going to write such a letter, why on earth would I type it?'

'Are you saying you didn't write this?'

'Yes. That's exactly what I'm saying. I wanted a divorce. She was the one who didn't.'

'Can you think of anyone who might have the slightest motive for writing this and pretending it came from you?'

'Of course I can. The person trying to frame me for Henrietta's murder.'

'Who? Who might have any motive for killing your wife? Or who hates you so much as to kill an innocent woman, just to frame you?' That, Charles is unable to answer. Wheatley continues: 'You were seen to leave your house last night immediately after a violent row with your wife.'

169

'Yes, that's right. Although it wasn't violent other than in the sense that she screamed and shouted at me.'

'You were then seen to drive off, in such a hurry as to smash the side of your Jaguar on the garage doorpost. You wife was found dead half an hour later.'

So someone *could* have entered via the garden doors without doing damage, thinks Charles. 'Drive off? I didn't drive off. I *walked* back to the station.'

'You did not, Mr Holborne.'

'I did.'

'Why should you do that? You had the car.'

'I didn't have the car. It had broken down and I had to use the train.'

'Where's the ticket?'

Charles sighs. 'I threw it away at Marylebone. And before you ask, I paid cash.'

'How unfortunate. So you say the car isn't working? Your Jaguar motor car?'

'I do.'

'Your Jaguar, registration plate BHA 402, was found this morning by police officers from Snow Hill Police Station outside the Temple. It drove perfectly. It is now sitting in the yard of this police station.'

Charles stares at his interrogator in open-mouthed disbelief.

'Do you wish to make any comment?' asks Wheatley, an unpleasant triumphant smile on his thin lips.

'I ... don't understand... That can't be right. You must have made a mistake.'

'Why don't you start telling us the truth, Holborne? Surely, a man with your training can see how hopeless it is? What did you do with the knife?'

'I didn't do anything with any knife. I never had a knife. We argued, I was told to get out. I walked up the lane and cut across the fields to the station. I didn't kill her!'

'You were still wearing the muddy shoes when you were brought to the house. I suggest you wore them when throwing the knife away in the fields behind your house before driving off.'

'No! I wore them across the fields, yes, but I never had any knife.'

The Superintendent looks at DC Sloane, who shakes his head. He continues: 'I propose ending this interview now pending further enquiries. You will have to remain here. One last matter: we have been unable to find a copy of your wife's will. It's supposed to be in safekeeping with a solicitor, but we don't know who. Do you know where we can find a copy?'

Charles frowns. 'Yes. There's one in a safety deposit box at Midland Bank in Fleet Street. I have a key and a combination number.'

'Thank you. Where are they?'

'At the flat in Fetter Lane.'

'Oh, yes, the bachelor pad. We'll have a chat about that in due course.'

'It's not a "bachelor pad". It's somewhere I can sleep when working late, that's all.'

'Come on, Holborne, this is the swinging sixties, right?'

'No one else has ever slept there except me.'

'Who said anything about sleeping?' interjects Sloane with a smirk.

Wheatley glances sharply at him and returns to his earlier theme. 'Where can we find the key to the safety deposit box?'

'I think it's in a little Chinese jar on the windowsill. I'm not sure though, as I haven't used it in a while.'

'And the combination?'

'I can't tell you. I only use the box once in a blue moon, so I have the number written down.'

'Where?'

Charles thinks quickly. 'In the flat somewhere. I'd have to look for it.'

'We're proposing to search your flat this evening. Whereabouts shall we look?'

Charles shrugs. 'I wrote it down somewhere disguised as a telephone number.'

Wheatley studies Charles's face, weighing him up. 'They tell me that people in your profession value integrity more than anything else.'

'What of it?' asks Charles.

Wheatley pauses before answering, still searching Charles's face. 'All right,' he concludes. 'There's no time like the present. We'll go now, and you can come with us. Sloane, get him something to eat. We don't want him saying the interrogation was unfair, or he was so hungry he'd admit to anything.'

Superintendent Wheatley leaves the room and Charles is taken back to the cell. Once there, for the first time since the day began, Charles permits himself a small, weary, smile.

Charles climbs out of the police car onto Fetter Lane, hampered by the handcuffs on his wrist which attach him to a young uniformed officer. The road throngs with people, cars parked on the pavement, vans double-parked — the usual late afternoon clamour.

A cold hamburger and soggy chips arrived in Charles's cell within a half an hour of the interview ending and Charles bolted them down as fast as he could, but then nothing happened for over an hour and he returned to pacing his cell. Once on the road his impatience was almost intolerable. It was essential they reached London while it was still busy. Finally, after fifteen minutes of crawling traffic, Wheatley directed DS Bricker to put on the siren, and they completed the rest of the journey in half an hour.

Charles and the young officer wait while Wheatley and Bricker get out of the front of the vehicle.

'Well?' asks Wheatley.

Charles indicates the entrance and the group crosses the road. As they sidle between stationary taxis, Charles sizes up the two men ahead of him. Wheatley is quite tall, but Charles doubts he's a fighter, more cerebral, and probably past it anyway. Bricker, on the other hand, is a different prospect. Although slightly shorter, the sergeant's in his thirties and probably weighs in at fifteen stone. His thick neck, the jacket that pulls taught over his shoulders and his gait — he walks lightly, on the balls of his feet —suggest a sportsman. He can probably handle himself, concludes Charles. He finally evaluates the young copper to whom he's attached: probably only a couple of years out of Hendon, and thin as a wisp. So, Bricker first. Charles is fairly confident. Although his last amateur fight was several years ago, he's kept himself fit, trains regularly and spars at least a couple of times a month. Another aspect of his life which finds — *found*, Charles corrects himself — disfavour with Henrietta.

Dennis, the concierge of Charles's building, recognises Charles immediately and is halfway into a salute when he sees the handcuffs. His hand freezes in mid-movement, leaving him looking like an uncertain signpost pointing right.

'Mr Holborne?' he asks.

'Not to worry, Dennis. Parking fines,' Charles replies. Dennis nods and smiles, and then does a double-take as he reconsiders Charles's response, leaving him looking puzzled. The group enters the lobby.

'It's the fourth floor,' says Charles. 'The lift'll take two.' He pauses, awaiting a decision from his guards.

'You go in the lift with Holborne,' decides Wheatley, speaking to the young copper to whom Charles is attached. 'We'll take the stairs. Wait at the top.'

The lift is a tight fit even with only two in it, and Charles and his escort have to shuffle round before they can arrange themselves for the button to be pressed. They arrive on the fourth floor only just ahead of the others.

'Keys,' demands Wheatley. Bricker fishes in his pocket for the plastic bag in which Charles's keys had been sealed earlier, and hands the bunch to Wheatley.

'Which one?' asks Wheatley.

'The small gold one, and the long Chubb,' replies Charles.

The door is opened and they file into the small living area. Charles gasps. He barely recognises the place. There are flowers in a pot that he doesn't own on the table. A huge pink fluffy duck sits in the corner of the couch, an inane grin on its face. The lampshade has been replaced with something frilly, and there are doilies on the arms of the armchair.

'Charming,' comments Wheatley, with heavy sarcasm. 'You were telling the truth; this is definitely *not* a bachelor pad.'

'Looks very feminine to me, sir,' says Bricker.

'Maybe the handiwork of this young lady, sir?' adds the escort, picking up a photograph from the mantle. It's of a blonde, lots of bright teeth, lots of cleavage.

'"*To my Charlie, with love, Melissa*",' reads Wheatley from the bottom of the photograph. 'I see we've just found another motive. Or maybe even an accomplice, eh, Holborne?' says Wheatley.

Charles shakes his head. 'I don't suppose for one minute it'd do any good to say that all this stuff's been planted, would it?'

'I'm sure you can do better than that.' He calls to Bricker who has disappeared into the bedroom. 'Bricker: go downstairs and have a word with the porter; see if Melissa's a figment of someone's imagination.'

'Certainly sir. But look at this!' calls back the sergeant. He returns with a very skimpy nightie held aloft in one hand and a pile of women's clothes over his other arm. 'The wardrobe's full of women's clothes. This lot was on a chair by the bed.'

'I suppose now you'll say you're into women's clothes, eh, Charlie?' Charles notes how the respect has ebbed away as the evidence had stacked up against him. At first he had been "Mr Holborne", then "Holborne", now "Charlie". As far as Wheatley's concerned, he is now definitely dealing with a murderer, and murderers don't require courtesy.

The final piece of evidence comes to light as Wheatley goes through a kitchen drawer: a paying-in book for a Midland Bank account. It's in the names of "C. Holborne and Miss M. Maxwell". Wheatley turns to Charles, wags his finger at him and tuts slowly, shaking his head.

'Very careless, Charlie. I'm surprised at you. You should have known better than to do something official like this. Now, you see, I can go to the bank, and ask for the correspondence setting up the account. You'll hardly be able to deny an affair then.'

He smiles and shakes his head in mock sadness with an odd expression, seeming to convey something like: "I'd hoped for a worthier opponent".

'Sir!' calls a breathless Bricker, having just climbed the stairs. 'The porter's seen her come and go quite often. Got her own key.'

'That's enough for me,' says Wheatley with satisfaction. 'Get someone over and have this place fingerprinted. Now,' he says, addressing Charles. 'Where's this combination?'

Charles pulls his escort to the table and begins, with obvious difficulty, to go through the papers stacked on it. The other policemen watch him as he drops a sheaf of papers and bends down to collect them, dragging his guard with him. He painstakingly tries to reorder the papers. Then he drags the young constable into the bedroom, climbs on the bed, and starts going through a small bookcase fixed to the wall above it, flicking through books and dropping several in the process. The poor young copper is hauled this way and that, even falling off the bed once, dragging Charles with him. Charles makes the most of the pantomime.

'How long is this going to take?' asks Wheatley after several minutes.

'A while, I guess. It's very difficult to move,' replies Charles, continuing his search.

'Unlock him,' says Wheatley wearily. 'He won't get past three of us in this small space.'

The young escort reaches into his pocket and extricates the keys to the handcuffs. Wheatley is standing with his back to the bedroom window, watching intently, and Bricker is directly behind Charles in the doorway. The escort releases the cuff on

Charles's wrist and is about to unlock himself when Charles spins round and with all his strength catches Bricker with a perfect right-handed uppercut on the underside of the sergeant's chin. The blow snaps his lower jaw closed with such force, the sound is like a ceramic tile breaking. The policeman's eyes roll up, his knees buckle and he drops in the doorway. Charles instantly recognises the look from many a boxing match; Bricker's out of it. He continues in his spin and grabs the trailing end of the handcuffs still attached to his escort. He yanks hard, twirls the man around forcibly, and pulls the officer's own arm round his throat. He heaves with all his might and the young man chokes, his face suddenly red.

'Don't come anywhere near me,' Charles threatens Wheatley, 'or I'll break his neck!'

The superintendent hesitates for a second.

'You'd better believe I can do it,' assures Charles, calmly.

'Where d'you think you're going?' challenges Wheatley. 'You won't even get out the building. Even if you do, where then? You're no criminal, Charlie. You're just making a fool of yourself.'

Charles backs out of the living room and onto the landing, keeping his grip as tight as he can. The escort's face is turning purple. The lift is still there. Charles backs further away to the stairs, Wheatley inching after him cautiously.

'Superintendent,' orders Charles. 'Get in that lift, if you'd be so kind.' Wheatley pauses but does as he's told. 'Close the gates and press the alarm button.'

As the button is pressed, a bell sounds in the lower reaches of the building. The lift is now immobilised until the alarm is shut off from below, and Charles knows from previous experience that even if Dennis is in the building, the task will take him close to five minutes.

Charles backs onto the top step of the staircase, takes a deep breath and shoves the escort forward. He then turns and races down the stairs.

He takes them two at a time, hearing footsteps almost immediately behind him. He stumbles, regains his balance, stumbles again, but keeps going, his hands on the rails to each side. As he reaches the first-floor landing, he runs headlong into Dennis, on his way up to investigate the alarm bell. He bundles the porter over, leaving him gasping on the landing, hoping that his body will slow up any pursuers for another second.

Charles bursts into the street and turns immediately left. He sprints across Fleet Street, oblivious to the screech of tyres and blaring of horns, and into Sergeant's Inn. He jumps down the steps and through the arch into the Temple proper. Footsteps thump behind him, but not as close. He turns sharp right, runs across the open courtyard and turns right again by Temple Church.

Charles races the twenty yards across Hare Court, barges through a group of startled barristers just returning from Inner Temple Hall, and bounds up the steps into number 2. He chances a look over his shoulder and sees the young copper about sixty yards back, half way across the courtyard. Charles was a pupil here and knows the steps lead to a landing which also serves chambers in Middle Temple. On the far side of the landing is another short staircase, leading back down into Middle Temple Lane. This is his one advantage; he knows the Temple like the back of his hand whereas Buckinghamshire officers do not. He leaps the flight of steps down into Middle Temple Lane and turns left, effectively going back on himself. He feels the beginning of a stitch in his chest but presses on, his breath coming in short ragged gasps. He reckons he has about ten seconds to round the next corner. If he makes the corner without pursuers emerging from Hare Court, they'll have three potential routes to choose from. He counts down as he sprints: 6 ... 5 ... 4 ... 3 ... made it! Hugging the wall, he runs through Fountain Court and out of the night gate, leaving the Temple and passing the Devereux Public House where he has spent so many Friday evenings standing in the sun, chatting to other barristers with a beer in his hand. That last turn, he thinks, will give them three further options.

He emerges, sweat streaming down his forehead, onto Essex Street and runs straight into a taxi pointing towards the Embankment and pulling away from the kerb. He leaps in.

'Waterloo East!' he shouts. 'I've got four minutes to make a train!'

'Right you are, guv,' replies the cabbie, and away they sail.

CHAPTER SIXTEEN

'What time d'yer make it, mate?' asks Charles through the screen. He deliberately softens his accent, slipping into the Cockney he worked so hard to eradicate, in case the cabbie is asked about a posh fare.

'4.58,' replies the cabbie over his shoulder. They are going over Waterloo Bridge. 'When's the train?'

'Five,' replies Charles.

'Then you've had it, aintcha? It's gonna take more than that from 'ere. There's always a jam at the other end of the bridge.'

'Yeah, you're right. Tell you what: turn left at the end of the bridge and try London Bridge Station. I might just catch it there.'

'Righto.'

Charles hopes that even if anyone had been near enough to hear him ask for Waterloo, which he doubts, the change of direction will finally throw them off the scent.

They make good time to London Bridge.

'Don't bovver wiv goin' inter the station,' says Charles to the back of the cabbie's head. 'Go right inter Tooley Street. If I've missed it, we can go on to New Cross, the next stop.'

The cabbie regards him with narrowed eyes through the rear-view mirror. Charles holds his breath for the answer.

'Fair enough,' answers the cabbie eventually. 'At this rate, I might as well take yer all the way 'ome!'

The cab turns right and pulls up by the steps running up to the station.

'Won't be a sec. I can see the board from the top of the steps,' calls Charles, and he runs up the stairs. For a man who prides himself on his honesty and integrity he realises with a shock that he's lying and cheating as well as any of his clients; probably better than most. He doesn't like to bilk the innocent cabbie out of his fare but he's penniless and has no choice.

He walks swiftly onto the station concourse, crosses the front of the platforms and exits the station by the far door that takes him out onto St Thomas Street. He walks off down the road and onto the High Street.

His first problem is money, or the total lack of it. He stops in a doorway and goes carefully through his suit pockets. He always used to lose tickets in this jacket because there are so many little hidden pockets. Maybe ... just maybe... Yes! He feels a coin in a tiny pocket inside one of the others. He takes it out: half a crown; enough for a bus fare and a sandwich, maybe a cup of tea.

He sees a bus approaching and decides to change direction again. He crosses the road, runs to the next stop, flags it down and climbs on. It's going towards Mile End; his old hunting ground. With a flash of insight Charles realises where he needs to go, and it's somewhere he hoped never to set foot.

The Krays' acquisition of the Regal Billiard Club on Eric Street, Mile End, marked the beginning of their rise to becoming London's pre-eminent gangsters. It became their HQ, meeting place, labour and information exchange and watering hole rolled into one dimly-lit, smoky venue. It was often the first stop for anyone released from prison; the safe haven of choice for villains on the run or with stolen goods to hide; and the place to recruit personnel for the next robbery or burglary. It was also a circus, of which Ronnie Kray was the undisputed ringmaster. Reggie was the twins' businessman, with a nose for a business opportunity and an eye for profit, but Ronnie was a showman. It was Ronnie's antics that made the Regal *the* place to go for a good laugh or a bit of excitement, like a Saturday night battle with a rival gang.

Charles has never been inside the hall before, but like anyone in the East End who numbers burglars and con artists amongst their acquaintances, he knows where the Krays are usually to be found.

Charles steps off the bus and looks across the road. On the corner is a forecourt of used American cars with prices in their windscreens. He threads his way through them and walks the short distance down Eric Street to the billiard hall. He hesitates, looks around to make sure he's not being observed, and climbs the few steps to the door.

The club is in virtual darkness, with lights illuminated above only two of the billiard tables at the far end. Two men play at each, and a couple of others line the walls, watching. A man in shirtsleeves is wiping the bar. There is a huge bear of a man in shirtsleeves and waistcoat with his back to the door, in the act of hefting a beer barrel. He's about six foot two and weighs no less than twenty stone, and his stand-up mop of dark hair makes him look bigger still. He hears the door open and turns, the barrel in his arms.

'Hello, Chunky,' says Charles. 'Didn't know you were out.'

Charles has known Chunky Morgan, a long-term associate of the Krays, since he was a teenager. Shimon Cohen, Millie Horowitz's cousin, used to be an "uncle", a pawn broker, in Bethnal Green, and as children Charles and David used to play in the yard at the rear of Shimon's shop. Chunky's family home backed onto the yard.

'Do I know you?' asks Chunky, eying up the well-dressed interloper suspiciously.

'Course you do. It's me, Charlie Horowitz.'

There's a long pause before the other answers. 'Fuck me, Charlie. I ain't seen you in a lifetime. How's yer luck?'

'Not too good, Chunky. That's why I'm here. Are the twins around?'

A voice comes out of the shadows. 'I'm here, Horowitz.'

Charles peers into the gloom. At the far end of the bar, in an armchair angled so its occupant can see both the entrance and the length of the club, sits Ronnie Kray. He wears an expensive suit, the jacket slung round the back of the chair, and wide braces over a white shirt. The tie looks like silk, and the matching tiepin and cufflinks look like diamonds. The persona is calculated: Hollywood Chicago-style gangster.

An Alsatian dog lies on the floor by the side of the chair, panting, its tongue lolling. Charles approaches cautiously.

'Can I have a word with you and Reg?'

'Must be something important,' sneers Ronnie, 'to bring a big shot brief down here from up West.' Charles wishes he were able to talk to Reggie, who is usually more amenable than his unpredictable brother. 'Reg ain't here. But you can talk to me if you want. Come on in. Drink?'

'I've got no cash.'

'Nah. My treat.'

'Scotch then, if you've got it.'

'We got everything. It's a bar, ain't it?' Ronnie nods to the barman.

Charles walks further into the club, aware that the click of billiard balls has stopped and his progress is being observed by everyone. He stops just short of Ronnie Kray and leans on the

183

bar. The barman slides a glass towards him and Charles knocks back the drink in a single gulp.

'So,' says Ronnie from his armchair, 'a barrister without cash. That's a new one.' He's smiling. *Does he already know?* wonders Charles. Ronnie has a disconcerting way of looking at people, as if staring past them, and a reputation with some of the more gullible East Enders as a mind-reader. Charles knows there are no supernatural powers involved: the Krays have an intuitive understanding of people and their motives; they also have numerous police officers on their payroll and word could easily have reached him.

'I'm in a bit of trouble, Ronnie.'

'So I hear.'

'You know, then?'

Ronnie smiles again, and he seems genuinely amused. 'We keep ears on the police radio. Seems like you're on the run. Considered dangerous, too.'

'Did they say what for?'

'No. Just "escaped from custody". Tut-tut, Charlie. I bet you thought you'd put that all behind you. Can't imagine this'll do much good for your career development.'

'Probably not. But right now, I need a bit of time to regroup and think things through. And a loan, maybe a pony. Can you help?'

Ronnie stares at Charles for a moment and then stands. He approaches Charles until their faces are only an inch or two apart. He's slightly shorter than Charles, and he used to box in a lower weight division, so man-to-man in a boxing ring Charles would have no reason to fear him. But the Krays' penchant for extreme violence, their lack of restraint, both with and without weapons, makes Charles extremely nervous.

He steps back half a pace, relaxing his arms by his side, readying himself for whatever might come.

'I'm really sorry, Charlie,' says Ronnie, leaning forward so his face is again uncomfortably close to Charles's, 'but my professional rules make that impossible.' His broad smile reveals white teeth but, now, no mirth.

'What, nothing?' asks Charles softly. 'Even a spot of cash?'

'Not even for old time's sake.'

'Right.'

'Best fuck off up the Temple; see if any of your posh friends'll help you out.' Ronnie Kray reads Charles's expression perfectly. 'What? Posh friends won't come through? P'raps you shoulda thought of that before now.'

Charles turns to leave, but a thought occurs to him. 'You'll keep schtum?'

Ronnie's face darkens. 'You ain't calling me a grass now, are you, Horowitz?'

'Just asking.'

'You should know better. I won't do you no favours, but I'm no grass. Anyway, this'll be interestin', seein' how far you get. I've got a fiver on you being arrested by the morning.'

Rachel steps out of the door of the Whitechapel Gallery, followed by another young woman. Charles watches from the shelter of a closed shop doorway on the other side of the street. The two women chat for a moment, wave and separate. Rachel heads towards the station. Charles crosses the road swiftly and approaches her from behind. He grabs her elbow.

'Rachel.'

She turns and smiles. 'Hello. What're you doing here?'

Charles leans forward, speaking urgently. 'I'm in trouble and I need your help.'

She becomes very still. Her eyes search his face for a moment, and then she nods. 'Let's go to my place. You can explain there.' She scans the street. A bus is approaching from the direction of the city. 'Quickly!' she urges, setting off at a jog towards the bus stop.

They get on and, without asking, Rachel pays for both of them. She takes him upstairs to the front of the bus where there's an empty seat. Charles sits on the aisle, looking at the pavements as they flash by. After a few minutes he seems to relax a little, but Rachel sees him wipe away beads of sweat trickling from his temple.

Fifteen minutes later they are walking along a quiet residential street in Hackney as dusk falls. Entire families of Hassidic Jews pass them. Charles remembers that it's Friday night, the start of the Sabbath; they're all off to synagogue. He has no use for synagogue but he wishes fervently that he was doing a normal, family thing without a care in the world. He is led to a three-storey terraced house and Rachel opens the door.

'Come in.'

Charles catches a glimpse of a lighted kitchen at the back of the house and a woman stirring something on a stove as he follows Rachel up two narrow flights to the next floor, where she unlocks another door and shows him into a large square room overlooking the back garden. It contains a double bed with a cheap plywood bedside table, a sink in the corner of the room and a heavy oak sideboard which once belonged in a Victorian dining room. A single wooden chair, once part of a different dining set, is piled with books. There's no wardrobe, and Rachel's clothes are hung on an open rack on hangers. The room smells damp.

'You can sit on the bed,' she says. She hangs her coat and bag on the back of the door, shuts it behind Charles, and starts filling a kettle which she places on a small two-burner electric hob on the sideboard. 'I've only got tea.'

'Tea's fine.'

'OK. What on earth is the matter? Is someone *chasing* you?'

'Can you leave that alone for a minute? I need you to sit down.'

Rachel glances sharply at him, but she turns off the hob, lifts the books from the single chair onto the floor, and draws it up two feet from Charles.

'I'll tell you what the headlines will say tomorrow,' starts Charles. He takes a deep breath. 'They'll say "Leading Barrister Murders Wife And Escapes from Police".' He hears her sharp intake of breath and he forges on. 'Underneath it will explain how I viciously cut her throat; how I did it for the money; how I was having an affair with some blonde floozie; how I killed Henrietta to stop her divorcing me; how the evidence against me is overwhelming. And how I am very dangerous and any member of the public seeing me should immediately call the police.'

There's a long silence when he finishes.

'And will any of it be true?' Rachel asks in a small voice.

Charles doesn't answer immediately. He leans towards her, and Rachel flinches and shrinks back in her seat. He reaches out to hold her shoulders at arm's length, feels her freeze with fear, and looks straight into her eyes. He measures every word carefully, pouring sincerity into each one as he speaks.

'Henrietta is dead. I had to identify her body. That's true. Beyond that, not a single word of it, Rachel. I swear on everything I hold dear, not a single word.'

Rachel looks deep into Charles's eyes, and he tries not to look away.

'Tell me,' she demands. 'Everything.'

Charles does: the problems with his marriage, the row at the house, his arrest, the trip back to London with the police, what they found at the flat, and his escape. Then he tells her about Wheatley and his methods, and how trying to persuade him that the evidence stacks up too neatly would be a waste of time. Rachel sits motionless on the chair, occasionally asking questions but for the most part listening intently. Her face doesn't betray any emotion and Charles can't tell if she believes him or not. When he finishes, she turns her head to gaze out of the black curtainless window over the gardens and rooftops, and says nothing. Charles sits on the edge of the bed, waiting for a long time.

'Well?' he asks finally.

'Can I see the bump on the back of your head?'

He stands and turns his back to her. 'There,' he says, probing carefully and parting the hair.

She too stands and explores gently with her fingers.

'OK. Sit down again,' she commands.

'Do you believe me?'

She pauses before replying. 'I did wonder if you had concussion and were having hallucinations or something. And I've been reminding myself that you're very clever, used to dealing with liars and spinning stories for juries, and you're probably a very good liar yourself. But … yes, I do believe you. If you take my advice, you'll hand yourself in. By running off like that you've confirmed your guilt in their eyes.'

Charles sits back on the bed and rubs his eyes. He's exhausted, but there would be little chance of sleep that night. 'I know. But someone's gone to a lot of trouble to set me up, and all the evidence points to my guilt. The police aren't listening to me; they have closed minds. Especially Wheatley.'

'Are you sure you're not mistaken, Charles? Policeman don't do that sort of thing, do they?'

'You have no idea, Rachel. There are departments in the Met that are institutionally corrupt. There are so many taking bribes and bending the rules, it's difficult to find an honest copper.'

Charles tells her about a couple of cases in which he did battle with Wheatley; how the man would plant evidence here, fabricate a confession there. She listens patiently.

'Everyone in the business knows about him,' he concludes.

'But was your client guilty?' she asks.

'Well, the jury said so. Maybe he was, despite the false confession. But I do know this: he was beaten black and blue by Wheatley before he confessed. That man's methods stink. He sets himself up as judge and jury, makes his decision and then creates the evidence to support it. There's no way I'll get a fair hearing from him. If he thinks he's got a watertight case he won't let it unravel it by looking elsewhere. He likes things neat and simple; it's good for his career. If anyone's going to prove my innocence, it has to be me.'

'I think you'll just make things worse.'

'How can it be worse? I'm facing the hangman! And that's the thing so far as you're concerned.' Charles pauses. So far he's banked on her not turning him in, but this is the crunch. 'If you help me, you'll be an accessory.'

'Which means?'

'I think we have tonight before you're at risk. My escape was too late for the late editions, but it'll be all over the papers by morning. After that, you can't be seen to assist me. If you do, after you should've known not to: prison, probably, if I'm convicted.'

'And if I help you right now?'

'You'd have to lie. Say you knew nothing about it; you just bumped into me.'

She considers that for a long time. 'What do you want me to do?'

'Firstly, I need some money. Secondly, and this is the tricky bit, I have to get into Chambers. I need my notebooks.' Rachel frowns, puzzled. Charles explains. 'Barristers all use these blue notebooks. Foolscap light blue notebooks. Every case I've ever done is recorded in them. I date and number them. I've got the names, addresses, and *modus operandi* of hundreds of active criminals, most of whom I've defended. It's a directory of crime. And most of them have cause to thank me. So I need the notebooks. I don't know if the building's being watched. But...' Charles hesitates. 'But … if you decided to go for a walk through the Temple, you could find out for me. If not, I'll try to break in. I doubt they'll be looking for me there; they'll think I'd try to get as far away as possible. But I can't take the risk of just walking in.'

Rachel and Charles enter the Temple from the Embankment entrance by the new Queen Elizabeth Buildings. It offers a more open access than the Victorian alleys off Fleet Street, and Charles should be able to detect if the entrances are being watched. The sky is overcast and the Temple even more shadowy than usual. The ancient courtyards seem deserted; the only person to pass them is the lamp lighter on his way home. Charles points Rachel in the right direction and she leaves him at the corner of Essex Court and Middle Temple Lane. Charles backs into a nearby doorway to wait. He would have been completely invisible to anyone passing, but in fact no one passes him at all. Rachel only has to walk 200 yards or so to the door of 2 Chancery Court and Charles expects her to return within a couple of minutes.

Two minutes become five and five become ten. By fifteen minutes Charles's anxiety has reached breaking point and he convinces himself that Rachel must have been arrested. He's on the point of emerging from the shadows and walking the remaining distance to Chancery Court when he hears muffled footsteps approaching. He retreats into the shadows and watches a figure emerge, almost bent double with a heavy burden. The figure approaches, passes Charles and hesitates, looking around the dimly lit square. Charles steps out and Rachel whirls round.

'Oh, there you are. It was all clear, the lights were on and the doors were wide open. Here —' she unslings from her shoulder a red robes bag — 'I think I got them all.'

'But how on earth did you —'

'The cleaner was at the back, emptying the bins. Your room was obvious, police tape across the door, so I ducked in. Your blue notebooks were on the shelf behind your desk, right?'

'Yes!' responds Charles, astonished.

'I think I got them all. They're bloody heavy, aren't they?'

'Yes, let me take that. We need to get out of here.'

Charles takes the bag, pulls the cord tight and hoists it onto his shoulder. They retrace their steps to the Embankment.

'What took so long was finding something to carry them in, but I found the bag hanging on the back of the door. It's got your initials on it.'

'Perfect. I think you're amazing,' he says. 'But that was really dangerous. Are you sure you weren't seen?'

'There were definitely no police, and the cleaning lady was vacuuming in the basement when I slipped out. I don't think anyone saw me at all.'

'Amazing,' repeats Charles, and he puts this free his arm round Rachel's shoulder and pulls her towards him. It's intended as a friendly squeeze, but she turns her face to his, puts a hand behind his head and pulls it down to her. It's awkward because they're still walking, but her lips touch his and they stop. The kiss is brief, but their faces remain inches from one another.

'My heart was pounding so hard I thought it would burst through my ribs,' she whispers. 'It's the most exciting thing I've ever done in my life!'

CHAPTER SEVENTEEN

Rachel places a plate bearing a sardine sandwich on the chair next to Charles's third cup of instant coffee and sits on the edge of the bed, watching him work. Charles lies on his front, poring over the notebooks, making notes on a sheaf of blank pages torn from the current one. Rachel's glance lingers on his broad shoulders and the curly hair at the nape of his neck. Every time he finishes a notebook, he reaches over and drops it onto the growing pile on the floor beside the bed, and Rachel studies the muscles under his white shirt as they ripple, like the uncoiling of a huge snake.

Charles picks up the next notebook and checks the date and number. Then he reaches over to the remaining pile and fans them out, running his finger across the neat numbers written in black ink in the top right-hand corner of each cover.

'There's a gap,' he concludes. 'At the end of 1960. Is there any chance you missed one or two?'

Rachel shakes her head. 'No. The shelf was empty when I left.'

Charles checks the numbers again. 'Well, there's definitely … one … two missing.'

'Could they be anywhere else?'

'Not that far back. November 1960…' Charles swings his leg round and sits upright. 'What was I doing at the end of 1960?' He shrugs. 'Never mind, there's plenty here.'

Rachel stands. 'I know you've a lot to do, Charlie, and nowhere else to do it. But I have to go to sleep. It's almost two.'

Charles looks up from his notes. 'Is it really? I'd not realised the time.'

'I don't know how you can concentrate when you're so tired.'

'I'm used to it. "Burning the midnight oil" they call it at the Bar. I do it once or twice a week.' He looks up at her, and then at the bed littered with notebooks. 'Ah, I see.'

'Yes. It poses a problem. Would you be able to work on the floor just using the bedside lamp?'

'I should think so.'

'Then I'm going to get changed in the bathroom and go to bed.'

Charles looks around and realises there's nowhere for him to sleep but the floor. 'Right. I'll be fine on the floor,' he offers, standing.

'I have no spare bedding.'

'I'll manage. It's not cold.'

'Well … Charlie, look … it's a big bed, and I'm only little. Once you finish, I have no problem with you getting in … but…'

'Of course. On my honour.'

'I know what lots of people are getting up to nowadays, but … I'm not one of them. Nice Jewish girl, remember?'

'Understood.'

'Got enough coffee to keep you awake?'

Charles picks up the jar, bought from a corner shop on their return journey to the bedsit, and shakes it. 'Plenty.'

He finishes at almost 4 a.m. He undresses, looks at Rachel in the bed, and replaces his underpants. He slips into bed beside her, careful to disturb her as little as possible. She started on one side of the bed but has since migrated to the centre, so Charles lies as close to the edge as possible, curling his body into the same shape as hers so they won't accidentally touch. His face is only inches from the back of her head. Her short dark hair fans over the pillow and the moonlight from the uncurtained window illuminates her slim shoulder protruding from the sheet. It looks unnaturally white. Charles watches it rise and fall with her regular breathing. He is suddenly conscious of the fact that, for the first time in years, he is sharing a bed with someone other than Henrietta. Rachel is a stranger — lovely, desirable and astonishingly generous — but a stranger nonetheless, and Charles is suddenly overwhelmed by waves of loss. His breath catches painfully in his throat as a sob rises in his chest. He slides his legs back out from under the covers to sit on the edge of the bed, his feet hard against the cold lino and his body rigid as he tries not to disturb the sleeping woman behind him.

Hot silent tears spill down his cheeks as, for the first time, he allows himself to be overborne by waves of loss, fear and dislocation. He cries silently, his huge shoulders shaking uncontrollably. He feels a cool hand on the back of his neck.

'Lie down,' says Rachel softly. Charles shakes his head vigorously but can't trust himself to speak. 'Lie down,' she commands again.

Charles does as he's told, facing away from her, knees drawn up to his chest. He feels Rachel's body as she curls into his and strokes his hair.

'Hush,' she whispers.

As Rachel's soft hand strokes, Charles's sobs gradually become less frequent. She listens to his breathing becoming lighter, and after a few minutes he is asleep.

She moves away slightly and props herself up on her hand, staring at the stranger in her bed. Charles turns over, still asleep, and now lies on his back, his muscled arm hanging out of the bed. Rachel notices for the first time his dark curly eyelashes, almost as long as a girl's. Her eye travels down his neck to the rise and fall of his enormous barrel chest with its central patch of black curls. Rachel has has boyfriends in the past — she's no virgin — but they were boys compared to this powerful, very masculine man. She's tempted to lean over and kiss his full lips as he sleeps, but she resists. She knows how exhausted he is and, despite his apparent confidence, how frightened. She divines that the one relationship in which this man has placed all of his trust, his relationship with the law, has failed him, and it's that as much as losing his wife that's left him completely disorientated. She also knows what might follow if she succumbs to the temptation to place a kiss on those lips, and she's not sure how she would feel about that. As she reminds herself, within days he'll probably be in prison, maybe even sentenced to hang. She believes Charles is innocent — she trusts her own judgment of people — but even she can see how the case against him looks impregnable. It's plain foolish to become romantically involved with someone in his position. She lies down again and settles herself once more to sleep.

Some hours later, Charles's eyes open and he is suddenly and completely awake. It is still night, but there is now a blue tinge to the dark rectangle of the window which heralds the dawn. He reaches over gently, feeling for his watch on the floor beside the bed. Rachel stirs, turns towards him sleepily and jumps, her eyes also now wide open.

'Sorry!' she says. 'I'd forgotten you were here.'

Charles smiles. 'It must be really weird waking up to find a hunted man in your bed. I'd do the same if our roles were reversed. What time is it?'

Rachel leans over the edge of the bed to look at an alarm clock also on the floor. Charles watches her nightie ride up and expose most of her buttocks.

'Just gone six.' She lies on her back and pulls the bedclothes up under her chin.

'OK. I'll get out of your way,' says Charles, swinging his legs down and sitting up. 'Can I use the bathroom?'

'Yes; it's directly opposite. I share with Nina in the attic room above, but she's on nights this week. She won't be back for an hour. Use the towels on the left.'

Charles leans over Rachel. 'You've been wonderful, Rachel. Whatever happens … thank you. From the bottom of my heart, thank you.'

She smiles. Then: 'Oh, I've just remembered: you asked for some money. I haven't got much, but there's fifteen pounds in the sideboard drawer. I needed another seven and six for next month's rent anyway, but I'm never going to find it, so you might as well have what I've saved.'

'Thanks. I promise I'll repay it.'

Their eyes lock again, and this time Rachel sits up and takes Charles's head in her hands and kisses him hard on the lips. Then she shoves him away with a grin.

'That's all for now, Charlie. If you get out of this mess … then we'll see.'

CHAPTER EIGHTEEN

Superintendent Wheatley is still seething at Holborne's escape. Despite managing to persuade the Met and the City police to set up roadblocks at both half a mile and one-mile radii from Fetter Lane within twenty minutes, somehow Holborne slipped through. It's extremely frustrating, but Wheatley is confident that it's no more than a temporary setback. An almost unrecognisable photograph of Holborne appeared on the television news that night, but the morning papers have something more recent splashed across the front pages, and it's only a matter of time before someone recognises him. How long can a man like that survive on the run, with no money and no passport? Especially in such a high-profile case: a barrister and a Viscount's daughter? It's *made* for the tabloids! They'll be running it for weeks, months probably.

So Wheatley has returned to the scene of the crime with seven officers who are now in the process of going through every scrap of paper in the place to build a picture of Holborne's life. Usually within twenty-four hours they'd have a list of friends, acquaintances and contacts where he might have sought shelter. But — and this is odd — Holborne seems to have been almost completely unconnected. Enquiries with his parents and brother reveal reliably that he hasn't been in touch with them for almost a decade, and all the contacts turned up at Putt Green are those of the wife. Wheatley begins to get the flavour of the Holbornes' marriage and is not at all surprised it was failing. Holborne's a loner and, as Wheatley assures himself, possessed of just the sociopathic profile he'd expect of a cold-blooded murderer.

It is Wheatley himself who happens to be at the foot of the stairs when the doorbell rings. He opens the front door to find a man in oily overalls on the doorstep.

'Where's the car, mate?' asks the man cheerfully.

'What car?' asks Wheatley.

'The Jag. I was told it'd be in the garage, but it ain't.'

'Who told you it would be in the garage?'

'My guvnor. I've come to collect it.'

'Can you explain please, sir? Who are you?'

'Roger, from Breck & Co.'

'Well, Roger from Breck & Co., who exactly asked you to collect the Jag?'

'Look,' says Roger, very patiently, because he was clearly dealing with an imbecile, 'Mrs Holborne rings us up on Tuesday or Wednesday, or whenever it was, and says that the Jag won't go and would we book it in for work, right?'

Wheatley glances swiftly over his shoulder and escorts the mechanic away from the front door. He walks him to the end of the drive, where a tow truck is parked next to one of the police vehicles, engine idling.

'Go on.'

'Well, we were so busy that we couldn't do it till today. My foreman asks me to come and collect the car and leave a courtesy car, which I have. Over there.'

Wheatley looks across the road where another man stands by the open door of a grubby Ford Anglia.

'But the Jag isn't there,' concludes Roger.

'OK,' replies Wheatley. 'We have the Jaguar and it's now important evidence in an investigation. So it won't need repairing.'

'What about the Anglia?'

'Didn't you watch TV last night?'

Roger shakes his head. 'We ain't got one.'

'OK. Well, Mrs Holborne won't be requiring the Anglia, thank you very much.'

'I can go then?'

'Yes. One thing less for you to do today.'

'Suits me.'

Roger walks across the road to tell his colleague, who gets back in the Anglia, and starts up. Roger climbs back in the tow truck and the two vehicles depart. Wheatley watches them disappear. It might mean nothing — cars, especially Jags, do develop intermittent faults — but Wheatley isn't going to waste police resources investigating a peripheral issue. Even if — most especially if — it might confirm Holborne's story that he couldn't have driven off after the murder.

Charles steps out of Covent Garden Tailors, having spent over half of Rachel's loan. He now wears narrow Hepworth trousers, a white cotton shirt with a narrow black tie, a boxy black leather jacket, and a trilby. With his new Mod haircut and his big-framed glasses containing clear glass he looks like a darker version of Michael Caine. He pauses to look at his reflection in a shop window. Those who know him well would have no difficulty recognising him on a second look, but he looks sufficiently different from the photograph on the front pages of the newspapers that he should be able to move undetected around London, as long as he's careful. He pulls his collar up, lowers the hat over his brow and heads towards the Strand.

It takes Charles fifteen minutes to reach the corner of Fetter Lane and Fleet Street. He enters Oyez, the legal stationers on the corner, and while pretending to read one of the law books, observes the entrance to his apartment for a few minutes. A single bored police officer stands by the door. He wears the dark blue uniform of the City of London Police, which probably means he knows little about the case, but Charles isn't going to take any chances; he waits.

After ten minutes, Charles realises he'll have to move. The shop assistants have been glancing in his direction for a while and he can't afford to raise suspicions. He returns the book to the shelf but, as he's about to leave the shop, the front door of the block opens and Dennis appears. Charles turns his back slightly as the concierge walks past him on the other side of the window. Charles calls "Thank you" to the shop assistants, opens the door and follows.

Dennis has a small paper bag in his hand and a newspaper under his arm. He dodges the traffic on Fleet Street and walks into the Temple through Sergeant's Inn gate. Charles follows him past the *Clachan* pub, along Kings Bench Walk and out of the Tudor Street exit. Dennis jogs through the traffic on the Embankment, sits on a bench overlooking the Thames, opens the newspaper on his lap and takes a sandwich from the paper bag. As he eats, he follows the progress of a large launch cruising past him on its way downstream. Charles crosses the road behind Dennis, puts his hand in his jacket pocket and creeps up silently behind the bench. He places his leather-covered finger on the back of Dennis's neck.

'If you move a single inch, Dennis, I'm going to blow your fucking head off. Do you recognise my voice?'

Dennis chokes on cheese and pickle and it takes him a few seconds to answer.

'Yes, Mr Holborne, sir.'

'Don't turn round. Just carry on watching the boats and listen carefully. I have a few questions. That blonde woman who you saw coming in and going out of my flat.'

'Miss Maxwell?'

'You know her name? OK. Did you ever see her arrive?' Dennis nods, the sandwich clutched tightly in his right hand. 'Did you notice a car?'

'Yeah. A big gold Mercedes.'

Charles raises his voice to be heard above two buses thundering past behind them. 'Did she arrive alone?'

'Yes.'

'Never saw anyone with her?'

'No.'

'Did you ever speak to her?'

'Once, when I helped with her shopping.'

'Explain.'

'She had stuff for the flat, you know, lampshades an' all. An' that enormous teddy or whatever it was. I kept an eye on the car while she went up and down cos otherwise she'd've gotta ticket.'

'I don't suppose you remember the registration number, do you?'

'I do actually. It was flash: NF 777.'

Charles raises his eyebrows in surprise, finding a new respect for his observant porter. 'Do you know anything else about her?'

'No, honest, Mr Holborne, not a thing. I'd tell you if I did.'

'OK, Dennis. Now, listen to me very carefully indeed.' He waits for a lorry to pass behind them before continuing. 'You know they say I killed my wife, don't you?'

Dennis nods.

'The police reports don't say how I'm supposed to have done it.' Charles pauses for effect. 'My wife's throat was cut from ear to ear. Her head was hanging by a thread of skin.'

Charles sees the man's hands trembling in his lap.

'If you say one word, I will come back and do to you *exactly* what I did to her. Do you understand?'

Dennis nods again, vigorously.

'Got your house keys on you?'

'I think so.' He pats his jacket pocket. 'Yes, sir.'

'Your Brenda lives in Westcliffe, doesn't she? So as soon as you finish your lunch, you're going to take a two-week holiday to visit her and the baby. If anyone asks, the stress of what's happened has been a bit much. Don't go back to Fetter Lane. Go straight home and pack a bag and get the next train to Westcliffe. Make it a nice surprise, and don't tell her anything, either. Do you completely understand what I've said?'

'Yeah, sir, really, I do!'

'Tell me.'

'I'm gonna finish me sandwich and go back to Poplar, pack a bag and go visit my girl in Westcliffe. I'm gonna say nothing to no one about this conversation or seein' you. If I do, you'll … you'll come back and…'

'Exactly. Remember, Dennis, I'm facing the rope for one murder anyway. They can't hang me twice. So I've nothing to lose.'

'Yeah, I geddit.'

'Right. I'm going to go now. I want you to wait there without moving for five minutes. I'll be watching. You just finish your lunch and read the football results.'

'Got it.'

'Oh, and while I'm here, did the Hammers win last night?'

'No. They lost two nil.'

'Bad day all round,' says Charles quietly, and he runs back across the road, leaving Dennis still talking through the match to himself.

Charles walks swiftly into the basement car park at Shoe Lane and locates the old Austin Healey. He hasn't got around to registering it in his name so, other than Simon Ellison, no one in the world knows he owns it, and Ellison's out of town on a case.

Breaking in is no difficulty; he just lifts the corner of the soft top and opens the driver's door from the inside, but how to start it? The keys were at Fetter Lane and have now surely been seized by the police. During the Blitz he and his cousin Izzy hot-wired vehicles on a couple of occasions, but that was twenty years earlier. Even if he could remember how they did it, car wiring must surely have changed in the interim.

He sits in the driver's seat, takes his sheaf of notes from his jacket pocket and leafs through them until he finds a passage of cross-examination. One of his early clients was charged with hot-wiring six cars in twenty minutes so his mates could each have one to race along Southend seafront. Part of the Crown's case had been to prove that it was possible, and Charles still has notes of his cross-examination of the police vehicle engineer.

Charles flattens the sheets of paper on the passenger seat, takes a pair of scissors borrowed from Rachel from his pocket, and dons his new leather gloves. He pops and lifts the bonnet, disconnects the battery cable and locates the power wires running up the steering column through the bulkhead. He returns to the car and lies on the seat with his head under the steering column. Taking a deep breath, he starts cutting through the power cables. The scissors are too small and it takes some time, but eventually he gets through them and twists the ends together to complete the circuit. He refers again to the notes and locates two other brown wires going to the ignition. He cuts them both and makes sure they're not touching. He exits the car again and reconnects the battery. Immediately, the radio starts crackling; a good sign. He returns to the car to check that he's followed the notes correctly. Then he pulls the choke out, bends into the foot well and, using his hand, pumps the accelerator pedal twice.

'Moment of truth, Charlie,' he says softly to himself. He twists round and, with his torso and legs hanging over the sill and half-lying on the seat, touches the two bare wires together. The engine starts first time.

'Thank you, Simon!' he exclaims. Without Ellison's tinkering with the points, he knows she'd never have started.

Charles jumps out and slams the bonnet. He returns to the car and manoeuvres it slowly up the exit ramp. It's a lovely day, with white clouds scudding across a blue sky, a perfect day for driving with the hood down, especially as the interior of the car smells unpleasantly of damp, but with reluctance Charles decides against it. Better not to be seen. He turns left onto Fleet Street and heads east.

Charles slows to 15 mph, moves the gear lever into third, lets the clutch out sharply and allows the car to stall. He then disengages the clutch and coasts gently into the kerb. He is outside a shop on Leytonstone High Road. He checks the numbers of the shops and looks again at the notes. Right number, wrong place.

'Bugger,' he swears quietly. What he expected to be a car showroom is now a kitchen and bathroom centre. He climbs out of the car and enters. The place smells new, of freshly-sawn timber and plastic.

'Can I help you, sir?' asks a young salesman. Charles judges that he's about twenty-two years old, also evidently a Mod, with a mass of pink and yellow pimples from forehead to chin. Less Brylcreem might help, Charles observes to himself.

'Aye, mebbe,' he answers, adopting a Scottish accent. 'What happened tae the car dealership that used tae be here?'

The boy shrugs, uninterested. 'Was there a car dealership? I dunno. I only started last week. Mr Wilson!' he calls.

An older man's head appears above a half-assembled bathroom cabinet, a screwdriver in his hand.

'What?' he answers irritably.

'This geezer wants to know what happened to the car showroom.'

'Well, it ain't here, is it? He sold up, the Arab.'

The youngster turns to Charles, and shrugs again. 'Sorry, mate, can't help you.'

Charles reaches into his pocket and comes up with a pound note. 'Would you look in the office and see if there's anything that says where I might find him? His name was Kharadli.'

The lad regards the note, which represents a day's wages, looks sharply over his shoulder at his boss, and whisks it from Charles's fingers. It disappears into his jacket pocket. 'Wait there,' he says quietly, and he walks swiftly to the office at the rear of the showroom.

He emerges a couple of minutes later with a scrap of paper.

'That's the forwarding address for 'is post. Should still be good, we only started fitting out the place last month.'

'Thank you.'

The address is in Leyton, a mile away, and is a breaker's yard. Outside the yard stands an old blue Rolls Royce. Charles parks just round the corner where he can watch the yard unobserved. The gates are open but there's no movement inside, and no customers Charles can see. The difficulty is that anyone might emerge from behind the piles of rusting car chassis or vans with flat tyres and collapsed axles. A large dog is tied by a rope to a hook on the wall of a prefabricated office. It gnaws at a bone between its paws and seems unconcerned.

After fifteen minutes, Charles reaches a decision. He gets out of the Healey and crosses the road towards the gates. The dog pauses in its chewing and watches Charles's approach, but makes no sound or movement. Charles steps carefully into the yard, trying to avoid oily puddles, and the dog leaps to its feet, barking and straining at the rope. A slim, handsome, dark-skinned man in his fifties emerges from the office, stepping out onto a small metal landing but not descending the steps. Charles notes his expensive leather shoes and mauve silk socks, and wonders how long the shoes will last in this environment.

Charles skirts the dog and approaches the office, his right hand held stiffly in his jacket pocket. Kharadli is no fool and has plenty of experience dealing with members of the criminal fraternity. When Charles represented him, he was one of London's major suppliers of ringed vehicles for both criminal enterprises and onward sale to unsuspecting punters. Charles doesn't expect for one minute to frighten him with a stiff finger in his jacket, but he holds no other cards.

'Mr Kharadli?'

The Arab looks down at him suspiciously. 'Who asks?' His eyes move to Charles's jacket pocket and then up to Charles's face, amusement in his eyes.

'You don't remember me? I'm Charles Holborne. I represented you in court some years ago now. Two cases, at the end of 1958? Remember?'

Recognition gradually dawns and Kharadli's face breaks into a smile.

'Yes, I remember! How are you?' He frowns suddenly. 'Wait one minute,' he says. 'You're in big trouble with police, yes? You killed your wife?'

Charles moves closer to him. 'Can I talk to you, just for a minute?'

Kharadli backs off, shaking his head. 'I don't know...'

'Mr Kharadli, when I represented you, the police were saying you'd done all sorts of things, but I didn't believe them,' lies Charles. 'We both know that the police say many things which are not true.'

Kharadli's retreat halts while he considers this. 'This is true, my friend,' he replies, brightening immediately. 'Anyway, what do I care that you killed your wife? Maybe she deserved it.' He laughs loudly. 'Come in!'

Charles follows him into the office, a smell of strong coffee greeting him.

Kharadli pours a tiny amount of coffee from a metal jug into two plastic cups and hands one to Charles.

'Take a seat. You like my new business?' he waves his arm expansively, indicating the muddy yard and piles of rusting metal. 'No money in ringed cars, always hassle, hassle, hassle. This is better. No one asks for money back! Now, how can I help you?'

Charles sips the coffee; it's good, sweet and strong.

'You used to have a policeman friend who could look up car registration numbers. I need to know who owns a particular vehicle, very urgently. It's to do with ... well ... you've obviously read the papers.'

'Yes. This should be possible. But why should I help you? Are you going to pay me?'

Charles shakes his head. 'I have no money to pay you.'

Kharadli leans back in his chair and sips his coffee, his handsome face still smiling lightly. There's a long pause. 'I like this situation, Mr Brief. You've never been on the wrong side of the law before, yes?'

'No,' replies Charles, untruthfully. 'Never.'

'It is different, is it not? Maybe this does you some good; to see life on the other side.' He pauses again. 'OK, I shall help you. Just once for … how you say … old time sake.'

He reaches for a telephone on the desk, dials a number, and waits. 'Is PC Compton on duty today? Tell him it's Mohammed.' There's a short pause. 'So, it's Sergeant now, is it?' says Kharadli cheerfully, giving Charles a thumbs up. 'Congratulations, my friend! Have you time to look one up for me?' He snaps his finger at Charles and shoves a piece of scrap paper across the desk to him. Charles quickly scribbles the number on it, and slides it back. 'NF 777.'

Kharadli snaps his fingers again and mimes writing, and Charles hands him the pen. 'Yes,' he says as he writes. 'Yes … got it. Thank you, Steve, much appreciated. You must come round to the house soon … yes, it's been too long. Bring the children, too … OK. Bye.' He replaces the receiver and hands the paper to Charles, who reads the scribble. 'Starline Model Agency, D'Arblay Street, W1.' Charles sighs, disappointed. A company car. Any number of people might have been driving it.

'That's all I can do,' says Kharadli. 'Now, Mr Holborne, I must get back to work.' He stands and holds out his hand. 'I do sincerely hope that everything works out for you, my friend, but please do not contact me again. One cannot be too careful who one is seen with.' He is completely serious.

Charles returns to the Austin Healey. He looks at his watch. With luck, he can get to Companies House before it closes.

CHAPTER NINETEEN

Peter Bateman, pupil barrister, and his flatmate, a trainee doctor at Guys, are just settling down to their grilled lamb chops when they hear the landlady's call from the foot of the stairs. Peter grimaces, but descends to find that Stanley has left a message, summoning him to Chambers where he is to prepare an overnight return for Middlesex Assizes. One of the other barristers has got himself part-heard on the Western Circuit and can't get back in time. Peter doesn't relish working through the night, but a brief, any brief, is a Godsend for a young man just starting at the Bar.

When he arrives, with indigestion, at Chancery Court, Peter finds the brief as predicted in Charles's pigeonhole with a note from Stanley: "*Court 2 Middlesex Assizes, NB 12 noon*" — not to be listed before noon. That at least is good news. If Peter finishes by the early hours, he might still manage a few snatched hours' sleep.

He opens the door to Charles's room where he usually sits, waiting for the pearls of wisdom to drop from his pupilmaster's lips. The City of London police tape that formerly barred entry has been removed, and Peter's been told it's safe to use the room. He sits at the desk facing Charles's, wondering where his murderous pupilmaster is. Peter is convinced there must have been some mistake. Six months of sharing a room with a man, travelling on trains with him up and down the country, burning the midnight oil, and you get to know him pretty well. Peter finds it difficult to believe Charles is guilty, whatever the newspapers say. And a cut throat razor?

Not Charles's style at all; far too crude and theatrical and, evidentially, suicidal.

He switches on the desk lamp and almost immediately notices something is wrong. The day before, when he was told to work in an adjoining room, he distinctly saw from the threshold the shelf behind Charles's desk, lined as usual with its series of annotated blue notebooks. They've been gathering dust there from the day he joined chambers. Now the shelves are bare. *Perhaps the police took them?* he wonders, *but what on earth for?* He looks at the back of the door where Charles's robes bag usually hangs. It too is bare. It's not unheard of for a barrister to borrow another's robes, if he has an unexpected court hearing for example, but the absence of the bag and the notebooks taken together is puzzling.

Peter picks up the telephone and dials Stanley's home number.

'Stanley, it's Peter Bateman. Sorry to trouble you. I'm in Chambers now. Do you know if the police removed any property from Mr Holborne's room?'

'Not as far as I know. An officer came yesterday with the fingerprint man, and when they finished they simply took down the tape. Why?'

'Mr Holborne's robes bag and all his notebooks are missing.'

There's silence at the other end of the line. Then: 'If you go to my desk you'll find a piece of paper on the blotter from the City of London Police. It's got the name of the officer who came yesterday. I'd like you to give Snow Hill a call just to make sure.' There's another pause. 'You don't think Mr Holborne might have broken in and taken them, do you?'

'The thought did cross my mind,' replies Peter. 'But I wouldn't want to get him into more trouble.'

'I respect your loyalty, sir, but I don't see how he could *be* in any more trouble. And this has caused very bad publicity for Chambers — I've been fielding press calls all day — so we need to distance ourselves from it. We have to be seen to be helping in every way possible. Give Snow Hill a call, and keep me informed of developments.'

'All right. Will do.'

Peter hangs up and goes to fetch the officer's name and telephone number. He hesitates, but then smiles as he takes Stanley's chair while he dials the number. The officer's off duty, but the duty sergeant gives Peter the phone number of someone at Buckinghamshire Constabulary, a DC Sloane, who might be able to help. Peter dials again.

'DC Sloane.'

'Hello, Detective Constable. My name's Peter Bateman. I'm Charles Holborne's pupil. I'm very sorry to trouble you, but I've just come into Chambers, and there's something odd which I think you should know.'

'What's that?'

'All his old notebooks from his criminal cases have disappeared, together with his red barrister's bag, you know, the one he used to carry his robes. Did you or one of the other officers remove them?'

'I'll need to make enquiries, sir, about the notebooks, but we've definitely not got his robes bag. That was last seen at Holborne's property in Buckinghamshire on the day of the murder. And it's blue, not red.'

'No, that's not right. He's never had a blue one, not since I've known him. I've seen him with his red one almost every day for the last six months. It was on the back of his door the day before yesterday. And he wouldn't be seen dead with a blue one, anyway.'

'Why not?' asks Sloane, puzzled.

'The blue ones you buy yourself. The red ones are given by a leader to a junior as a gift, to mark good work done on a case. Charles is very proud of his red bag. He'd never use a blue one.'

Peter waits, listening to the scratch of Sloane's pen at the other end of the line.

'You don't know what case it was for, do you?'

'Yes.' Peter smiles. 'You don't have to spend long in Charles's company to find out. It was his first murder. The Queen versus Sands and Plumber.'

'Has anyone taken a statement from you, Mr Bateman?'

'No. You're the first.'

'Well, it may be unimportant, but I'll send an officer over in the course of the next couple of days to take down what you've told me and get a signature. You're not planning on holidays in the near future, are you?'

'No. You can get me through Chambers.'

At almost exactly the same time as Peter is hanging up and starting his late-night work, Charles is standing in the dark, in the back garden of the Hackney house where Rachel has her bedsit. Her room is in darkness. He's undecided. The idea of sleeping in the Healey is distinctly unappealing but he has nowhere else to go. He's had to put petrol in the car and buy some food. And then the car radio died, and he was forced to buy a small transistor radio so he could pick up news reports of the investigation. It was more expensive than buying newspapers, but meant that he didn't continually risk being recognised by newsagents or paper vendors, all of whom had hundreds of copies of his photograph right in front of them. He now has less than £3 of the money Rachel lent him, enough for the cheapest of hotel rooms, but little else thereafter. In any case, he can't risk being asked to produce a passport.

Charles picks up a pebble from a flowerbed and throws it at Rachel's window just in case she's gone to bed early. It's a good shot, and the *clack* made by the impact would certainly have disturbed her, had she been there. The room remains in darkness and silence.

Immediately beneath Rachel's window is the sloping roof of the kitchen at the back of the house which Charles glimpsed the night before. The window of the kitchen is again illuminated and every now and then a middle-aged woman in hair-curlers and a dressing gown passes to and fro. Charles hears laughter from a radio or television. On the flank wall of the property, around the corner from the window, is a garden bench. Charles removes his fake spectacles and stows them carefully in his breast pocket. He climbs onto the bench, reaches up to the overhanging tiles and tests their strength. They creak dangerously and he desists, but there's a gap under the line of the roof and the soffit, and a very slight overhang of the roof beam. He gets a good grip on the beam and pulls; it holds firm. He reaches up again and hauls himself onto the kitchen roof, taking care to avoid standing on the edge, where his weight risks snapping the tiles. He tiptoes his way up the gradient to the top of the roof where it joins the wall. Rachel's bedroom window is now at waist height, an old wooden sash with no lock. He puts his hands under the lower sash and heaves upwards. The window slides up easily and Charles rolls into the room.

It is empty and smells of damp and Rachel's perfume. Charles doesn't want to move further than necessary in case his footsteps are heard from below. He slips off his shoes, takes one pace to the bed, and lies down carefully, fully dressed.

Rachel arrives two hours later. Charles is half asleep but hears her voice at the front door and her steps coming up the stairs. He reaches to the floor and turns on the bedside lamp, and Rachel sees him the moment she opens the door. She stops, but smiles, and immediately closes the door quietly behind her.

'I wondered if I'd see you,' she says. She removes her coat and hangs it on the back of the door. 'How did you get in?'

He indicates the window. 'You should have it looked at. It's decades since I did any burglaring, and if I can get in, anyone can.'

'You've been a burglar?' she asks, her voice shocked.

Charles hangs his head. 'And worse. It was during the war, and I was just a kid. I know a lot of people who did a lot of things they'd rather forget now.'

'I wonder if I'd have believed you about … Henrietta … if I'd known a bit more about you,' she says cautiously.

He stands and approaches her. 'I've told you nothing but the truth.'

She nods. 'I'm probably an idiot, but I do believe you. But you're a more complex man than I realised, Charlie Horowitz.'

'Yes, possibly. And I'm really sorry to turn up again, like this, but I'm almost out of money, and I've nowhere else to go. I said I didn't want to put you in any danger, and I meant it, so just say if you want me to leave.'

'No, it's fine. You can stay, although you'll have to be very quiet, as the house is full. You'll need to leave by, say, six?'

'No, I need to leave before then. I've got somewhere to be, but I could do with a bit of shut-eye beforehand.'

'Well, you can explain all that in a moment. We need to talk about your family,' she says, putting on the kettle to boil.

'My family? What about them?'

'Charles! They're frantic with worry!'

'I doubt it,' he replies, bitterly. 'They said *Kaddish* for me years ago.'

Rachel steps closer to him, examining his face carefully, her eyes narrowed. She shakes her head sadly. 'And you think that means they don't care?'

Charles shrugs and shakes his head sharply, an awkward movement, as if trying to throw something off. 'They made their position abundantly clear,' he says, breaking eye contact with her. She reaches up and gently turns his face back towards hers.

'You're wrong, Charles. They love you. Your father in particular misses you terribly. I see him in synagogue every week. You know he's never let anyone sit in your seat?'

'No,' replies Charles. He sighs. 'I didn't know that.'

'If you saw him, Charles, you'd know. He looks so forlorn. Anyway, newspapermen have been camping on their doorstep since the news broke and they can't even go out. Your brother thinks your parents' line is tapped.'

'They'd need a warrant, but it is possible I guess.'

'For heaven's sake, will you stop being a lawyer for a moment?'

'Sorry. So, you've spoken to them?'

'I thought someone should tell them you're OK. And that you're innocent! That's where I've been. I didn't want to risk calling, so I went round.'

'You did?' he exclaims. 'And?'

'They're relieved. To know you're OK, and that I'm … well, that I can do something to help.'

'Does Dad think I did it then?' asks Charles.

'How can you ask that? Of course he doesn't.'

Charles nods introspectively, turns and sits heavily on Rachel's bed.

'So,' she says, after a moment. Charles looks up. She's standing next to the open door of a tiny refrigerator he hadn't noticed before. 'I have four eggs and some cheese. Your choices appear to be scrambled eggs or omelette. Any preference?'

'No, either would be wonderful.'

'OK. Tell me what you've been doing. By the way, I like the new look.'

Charles wakes at 3:30 a.m. Rachel lies on her front, her left arm across his chest and her head snuggled into his side. He inhales her smell and watches the creamy bumps of her vertebrae rise and fall with her breathing. He slips out of bed quickly, his feet hitting the unheated lino.

He dresses hurriedly in the dark, opens the door a couple of inches and listens for a few seconds. Satisfied that the household is asleep, he creeps silently downstairs. The front door is unlocked and he steps into the cold night, closing the door gently behind him. He's managed almost four hours' sleep and feels refreshed and alert.

The street is deserted. He gets into the Austin Healey, shivers from the cold and damp, starts her up by touching the ignition wires together again and heads towards the City of Westminster.

The streets of Hackney are silent and almost devoid of traffic, but as he heads west it becomes slightly busier. There's still a fair bit of action in Soho. The less successful, or perhaps more desperate, toms still prowl the pavements looking for clientele, competing for the few late kerb-crawlers. Several of the clubs are closing and Charles has to swerve as a drunk ejected by two bouncers almost falls under his wheels. The men laugh and Charles watches in his rear-view mirror as one takes a half-hearted kick at the punter crawling out of the gutter.

Charles finds a space to park off Wardour Street and returns to D'Arblay Street on foot. Fitting snugly in the palm of his right hand is the final purchase he made the previous day, a shilling's worth of pennies in a cardboard tube, fresh from Lloyds Bank on Chancery Lane.

Two young women in costume and tall golden headdresses emerge in a gale of laughter, cigarette smoke and cheap perfume from the back door of a club, and step straight into a waiting taxi. The bouncer on the door watches Charles carefully as he passes, and then shuts the steel door with a clang. Charles hears shoot bolts being fastened behind him.

Charles rounds the corner and turns into D'Arblay Street, looking for the Starline Model Agency. Parked right in front of him, outside a strip club, is the gold Mercedes, NF 777. A flashing pink neon sign over the club's facade informs Charles that inside he will find "Live Naked Acts". A big yellow poster over the blacked-out windows further confides that, although this is a private members club, as a special offer he may purchase membership in the foyer for only ten shillings. Photographs of scantily-clad women in improbable poses are displayed on a board on the pavement.

Two large men stand by the front entrance. Charles notices that they're unusually alert for this time of the morning, when Soho is normally heading for bed. They constantly check up and down the street and their hands move nervously.

Charles continues slowly past the club, feigning interest in the photographs of the strippers. As he passes the door he sees, to the right of the foyer, a staircase leading to the first floor and a sign for the Starline Model Agency, with an arrow pointing upwards.

Charles's presence seems to make the two men on the door even more uneasy. One, a giant of a black man with a gold ring on each of his ten fingers, takes a step towards Charles. Charles assesses him. At over six feet four and eighteen stone he is almost six inches taller and three stones heavier than Charles. Charles wonders what would happen if he had to force his way in. Just bounce off him, he concludes.

'We're closing,' the giant says in a Jamaican accent, looking down on Charles. He leans even closer to Charles's face, and Charles smells aftershave, lots of it. 'Move on, man.'

'I'm not going to the club,' replies Charles, stepping back slightly, and smiling. 'I need to speak to Mr Fylde.'

'Who's asking?' asks the other man from behind, an extremely fat white man with an improbable blond quiff and an earring in each ear.

Charles turns. 'Tell him it's Charles Holborne.'

The two men look at one another.

'Put your hands against the window,' orders the white man. Charles complies and allows himself to be frisked expertly. 'He's clean,' concludes the man, stepping back. The roll of pennies remains undetected.

'You sure pick your time,' comments the Jamaican, but he goes inside. Through the door Charles watches him lift a telephone in the ticket booth and press a button. A second later, ringing can be heard from the office above the club and Charles looks up at the window which casts a rhomboid of yellow light on the pavement.

Charles watches the conversation and after a moment the Jamaican hangs up and returns to the pavement. He nods at Charles strangely, his head going up rather than down. 'You can go up.'

The two bouncers watch Charles carefully as he enters the small lobby. It smells of cigarette smoke and stale beer. At the far end is a black curtain from which emanates muffled bump and grind music. A bored hat check girl wearing tight golden shorts, a bustier and goosebumps watches from behind the counter as Charles climbs the stairs opposite.

Charles finds his eyes travelling up the shapely legs of a female descending the stairs towards him. Good legs, he thinks, though not as toned and muscular as Rachel's. His eyes travel further up the girl as the gap between them narrows and is greeted by a pair of bouncing brown nipples. The bare-breasted dancer pauses in her attempt to pull on a gold lamé waistcoat and stops a couple of steps above Charles. Charles eyes move further north to be met by a sarcastic grimace which might, earlier in the evening, have been a reasonable facsimile of a smile.

'Piss off, pervert,' she says in a weary voice, and pushes past him, tucking a heavy breast into place through an armhole.

At the top of the flight is a wooden door with a brass plaque on it proclaiming the premises of the "Starline Model Agency" and, underneath that in smaller writing, "Mr N Fylde, Managing Director"; the name Charles found listed at Companies House, and presumably the usual driver of the gold Mercedes, NF 777.

Charles knocks on the door. Another Jamaican accented voice from inside answers: 'It's open.'

Charles enters. He is surprised to find the office well appointed. Light grey carpet covers the floor and the walls are hung with classy black-and-white photographs showing scenes from the race track. In front of him stands a large mahogany desk behind which sits a short but powerful black man with a shaved head. He wears a light brown three-piece suit, the jacket of which is hung behind him on a hanger. A gold watchchain pulls taut across his waistcoated belly, and he sports a gold-coloured silk tie which Charles rather covets. A heavy gold chain hangs from his neck and his fingers flash and sparkle with rings. He's evidently counting the night's takings because, as Charles enters, he snaps a rubber band around a thick wad of notes, turns, and throws the wad into an open safe on the floor behind him.

'I thought you said we'd never meet,' says Fylde, rising from his chair and studying Charles. 'Anytin' wrong?'

'No,' says Charles. 'But there's a loose end or two, and I need a word with Melissa.'

'That's not possible,' replies Fylde, kneeling to the safe. Charles thinks he's locking it, but a second later Fylde stands and there's a pistol in his hand, and it's pointing at Charles's chest.

'OK. Who da fuck are you, man?'

'Charles Holborne,' replies Charles.

'No, you ain't. De man I deal with talk different.'

Charles nods. 'That's because I'm *the real* Charles Holborne. Look at your newspaper.' Charles indicates the *Evening Standard* at the end of Fylde's desk. His photo takes up the top half of the front page. 'Whoever you dealt with set me up. And used you and Melissa to do it.'

Fylde's eyes flick to the newspaper and back at Charles, who has taken off his glasses and put them in his pocket. Fylde shrugs. 'That ain't —'

There's a sudden explosion from downstairs, a woman's scream and the sound of glass shattering. Footsteps thunder up the staircase and Charles backs behind the office door at the same instant as it crashes open. From behind the door, through the narrow gap afforded by the hinged edge, he sees on the threshold a short man in a black suit, dark overcoat and a trilby hat, pointing a sawn-off shotgun at Fylde.

'Put that peashooter down,' he orders Fylde, 'or I'll put daylight through you.'

Fylde hesitates for a moment and slowly lowers his right hand, placing his pistol on the desk.

'Now move to the side.'

Fylde does as instructed. A second crash echoes up the staircase from the foyer. The man in the black suit calls over his shoulder, his eyes not wavering from Fylde.

'You OK, Jackie?'

There's no response.

The man in the suit takes half a step into the office. Charles nods at Fylde, who raises his eyebrows almost imperceptibly. Charles launches his considerable weight with all his force into the door and, at the same instant, Fylde ducks. The shotgun explodes, bringing a shower of plaster and dust from the ceiling, but the force of Charles's unexpected charge knocks the intruder to one side. Charles rams the door again with his shoulder, hearing a whoosh of air from the chest on the other side of the door as it's compressed between the door and the door jamb. Charles pivots around the leading edge of the door but he isn't fast enough and the other, balance regained, steps back half a pace to give himself room to fire again. Charles has no time. He throws a left jab and a straight right with the roll of pennies, using all the weight he can muster. The right lands just under the intruder's left eye, the blow snapping his head sideways. His eyes roll up, his knees sag and he folds onto the grey carpet like a marionette with its strings cut. Charles neatly catches the shotgun before it hits the ground.

The fat doorman appears at the head of the steps, wheezing, blood trickling from his scalp. He holds a pistol in his hand. Fylde has regained his feet and his pistol.

'You OK, boss?' asks the doorman, eying Charles suspiciously.

Fylde crosses the room with surprisingly light steps and rolls the unconscious man onto his back. He turns slowly to look at Charles with surprise.

'I am now. How many were dere?'

'Three. Kimani got one outside, but got hisself hurt, a knife wound in his side. The third did a runner when he 'eard the gunshots.'

'OK. Drag dis one out, and search dem both. Then tie dem up in the van. After dat get a cab and take Kimani to hospital,' orders Fylde.

'What about this geezer?' asks the other, pointing at Charles, who is brushing dust and ceiling plaster off his new jacket and trousers.

Fylde looks Charles up and down. 'I tink we OK, yes, Mr Holborne?' He holds out his hand for the shotgun. Charles turns the weapon over once, shrugs, and hands it over.

'Too noisy for my taste,' he says.

'Yeah,' says Fylde to the doorman. 'We OK.'

The doorman starts dragging the unconscious man feet first towards the stairs.

'Hold on a second, please,' says Charles. Charles pats the man's inside pockets and from one breast pocket takes out a pistol. He searches again and from the other pocket he withdraws a black leather wallet. Inside are ten brand-new £10 notes. He pockets five, replacing the others. 'Cleaning expenses,' he explains, and he tosses the wallet onto Fylde's desk. 'No objections?'

Fylde shrugs and shakes his head. He nods at his employee and the unconscious man's head disappears out of the door and can be heard thumping on each step as he is dragged by his feet to the ground floor.

'What was that all about?' asks Charles. 'It looked as if you were expecting it.'

'The Krays,' replies Fylde shortly. 'I won't pay for their protection.'

Charles laughs grimly. 'My credit with Ronnie is getting worse by the day.' Fylde looks questioningly at Charles, but he waves away the query. 'Not important,' he says.

Fylde brushes dust off the edge of his desk and leans against it, assessing Charles. 'You really dat steppa? The one all over de papers?'

'Steppa?'

'Escapee.'

'Yes.'

Fylde regards Charles carefully. He shakes his head slowly and sniffs. 'OK. I's very busy, as you can see. So, here's the story.' He speaks swiftly as he busies himself with clearing his desk and locking the safe. 'A geezer phone. He say he want a girl to fake adultery, you know? So de wife can get a divorce?'

Charles nods. There's a thriving market in providing the evidence necessary for divorce grounds: hired co-respondents, photographers and hotels that look the other way.

'If me agree, a motorcycle courier will come in twenty minutes with a monkey. All me have to do is supply one classy tom to pose as de mistress a few time. Got to be white, drive a flash car, speak well, and dat. Just go in and out dis flat a few time, you know, be noticed? And another monkey tomorrow, if it all go well.'

'And access to the flat?'

'Same courier, next day, brings a key and a timetable, when to go, when not to go.'

'Who was the man?'

'Me never see him, but he was white, spoke like you. But not your voice. I can leave a message at an answering service if I need to … for Mr Holborne.'

'And the girl's real name?'

Fylde focusses all his attention on Charles again. 'I ain't lettin' you hurt her. Girl just doing a job.'

'I'm not going to hurt her. Not my style.'

Fylde considers. 'Shirley Lovesay.'

'Is she here?' demands Charles, suddenly hopeful.

Fylde shakes his head. 'On de Costa. Geezer pays her to lie low. I 'spect her back in de club on Monday.'

'Did she ever meet him?'

'I don't know man, maybe. He give her a few tings to take to your place. Now, I got to attend to business.'

'Last question: where does she live?'

'Las' house on Grafton Road, Kentish Town. Next to de pub.'

'Thank you. I'll leave you to clear up.'

Charles turns to leave, but Fylde calls after him, 'Maybe you need a change of career, Mr Brief Man! I can use someone like you.'

Charles turn and smiles. 'I'll let you know.'

CHAPTER TWENTY

Charles sits in the Austin Healey, checking out his newly acquired pistol and considering his next move. The pistol is American, a stainless-steel AMT Backup made in California. The serial number has been filed off but it's been well maintained. Charles checks the magazine: full — six gold-coloured rounds of 0.38 calibre. It's small and Charles finds it fits snugly in the breast pocket of his jacket without any obvious bulge. He takes it out again, turning it over. Not much use at a distance, but as a concealed backup, it's perfect. He wishes he had time to find somewhere to test fire it.

Charles turns his attention to Fylde's story. Wheatley isn't the sort to be interested in loose ends when he already has a nicely packaged prosecution, but even he can't ignore the pimp's evidence of another man posing as Charles. Of course, that assumes Fylde will give a statement — unlikely, given his profession. There's the evidence of Dennis, but he just confirms that "Melissa" moved things into the flat, which is just as consistent with Wheatley's case. To have any chance of persuading Wheatley to take his story seriously, Charles needs a description of the man posing as him and *that* means waiting until the blonde, Shirley, returns from the Costa Del Sol. If she'll meet him and co-operate, which also isn't certain. So he has to wait at least four days on the chance that Shirley can give a description, and is prepared to do it.

It all feels too tenuous, and in any case Charles doubts he'll last another four days at liberty before the police catch up with him. He won't go back to Rachel's flat; she's already risked too much for him. There's only one other place where he might

226

turn, and that's Izzy's in Shadwell, but he hasn't seen the lighterman in nearly fifteen years, and is embarrassed to ask for help now. Anyway, he's not sure his formidable aunt Beatrice, Izzy's mother, wouldn't turn him in anyway.

He's at a loss to decide what to do next. In fact the only things of which Charles is absolutely certain is that, firstly, he's famished and, secondly, courtesy of the Krays' shooter, he's flush. He glances at his watch. Where to get a decent meal in London at quarter to six in the morning? He smiles to himself, starts the engine and drives east, back towards the City of London.

The streets are getting busier but it takes Charles only fifteen minutes to reach Smithfield's meat market. He turns off Farringdon Road and parks in West Smithfield. Under the dome of the new market there's a jam of unloading lorries, porters and men with bloodied overalls and carcasses hefted across their shoulders. Charles has to sidestep swiftly as he is almost run down by a man trotting across the cobbles carrying half a cow. Charles crosses the central courtyard to *The Fox* and pushes his way through the heavy doors. The pub is half-full of market traders and drivers. The smell of frying steak and beer makes Charles's mouth water immediately.

The Fox is one of half a dozen pubs that opens at 4 a.m., specifically for the meat market. Charles discovered it while on one of his insomniac walks around the city's deserted streets, shortly after the rebuilding of Smithfield finished the previous year, and loved the slice of London underbelly it revealed.

He pushes his way to the long wooden bar, attracting a few glances as he does. A man takes his order for a rare steak sandwich and chips and pulls him a pint of mild. Charles threads his way through the butchers and porters to a small wrought iron table in the corner of the bar. He sits facing into the corner of the room, pulls up his collar and tries to look inconspicuous as he focuses on his next step.

He is stuck. He can think of nothing to do but lie low until Monday and then hope he can speak to Shirley. Perhaps, now he has money, he could check into a hotel, maybe outside London?

A harassed waitress brings his steak and a large pot of mustard and hands him some cutlery rolled in a paper napkin. Charles is working his way through his wonderfully bloody steak sandwich when he looks up. In the mirror facing out onto the bar he spots a man staring at him. He's middle-aged, with a few strands of sandy hair combed across a mottled pale scalp, and a day's growth of stubble on a doughy chin. A rollup stuck to his lower lip bobs up and down like a conductor's baton as he talks from the corner of his mouth to another man at his elbow. He wears a donkey jacket over a blood and fat-streaked knee-length apron and heavy Wellington boots.

Charles considers reaching for the pistol in his inside pocket, but decides against: it would bring things to a head too quickly and, if possible, he wants to finish his breakfast. Instead, he alters his grip on the steak knife, ready to use it as a weapon if necessary. He manages to eat a couple more mouthfuls before a voice sounds above him.

'All right if I sit down, mate?'

It doesn't look as if he's about to be grabbed immediately so Charles mutters, 'Free country,' through a mouthful of cow, and indicates the chair opposite with the knife. The man pushes past the table and lowers himself onto the seat opposite Charles.

'We've met before,' says the man, keeping his voice low and not making direct eye contact with Charles.

'We have?'

'Coupla years back. You represented me brother at the Bailey. Del Plumber.' He speaks through lips that barely move and Charles has to concentrate to catch the words over the hubbub in the bar.

Charles tenses. There is no denying now that he's been recognised.

'You won't remember me,' says the man. 'We only met the once, just before sentencing, and you was busy. But I remember you. And I know you're in a spot of bother.'

'I'm tooled,' warns Charles. 'And not just the knife.'

The man looks Charles in the face for the first time. 'Easy … easy! If I was gonna grass you, why'd I come over?'

'What then?'

'Del's in trouble —'

Charles interrupts. 'Well, perhaps you've clocked that I've got problems of my own right now.'

'I know that. But I wonder if they're not connected. You hear about Robbie Sands?'

'Sands? Derek's co-defendant? No. Why?'

'He's out. Ten days ago. Started a ruckus with a nonce and did a runner on the way to hospital.'

'What makes you think he's connected to my … troubles?'

'He's been bothering Del. And your name was mentioned.'

Charles's hands cease moving. He studies the other man's face. He hasn't seen Plumber in two years, but there is indeed a similarity with the man before him; the same height, colouring and fleshiness, although this brother's not turned to flab in the same way as Plumber. The man looks at him frankly, awaiting a verdict. Charles decides that he's telling the truth.

'What're you going to do?' asks Charles.

'About seeing you? Nuffin'. Not my business. I keep straight, but I still don't talk to rozzers. The family'd never forgive me.

But go and see Del, eh? He's in a right state. He wants to get away, but there's no way.'

'Why not?' asks Charles, but the man doesn't reply. He pulls a Rizla cigarette paper from a packet and starts writing on it with a stub of pencil taken from behind his ear. He slides it across the table.

'That's the address. Have a shufti.'

Without another word he stands and brushes past Charles, causing the table to wobble and some of Charles's beer to slop over the edge of the glass. Charles watches him in the mirror as he rejoins the man he'd been talking to, laughs and slaps him on the back and then disappears through the throng. Over the heads of the traders and butchers, Charles sees the door of the pub open and close again. He looks at the wafer of paper in his hand. The address is in Limehouse, only a mile or two further east. Charles pockets it and resumes his breakfast.

Charles brings the Austin Healey to a halt outside a Georgian house in Narrow Street, Limehouse. He can smell the river on the other side of the houses, less than 100 yards to his right, and two seagulls screech, flap and squabble over something dead in the gutter opposite him.

The pavements are quite full as people hurry to work, and more than one person notes the Healey and looks into its windows as they pass. Charles needs to move. The house he is looking for is two doors down from *The Grapes* pub. He approaches a faded blue door, tacked to which is a dog-eared index card with a message in block capitals: "PLEASE KNOCK AND WALK UP." He knocks, flakes of peeling blue paint falling to his feet as he does so, turns the handle and opens the door cautiously. A narrow wooden staircase faces him. He climbs to a small landing from which a half-glazed door opens. A radio can be heard playing music through the door. He knocks on the glass and waits. There's no answer so he pushes the door open to be assailed by the sharp odour of urine. He wrinkles his nose. He's in a large kitchen. This is a poor household but, despite the smell, it's immaculately clean and tidy. The room was once rather elegant, with tall ceilings, a large intact plaster ceiling rose and an imposing fireplace now housing an electric two-bar radiator. The floor is covered in lino and there's a scrubbed pine kitchen table. The previous night's dishes, washed, sit on a metal drainer.

Charles follows the sound of the radio which emanates from another room leading off the kitchen. He knocks on the door, twice, with no response, so he opens it slowly.

The room beyond is in darkness and here the smell of urine is at its strongest. Charles pauses to allow his eyes to become accustomed to the gloom. There's an unusually high narrow bed against the far wall, and a hoist attached to the ceiling hanging over it. The curtains are closed. Then Charles sees two dark shapes on the floor. He takes a couple of steps to the window and opens the curtain nearest him. Light enters the bedroom. Derek Plumber lies on the floor, unconscious, face down with his knees drawn up under him. His pyjama trousers are saturated with urine, and his right arm is outstretched, as if reaching for something on the dressing table. Beside him, on its side, is a wheelchair. Charles rights the wheelchair and bends to lift Plumber back into it. As he does so Plumber's pyjama legs flap emptily and Charles realises with a shock deep to the pit of his stomach that the man has no legs below the knees. He holds Plumber under the armpits, a deadweight. He changes his mind and instead of putting him into the wheelchair from which he might simply slide back onto the floor, Charles manages to swing him partially onto the bed.

From there he rolls the unconscious man into a more secure position. It's only as he is straightening Plumber that Charles recognises another strong odour in the room. It takes him a moment to identify it, so incongruous does it seem, and then he remembers the smell from Henrietta's dressing room: nail varnish remover.

Charles looks round at the dressing table against the wall; it's almost completely covered with bottles and boxes of medications, and Charles's eye is immediately caught by half a dozen ampoules of clear liquid and an open box of disposable syringes. Charles picks up one of the ampoules: insulin. He looks back at Plumber.

'You poor bastard,' he says softly. 'You couldn't reach.'

Charles returns to the bedside and tries to rouse Plumber, shaking him and slapping his face once or twice, but he knows he's wasting his time. His come across this in several of his personal injury cases: Plumber's in a coma from diabetic ketoacidosis, which explains the smell of nail varnish remover on his breath. He needs an ambulance, and quick. His breathing is fast and shallow and his face the colour of wet cement.

Charles races to the door, across the kitchen and down the stairs. He scans the road — no phone boxes — and spins round to the shut door of *The Grapes*. He hammers on the door with increasing urgency. Eventually a sash window on the second floor is thrown up.

'We're closed!' shouts a man in pyjamas.

'I know. Call an ambulance, quickly! The man two doors up needs help.'

'What, Derek?'

'Yes!'

'Righto!' says the man, and his head disappears back inside.

Charles retraces his steps to Plumber's bedroom. The ambulance station is just around the corner and he has a couple of minutes at most. For the first time he examines more carefully the otherwise very tidy home and sees that the bedroom is the exception. All the drawers and cupboards are open, contents strewn on the floor. Someone's gone through the room before me, thinks Charles. But what for?

A sudden noise startles Charles and he whirls round to see a short young woman in nurse's uniform enter the bedroom. She halts in surprise.

'Who are you? What's going on?' she demands. Then she sees Plumber. 'What have you done to Derek?' she shouts, brushing past Charles and going to the bedside. 'Oh, Jesus!'

'I found him on the floor with the wheelchair turned over. I got him back into bed and asked the landlord of *The Grapes* to call an ambulance.'

The district nurse is taking Plumber's pulse. 'Oh Jesus!' she repeats. She turns back to address Charles. 'Was it you on the phone last night?'

'Me? No.'

'One of his friends said he'd stay with him and that I needn't come. Said he was a doctor and he could do the insulin.'

'Not me. Was he a Scotsman?'

The nurse frowns at him. 'How do you know that?'

'Educated guess. That Scotsman was no doctor, believe me. Did Derek have anything of value here?'

'I doubt it, though he keeps his rent and housekeeping for the carers in the drawer over there.'

Charles follows her pointed finger and opens the bottom drawer of a small chest behind the door. He finds assorted underwear and two spare pairs of glasses, but no money. 'Not any more, he doesn't.'

The bell of an ambulance can be heard in the distance.

'I'll go and direct them up,' offers Charles. He goes back through the kitchen. As he is stepping through the door onto the landing, he registers a notepad by a telephone fixed to the wall, and a pen hanging from a piece of string next to it. He'd noticed neither before this moment. *You'd make a crap detective*, he thinks to himself, but he breaks his stride and steps back into the room. On the notepad are the initials "CS", a telephone number and an address in west London. Charles rips off the top page with the details and continues downstairs. As he emerges onto the pavement an ambulance is approaching from the far end of the street. He jumps into the sports car and speeds off in the opposite direction.

CHAPTER TWENTY-ONE

Detective Constable Sloane knocks on the door of Superintendent Wheatley's office and is told to enter. The room is neat and tidy to the point of obsession. The desk has two files on it, positioned perfectly parallel to the desk edge. Four sharpened pencils are placed in a line, like a musical stave, above one of the files. The Superintendent's coat is folded on a small table as if just unpacked from the cleaners, but Sloane knows that an hour ago Wheatley was wearing it when he came in. He folds it that way every time he removes it.

'I thought you ought to know this immediately, sir,' says Sloane, standing to attention in the doorway. He was once deemed to be slouching in the same doorway, and was bawled out for ten minutes.

'Now what?'

'We've just had a phone call from PC Blake, the local bobby at Putt Green. He's been away on honeymoon. The police house was supposed to be monitored by someone from the adjoining village but...'

'And?'

'He just got back and found a note from Mrs Holborne, saying that her husband's Jag had been stolen.'

'When?'

'The note's not dated, but probably early last week. The note said something about the car not running.'

Wheatley leans back in his chair and folds his hands across his stomach, staring at the ceiling. He shakes his head and opens his eyes. 'Forget it.'

'But it corroborates Holborne's story.'

'No, it doesn't. He probably got the car fixed to use for his getaway after the murder.'

Sloane frowns. 'But that doesn't make sense, sir. Why would he go to the effort of fixing a broken-down car? And surely he'd want to use a car that was *not* immediately linked to him. Doesn't it look more like someone *wanted* us to think it was Holborne?'

'I said forget it,' repeats Wheatley. 'We're stretched enough as it is without running round chasing loose ends. We've a cast iron case; leave it that way,' he orders.

Sloane stares at his boss for a moment and then nods. 'As you like, sir.'

The DC closes the door behind him and walks thoughtfully down the corridor to his desk. He sits for a moment staring out of the window, ignoring the ringing phones and banter going on around him. Then he lifts the phone.

'Ross? It's Sean. What was the name of that garage in Putt Green? On the other side of the green to the Holbornes' place?'

Charles pulls up at a telephone box. He opens the door — *Urine again*, he thinks, *apparently a recurrent theme in my life* — clears a space to stand amongst the cigarette ends, crumpled chip bags and other detritus on the floor, and dials the number torn from Plumber's pad. After a couple of rings a Scottish woman's voice announces that he has reached the Oaks Lodge Boarding House and Charles hangs up, satisfied. He returns to the car and drives the remaining couple of miles to the address, making a stop at a supermarket on the way.

He parks the Healey in a space on the suburban road, shifts down in his seat and pulls his hat low over his eyes. From his vantage spot he can see the stone steps leading up to the "Oak

Lodge Boarding House", a large double-fronted house in need of maintenance. A faded sign swings gently from a post by the garden wall informing the world that there are still vacancies but not for Irish or blacks. *You've forgotten the Jews*, he thinks to himself.

The weather has turned cold and blustery, and within an hour Charles has located half a dozen gaps in the roof of the Austin Healey where the wind whistles in. Sips from the half-pint of whisky snuggling in his jacket pocket, again courtesy of the Krays' shooter's donation, and two cheese sandwiches apparently made of cardboard keep him tolerably warm for the next few hours.

Dusk gathers over the Edwardian houses and the pavements become busier as people return home from work. The Scottish landlady closes the curtains on her ground floor sitting room, and smoke begins to emerge from the chimney, but there's no sign of Sands.

By 7:30 p.m., the clip-clop of women's heels has died away, their children have returned from school and their menfolk from work, and the streets are again emptying. Most of the houses now have lights in their rooms, some curtained, some shuttered and a few revealing the movements of their occupants as they go about their cooking, homework, television-watching and other domestic dramas.

Charles's legs are stiff and, despite the whisky, his hands and feet are cold. He swings his legs out of the sports car, closes the door quietly and crosses the road toward the boarding house. He climbs the steps and rings the bell.

The outline of a woman can be seen approaching down the corridor and the door opens a couple of inches.

'Yes?'

'I'm looking for a room. Just for a week.'

The woman looks Charles up and down. She has sharp, dark eyes, mean lips and straggly black hair streaked with grey. 'No luggage?'

Charles nods across the road. 'In the car,' he explains.

'Just you?' she asks. 'This is a respectable house,' she adds.

'Just me. And I can pay a week in advance, right now.'

'I've only got a single room left.'

'That's fine. Although I'd like to see it first, please.'

The woman sizes Charles up for a few moments longer and then opens the door fully to admit him. He enters the hallway and waits on the polished tiles for her to shut the door behind him. A coin-operated telephone is attached to the wall at the foot of the stairs.

'Follow me,' she says, and she leads Charles past a closed door from which emanates the sound of a television, and up the stairs. Charles plays a hunch.

'A colleague of mine told me about your boarding house. A Scotsman. I think he might be here now. His name's Robbie?'

'Mr Smith? That's his room.' She indicates a door on the first landing as they pass it. Charles glances down. A thin band of yellow light escapes from underneath the door.

They reach the head of the stairs and the landlady opens a door and stands back. Charles casts his eye around a small attic room with a single bed, a sink in the corner and a tiny wardrobe large enough to accommodate two or three hangers at most. Charles sits on the bed experimentally, bounces once and rises.

'This'll be perfect,' he announces cheerfully. 'I'll get my bag from the car, and pay you. Where can I find you?'

'Downstairs in the front sitting room. Just knock on the door. You'll need to register, Mr...'

'Collins,' replies Charles.

'Well, Mr Collins, the rent's six shillings for the week, with a further one and six security deposit. No food allowed in the room, no guests allowed after nine o'clock, and no female guests allowed at any time. Understood?'

'Perfectly.'

The landlady gives him one last searching look and returns downstairs, leaving the bedroom door open. Charles waits until he hears the footsteps reach the hall and the sitting room door close. He creeps back down two flights and stands outside the room below, pulling on his gloves. He takes the pistol out of his inside pocket and leans with his ear against the door. At first he can hear nothing except the occasional car passing outside and the ticking of a large clock from somewhere downstairs but, then, there's a new sound. It reminds Charles of a kettle before it boils, a low, steady bubbling. As Charles concentrates on the noise, it pauses. There's a different, gurgling noise for a second and then the bubbling resumes. Charles gently tests the door handle. It turns silently and the door moves inward slightly; not locked. Charles holds his breath, turns the knob fully and launches himself into the room.

There was no need for surprise. Facing the door is a small couch on which sits Robbie Sands, wearing an overcoat and a hat. He looks comfortable, his hands in his lap and his chin resting on his chest, as if he has just come in from a walk and is taking a rest. His chest rises and falls regularly. Where his weight creates a depression in the couch there is a pool of dark shiny liquid. Sands's overcoat is open and the top of his torso is a slowly expanding circle of dark red, in the centre of which is a black hole. It is just at the top of his sternum, slightly off centre and immediately below his left clavicle. With every gurgling breath another small gobbet of blood pulses out of the hole, runs down his saturated shirt, and joins the growing puddle in which he sits.

Charles takes a further step into the room and notes drips of blood leading from the door to the couch. So, he wasn't shot here. Another thought occurs to him, and he puts his head back out into the corridor. Bending down, he looks carefully at the carpet. It's dark brown in colour but, on careful examination, he can see further dark drips, heading not towards the front of the house, but towards another door overlooking the garden that he hadn't noticed on the way up. A fire escape?

He steps back into the room and closes the door quietly. The gurgling suddenly stops as the dying man coughs gently. Blood suddenly appears between Sands's lips, and his head lifts. He looks straight at Charles and his mouth widens into a black grimace. He tries to speak but the effort simply brings more blood from the hole in his chest and through his teeth.

Charles casts about looking for a weapon by Sands's hands but, finding none, moves closer.

'Too late,' whispers Sands.

'Why?' demands Charles, but Sands's head is slowly dropping to his chest again. The breath whistling through the hole in his trachea is now less regular, with longer pauses between each one. Charles grabs Sands's bloody chin and lifts his head. The Scotsman's eyes are half-closed but, for a second, they focus and he reaches up with a bloodied hand and grabs the sleeve of Charles's leather jacket. He seems about to say something, but the light dies from his eyes and with a final bubbling wheeze, his arm and head fall in unison.

Charles returns to the door, locks it, and sits at the table that overlooks the dark street below. He regards the dead man thoughtfully. One step behind, yet again. Not to mention the growing body count. Until a week ago, Charles had only ever once seen a dead body close up; one of the advantages of the RAF over the other armed services. Now they're turning up everywhere.

He stands and surveys the room. There's a massive old wardrobe, its mirror blotched with age, but a search reveals only a coat with nothing in the pockets and a small pile of clothes, a change of shirt and underwear, none of it clean. A spare blue blanket is folded on the floor of the wardrobe. On a shelf by the door is a bathroom bag containing shaving gear, toothpaste and so on, but nothing of interest. Charles balks at searching Sands's body, but he is about to start when he glimpses something dark by the end of the bed. Partly hidden under the trailing edge of the counterpane is a small brown leather attaché case. It looks like a narrow school satchel with two buckles fastening it. Charles pulls it out. Inside is a sheaf of papers, including a simple sketch of Putt Green with his own home marked with a large red asterisk, the layout of the house, and a blurry photograph of Henrietta. Charles's heart thunders in his chest; here it is at last: real proof.

He takes the photograph to the light hanging from the central ceiling rose to examine it more closely. It's unusually grainy, as if it's been enlarged from something much smaller. It shows Henrietta standing in a line with other young women, all wearing summer dresses. Some have hats and others are shading their eyes against the sun, which appears to be low and shining directly into their faces from behind the camera. Behind them is a section of a single storey wooden building with a veranda, and beyond that are tall trees in leaf. Charles has a vague recollection of the scene, but can't immediately place where the photograph was taken.

A lightning bolt of illumination suddenly strikes him, and he spins round and reopens the wardrobe door. He lifts out what he supposed was a blanket and turns it over. It's not a blanket; it's a barrister's robes bag, blue, and brand-new. It still has the Ede & Ravenscroft price label hanging from the cord which closes the mouth of the bag. Charles feels around inside, but it's empty. His investigation is suddenly cut short by a shout from downstairs. He throws the bag back into the wardrobe.

'Mr Collins? Mr Collins!'

Charles hurriedly slides the documents back into the leather case and replaces it, half-hidden, at the foot of the bed. He tiptoes across to the door, unlocks it, and sticks his head out. The landlady is calling from the bottom of the staircase. Charles closes the door behind him, and goes downstairs.

'I'm awfully sorry,' he says, 'but on reflection, I think I'll find somewhere closer to the centre of town. I've business in the City, and this is a bit far out for me. I'm really sorry to have troubled you.'

Without waiting for a response, Charles strides past her and out of the front door, closing it behind him. The woman watches him go and then runs upstairs as fast as her arthritic knees will allow to reassure herself that Charles hasn't stolen the furniture from her top room.

CHAPTER TWENTY-TWO

'Is that Buckinghamshire Police?'

'Yes. How may I direct your call?'

'I need to speak to Detective Constable Sloane. I think he's based at Aylesbury Police Station. It's very urgent.'

'Please may I have your name?'

'Charles Holborne. I'm wanted for the murder of my wife. And I have another murder or two to report.'

There's no sharp intake of breath from the young telephone operator at the other end of the line, which slightly disappoints Charles. *Remarkable sangfroid*, he thinks.

'Please hold the line, sir,' she replies calmly, 'and I'll put you through.'

It takes five interminable minutes and most of Charles's change before Sloane is located.

'Holborne?' he asks, without precursor, his voice echoing oddly down the line.

'Yes. Listen carefully. I'm going to have to trust you, Detective Constable.'

'You're going to have to trust me? And why would you be doing that?' asks Sloane. Charles thinks he detects a very faint Irish accent.

'Because I can't trust your Superintendent. I have proof of my innocence, but if I give it to him, it'll disappear.'

'What proof is that?' asks Sloane in a neutral tone.

'If you get your men quickly to Oak Lodge Boarding House, Ormiston Grove, Shepherd's Bush, in the front bedroom on the first floor you will find Robbie Sands, recently of HM Prison Long Lartin. He escaped ten days ago. He's dead, shot, and before you ask, no, I didn't kill him either. At the end of his bed you'll find a briefcase with the instructions he was given to enable him to kill Henrietta. It should have his fingerprints all over it. And with a little luck, if you check under the bonnet of my Jag, you might find some more there.'

'Where are you, Mr Holborne?'

'I'm in a call box in West London.'

'Don't you think it's time you handed yourself in?'

Charles laughs sardonically. 'Are you serious? I may have been a yard behind the murderer throughout, but at least I've been looking. I know how this works, Sloane, and I know your bastard of a Superintendent all too well. If anyone's going to break the seal on his "watertight case", it's going to have to be me.'

'We're not all as stupid as you think, Mr Holborne. We already know the Jag wasn't running, so it had to be fixed before you could make your supposed getaway. And we've also traced the owner of the girl's Mercedes, Neville Fylde — who I gather you've already … interviewed — and we know he was paid to make it look like you had a mistress. Was it you who put the hole in his ceiling?'

'Ceiling? Don't know what you're taking about,' replies Charles insouciantly, remembering at the same time Ronnie's Kray's assurance that, whatever else he was, he wasn't a grass.

'What colour's your robes bag?'

'What?' asks Charles, incredulous.

'You heard. What colour?'

'Red.'

'Your wife's murderer was seen to run off with a *blue* bag.'

Charles begins to think that Sloane, at least, is indeed no fool. 'Which you will find in the wardrobe of Sands's room,' confirms Charles. 'It's brand-new — the price label's still on it — and it has no barrister's initials stitched on it.'

'I'm telling you all this, Mr Holborne, to persuade you to come in. I assure you, I have more than just an open mind, and my guvnor is … coming round. But you must realise the danger you're in. You've done well so far, but you've been lucky. You're not trained for this; we are.'

'I've a got a few things to do first. But I promise I'll hand myself in when they're done.' There's something about the way Sloane refers to his guvnor which makes Charles suspicious. 'Are you recording this?' he asks.

'Of course I am.'

'And how many others are in the room with you, Sloane?'

There's a pause. 'Most of the team.'

Another dry voice adds: 'Including DC Sloane's bastard Superintendent.' *Wheatley*. It's his voice that continues. 'You told the switchboard you wanted to report "a couple" of murders. Do you want to tell us anything about the other one? Or are you keeping that one as a surprise?'

'Hello, Superintendent. Sands's accomplice on the Express Dairies robbery was a man named Derek Plumber. When I left Plumber's house in Limehouse this morning he was in a diabetic coma. I organised an ambulance and left him with the district nurse. I'm not one hundred per cent certain about this, but I think Sands deliberately kept him from his insulin.' Charles's voice accelerates as the pips start, signalling that he needs to put more money into the phone box. 'I'm not sure of the motive yet, maybe simply for money. And I have one further lead to —' At that, Charles's money runs out. He fishes in his pockets for more change, but changes his mind and lets the pips finish. The line is cut.

At Aylesbury police station, DC Sloane hangs up and switches off the tape recorder. He turns to face the room. Behind him sit or stand all the members of team he was able to round up to listen to Holborne's call. He'd made sure they were all in the room before he called Wheatley down. Only then did he have Holborne's call put through.

Superintendent Wheatley pulls another chair out from the desk and sits heavily. Twenty-four hours after the murder he had enough evidence to convict Holborne. Now, what looked like a simple collar is falling apart in his hands and, what's worse, half the team heard it, so he has no choice; he has to follow through on Holborne's information. What galls him most is that the arrogant Jew-boy has demolished the case against him by a combination of dumb luck and brute force.

'This is a waste of time,' Wheatley says. 'What's to say Holborne didn't give Sands all that stuff to do the job, and then shoot him to keep him quiet?'

'All that stuff to incriminate *himself*?' points out Sloane.

'And why tell us?' adds Bricker.

Wheatley looks round the room and meets the eyes of his junior officers. He sees a challenge in all of them, and accepts the inevitable. 'Bricker,' he orders.

'Sir?' replies the DS from the other end of the long table.

'Have we got all the elimination prints from Chancery Court yet?'

'All except three. One's confirmed as being in the British Caymans for the last month, so he's ruled out. Two others are here, but out of town on cases.' He fishes in his pocket for his notebook and flicks over some pages. 'Erm ... Jonathan Beardsley and Simon Ellison.'

'Where are they?'

'According to their diaries, Beardsley's in York on a three-week civil trial and Ellison's at the assizes in Wiltshire.'

Wheatley turns to Sloane. 'I assume you've had the Jag looked at? Seeing as you ignored my earlier orders about it?'

Sloane smiles cheerily at his Superintendent, trying to look fresh-faced and keen, rather than insubordinate. 'Yes. There were prints all over it belonging to Holborne and his wife, a couple from two of the mechanics at the local garage, and some half-prints from someone presently unidentified.'

'You think Sands was working with someone in Holborne's Chambers?'

'Well, sir, we know someone set him up to make it look as if Holborne had a mistress. They had to have access to the diary, to know where Holborne would be; they couldn't risk her running into him at Fetter Lane. And they had to have his keys copied. Both of which would be easy if they worked in the same office. There's no security of any sort and the barristers wander into one another's rooms all the time. So, yes, I'm thinking it was one of the other barristers. Several witnesses say that Mrs Holborne was, if you don't mind my language, a right tart. I'm pretty sure we'll turn up any number of motives.'

Wheatley sighs. 'All right. I'm not saying I'm buying it, but we'd better get down to the Temple. Make sure someone brings the dabs from the Jag. If it is one of the barristers, I suppose we'd best identify him before Holborne gets himself killed. Not that I'd shed any tears, mind, but still… Bricker, get on the radio. Get the City of London boys to bring in the clerk, Stanley Wigglesworth. Sloane: you and PC Redaway get to Shepherds Bush and see about Sands. Come on. Let's get on with this.'

CHAPTER TWENTY-THREE

Stanley arrives at Chancery Court just before 11 p.m. He has still to get over the shock of having one of his guvnors on the run, charged with the murder of his wife. Rita has never known him to get home so early, so assiduously has he been avoiding all his usual haunts for the last week. He can't bear the looks he receives whenever he meets other clerks. But then, to be called out of his bed just as he's settling to sleep, raced to London in a speeding police car still in pyjamas, and required to open up Chambers for more investigations, this time into *another* member of Chambers, well that was the final straw. 'I'm going to retire at the end of term,' he announced to Rita as he pulled a coat on over his pyjamas.

Superintendent Wheatley, DS Bricker and a third man get out of the car in which they've been awaiting Stanley's arrival. Bricker introduces Stanley to Wheatley and to the third man, named Reeves.

'Mr Reeves is a fingerprint specialist,' explains Wheatley.

'Who should have been off duty four hours ago,' adds Reeves, pointedly.

'Now, Mr Wigglesworth,' says Wheatley, ignoring him, 'can you let us in, please?'

Stanley leads the men up to the first floor and opens the main door.

'We need to see the rooms of Mr Beardsley and Mr Ellison.'

'They're both on the other side of the landing,' explains Stanley. 'I'll show you.'

Stanley unlocks the other door on the landing and leads the way to the far room. It's on the opposite side of the corridor to that of Charles and Peter, and has a view of a brick wall. He points to the desk facing the door. 'That's Mr Ellison's desk, Superintendent,' he says.

'And which is Mr Holborne's?'

Stanley points to the room opposite, and Wheatley and Bricker share a glance. 'Does anyone else use Mr Ellison's room?'

'Not usually, no.'

'OK, Reeves,' orders Wheatley. 'Off you go.'

'Nobody touch the light switch, please,' requests Reeves.

Reeves takes a torch from his pocket and enters Ellison's room. He goes to the desk, prowling round it, bending close to the surface, looking closely without touching anything.

'Hmm,' he says, turning on the desk lamp with a pencil and extinguishing his torch. 'The phone might be the best place to start.' He stands upright again and returns to the men watching him. He examines the door frame and then the light switch. 'And then the light switch,' he concludes.

Back at the desk, he opens his briefcase and takes out a small pot. He unscrews the lid to reveal a brush inserted into it, similar to those used by photographers to blow dust from their camera lenses. He lifts the telephone handset off its cradle by the cable and places it carefully on the desk blotter. The others standing at the threshold watch him silently. Reeves dusts a tiny amount of silver dust over the inside of the handset and examines the result.

'Lovely,' he says. 'We've a couple of quite decent ones.'

He reaches into his case and extricates a roll of tape. He cuts a small piece off with a pair of scissors and presses it firmly over the handset, repeating the procedure twice more and then gently lifting the prints off. He immediately attaches them to pieces of plastic card obtained from his case, and initials the cards with a pen. He then moves to the light switch, and starts again.

Wheatley's foot taps impatiently. 'Well?' he asks.

'What do you want me to compare them with?' asks Reeves. Bricker opens his briefcase and hands Reeves an envelope from which Reeves takes a further set of plastic cards. 'Is there another room I can use?' Reeves asks Stanley.

'Next door?' suggests the clerk.

'Fine.'

Reeves goes to the adjoining room, taking the plastic cards with him, sits at the desk, and turns on the desk lamp. Using a magnifying glass taken from his breast pocket, he inspects the fingerprints Bricker provided. Then he addresses his attention to the lifts he has just taken. Wheatley hovers over his shoulder like a vulture.

'You realise this is not supposed to be my job, don't you?' asks Reeves.

'I know. But didn't you used to be —'

'Used to be, yes. But that was almost eight years ago. Would you mind, Superintendent? You're distracting me, lurking behind me like that.'

Wheatley moves away and Reeves continues his perusal. Every now and then he jots something on the pad next to him. After about ten minutes, he switches off the lamp and sits back.

'I'm not a fingerprint expert anymore, you understand, and these are hardly the best conditions to work under ... but...'

'But?' demands Wheatley.

Reeves is not to be hurried. 'This wouldn't stand up in court, sir. You have to have a minimum number of identical features, and the prints marked "bonnet" aren't complete and they're not of the best quality —'

'Yes, yes, yes! I know all that!' shouts Wheatley. 'But this is extremely urgent! What's your opinion?'

'OK. There are no clearly inconsistent features between the prints here and those lifted from the car. As to common features, I can see six or seven in the thumbprint on the phone, and ten on the forefinger by the door. Yes. If you have to have an answer, I'd say that in all probability — no higher than that, understand? — they were made by the same man. Not enough to convict, though.'

'It's enough for me, especially if a rather high-profile barrister is about to be murdered!'

'What?' demands Stanley, shocked. 'Is Mr Ellison about be murdered?'

Wheatley turns to Stanley. 'I'm sorry, sir, I shouldn't have said that in your presence. No, he's not. But I need to know where he lives, right now.'

'Er ... er ... Chelsea somewhere... I've got the address in my room...'

'Bricker, go with Mr Wigglesworth and get the address. Then make him a cuppa and sit with him till you hear from me. He's not to contact anyone.'

'But —' protests Stanley.

'Sorry, sir, but I'm not taking any chances.'

Almost as soon as he leaves the boarding house in Shepherd's Bush, Charles remembers when that summer photograph was taken, and by whom. Simon Ellison had been the captain of the Chambers cricket team, and every year Chancery Court barristers used to play a motley group of clerks and ringers gathered together by Stanley. Two years earlier, Charles was

251

persuaded to play and, to his surprise, Henrietta asked to watch and help with the tea. The photograph of all the wives and girlfriends was taken by Jenny Ellison during the tea interval. Charles has seen the original on several occasions on the wall of Ellison's study.

As soon as he finishes speaking to DC Sloane, Charles drives to The Boltons, Chelsea. The home of Simon and Jennie Ellison is just around the corner in Gilston Road. Charles now stands in the tree-lined road, by Ellison's car. The bonnet is still warm. So much for the trial in Wiltshire.

Whoever employed Sands to kill Henrietta had to have access to Charles's room in Chambers, and to the photograph. Just to make sure, Charles sneaks past the wrought-iron gate at the front of the Ellisons' house and peers through the study window. The room is in darkness but Charles can see well enough to identify the photograph still in its accustomed place on the wall. He retreats round the corner to pace up and down under the dark trees in The Boltons, and to think. All his best jury speeches and cross-examination are developed like this, pacing up and down.

It all fits: detailed knowledge of Charles's movements and access to his keys for Fetter Lane, and Ellison's ability with cars — he had the skills to repair the Jaguar and replace it in the garage at Putt Green. But why? What was the motive? Charles has considered the possibility that Henrietta's affair was with Ellison — in fact, he remembers Michael Rhodes Thomas once saying something about Henrietta being seen at the Ellisons' home, which had puzzled him briefly at the time — but even if that were right, it still doesn't suggest a motive. A lovers' tiff? Possible, but unlikely.

So, with no obvious motive, Charles decides he needs incontrovertible proof; proof sufficient to convince the sceptical Wheatley and, probably, a jury. It's this which keeps him pacing up and down The Boltons for half an hour. Finally, the first glimmerings of a plan begin to take shape. He jogs back to the Austin Healey and drives to the Kings Road, stopping first at a tobacconist to get some change, and then at the next telephone box he sees. Again he dials Buckinghamshire Constabulary.

'DC Sloane, please.'

There's a delay. Then: 'I'm afraid DC Sloane is unavailable at the moment.'

'Is there anyone else from the Holborne murder enquiry team I could talk to?'

'I'm afraid they're all out of the moment, sir. Can I take a message?'

'No,' replies Charles, irritably. 'Forget it.'

He replaces the receiver without waiting for an answer and is about to leave the phone box when he has another idea. He reaches into his jacket pocket and pulls out the piece of notepaper from Plumber's kitchen. He dials again.

'Is that the Oak Lodge Boarding House?'

All Charles can hear is wailing at the other end of the line. A woman is crying, loudly. Perhaps Oak Lodge is no longer quite as respectable as it was, before bodies starting turning up in its bedrooms.

'If there's a policeman just arrived, I need to talk to him,' shouts Charles over the din.

That promotes a fresh wave of howls from the other end of the line, but Charles hears the phone being handed to someone else.

'Yes?' says DC Sloane's voice.

'It's me, Holborne,' says Charles. 'How long would it take you to get to the Temple?'

'Why?'

'I know who the murderer is, and I'm going to try to get a confession out of him in your hearing.'

'Now, Holborne, don't interfere. It's all under control, and you'll just get yourself hurt.'

'Be at Chancery Court by quarter past midnight, OK? Not earlier and not later. Don't use the lights, go straight to my room and once there, keep out of sight.'

'Holborne, don't be so bloody stupid! You're unarmed, and so am I!'

'Just be there. If you can get some backup, so much the better.'

Charles breaks the connection, returns to the Healey and drives to the Temple. As he passes Charing Cross station he sees the Wimpy on the corner and is suddenly awash with fatigue and hunger. Perhaps the whisky, on top of almost no sleep for three days, had been a poor idea. He stops long enough to enter the deserted shop and pick up a lukewarm burger and soggy chips, and bolts them down in the car. Then he completes his journey to the Temple. Rather than driving up Middle Temple Lane he parks on the Embankment as far from a streetlamp as he can manage. He doesn't want Ellison seeing the car. Having immobilised it, he opens the boot. Under the spare wheel is a rusty tyre lever. Perfect. He slips it inside his belt and strides off towards the Temple. Then, on an afterthought, he retraces his steps to the telephone box at the corner of Temple Place. Better to call from a payphone, rather than from Chambers. He delves into his pockets and comes up with just enough change to make one last call. He dials and while the phone rings, he checks the time: twenty-five to midnight. It takes a while for the phone at the other end to be picked up.

'Yes?' says Jenny Ellison's sleepy voice.

Charles presses the button to speak and the coins drop. 'Simon Ellison, please,' he says in a Scottish accent.

'At this hour? Who's speaking?'

Charles effects a wheeze and pants: 'Say it's Robbie Smith.' He hears Jenny speaking to someone else. 'It's a Scottish man … Robbie Smith? In a callbox.'

Ellison comes on the line. 'Who is this?' he demands angrily.

'It's me, Sands,' croaks Charles.

'You … you're…'

'No, I'm not. You winged me, but I'll live. I'm back at my digs. I want tae talk.'

There's no reply at first. Then, in a low whisper: 'I can't talk now. Sorry, darling, go back to sleep; it's work.'

'Meet me in your room at Chancery Court … one hour.' Charles inhales deeply as if fighting for breath. 'And bring money. I'll need at least a grand if you want me tae disappear. Can you do that?'

He waits for Ellison to find a phrase which won't give him away to his wife. 'Not quite, but close perhaps.'

'Bring what you can, then. I'll give you back the photo of Holborne's missus and the plan of the house … and if you dinna come, I'll post them to the polis. Oh, and bring Holborne's notebooks. I want them back on the shelf wi' the rest. They've go' my name all over 'em. Have you go' all that?'

'Yes,' whispers Ellison.

'And no tricks, Ellison. You'll no' catch me unawares again. I've got a gun, too, and it's a lot bigger than that wee peashooter o' yours. I'll be watchin' you all the way in. Just go straight to your room, and wait for me.' Charles gives one last cough for effect and, pleased with his performance, hangs up.

He runs up Middle Temple Lane. He reckons he has at least half an hour's start on Ellison, but he has to find a way in without keys; he'll need every second.

2 Chancery Court backs onto 3 Pump Buildings, another set of chambers, with a narrow light well between them. Charles has often wondered why the architect placed a window on the first floor landing of Chancery Court when its sole function appeared to be not to admit light, but a howling draught in the winter. His hope is that the draught means the window isn't secure.

A few lights shine from the upper storeys of some of the old buildings, but the courtyards of the Temple are completely deserted. Charles runs under the plane trees through the yellow gaslight. A thin mist drifts up from the Thames and carpets the courtyards in wisps of grimy white. Charles feels as if he's in a ghost story. He slows his footsteps as he realises that the sound of his running is making too much noise; he doesn't want the echoes disturbing any of the judges in their cosy flats on the top floors.

He skirts round the back of Pump Buildings, trying to orientate himself and find the window that overlooks Chancery Court's landing. There's a locked ironwork gate and, behind that, a service door for the other chambers. The gate is set in a tall wall reaching first floor level, where there's a ledge. If Charles can make his way along the ledge without falling, he'll be in the light well at the same height as the window. He just needs a way of getting to the top of the wall, but it's much too high to jump and haul himself up, and the gates have no cross bars to assist a climb.

He looks up and down the deserted courtyard; nothing. Then, on the far side of the car park, he spots a bicycle resting against some railings. He runs over to it. As long as it's not chained to the railings... No! It's an old bike, and the owner presumably took the view that the Temple is usually safe. Charles wheels the bike back to the gates.

He takes off his fake spectacles and stows them in an inside pocket. He moves the tyre lever to the back of his belt so it won't get in his way and, gripping the top of the gate, heaves himself up by standing on the bicycle seat. Within seconds, he's on top of the wall, hugging the side of the building. He inches his way around the ledge for ten feet, turns a corner, and finds himself outside the window. Feeling behind him for the tyre lever, he pulls it out of his belt and inserts it into the base of the sash window. The window slides up without any effort. Charles steps in. *Easy. I really would make a decent criminal*, he thinks.

Charles closes the window behind him and tucks the tyre lever back in his belt. The outer door leading to the rooms he and Ellison occupy is closed and locked. He expected this, but is nonetheless disappointed. His choice now is to force the door, which if seen by Ellison will certainly alert him to something being wrong, or hide, perhaps on the stairs above. The second option is not attractive; he'll be in plain view if Ellison happens to look further up the stairs. He decides on the former. With luck, Ellison won't notice any damage. If he does, he might still assume Sands got there first and broke in. It will also clear the way for Sloane to enter and take up position.

The outer door is solid oak, seasoned over centuries, with enormous studs and strap hinges covered in layer upon layer of paint. It also forms a very flush fit with the door frame.

Charles attacks the door with the tyre lever with all his strength for fifteen minutes, with no discernible result. He is almost ready to give up when one final shove produces a loud *Crack!* as the lock housing splinters. Charles opens the door fully flat against the wall, just as it would be during office hours, and hides the larger splinters of wood behind it. The inner door is simpler, and he forces the Yale lock at the first attempt. He stands back and surveys his handiwork. He doubts anything will look unusual to a cursory glance in the dark.

He goes to Ellison's room. There is nowhere to hide here, and he realises there's absolutely no chance of him surprising the other barrister. He looks into his own room briefly, but discounts that. If he shows himself to Sloane, he might get himself arrested before he can put his plan into operation. He tries the door opposite. This is the room of Gwyneth Price-Hopkins. Charles is surprised to find his entrance to the room partially blocked by upended desks, a table and stacks of chairs. The party! This is the furniture cleared from Sir Geoffrey's room. Charles also sees several bouquets of wilted and crisping flowers in assorted receptacles dotted around the room. The desk and one of the shelves bear a large display of greetings cards. Charles picks one up. It congratulates Gwyneth and her husband on the birth of their child. The baby must have arrived early and, in the knowledge that she'd be away for the next few weeks at least, the clerks haven't got round to moving the furniture back into what had been Sir Geoffrey's room.

Charles moves one of the desks slightly so that it impedes the door opening fully, and then returns to the corridor separating this room from Ellison's to evaluate the sight-lines. From a position standing at the threshold of Ellison's room it's impossible to see past the furniture into Gwyneth's room, even with her door open. On the other hand, properly positioned, Charles has a view of Ellison's desk.

It's the best that can be managed. Charles runs to the ground floor and opens the street door to Chambers from the inside, leaving it ajar. He takes the opportunity offered by the moonlight to check his pistol. Then he returns to Gwyneth's room to hide, and to wait.

As the minutes tick away, Charles's nervousness grows. The smell of dead flowers, trapped for too long in the closed room, is cloying, and somehow increases his agitation. He waits twenty minutes before he hears soft footsteps on the stairs. He checks his watch, angling it toward the little light coming through the window. Quarter past midnight exactly. The sound stops, but no one passes his position. The silence lengthens for so long that Charles begins to wonder if he imagined it, but eventually the footfalls continue. A shape passes Gwyneth's door. Sloane; not tall enough to be Ellison. Then a second man, bulkier, almost bald, goes past. Good; reinforcements. Charles hears the floorboards creak and the sound of his room's door opening against carpet, and then silence.

The building settles into complete stillness again. Charles strains his ears, but he can hear only the wind in the trees from the courtyard outside and, once, a lonely ship's horn drifting up the Thames.

When he does next hear a noise from inside the building, it's so close that he jumps. A floorboard creaks right outside Gwyneth's room and Charles realises that Ellison has made it all the way into the building a good deal more quietly than the police. *Now I know why they're called "the Plod"*, he thinks. Through the crack in the door Charles watches Ellison's shape approach the half-open door to his own room. He moves with extreme caution, his right hand in front of him, and although

Charles can't see a gun, he recognises the pose. Ellison prods the door gently with his free hand and it swings inward silently until its brass handle bumps gently on the adjoining wall. He waits, listening intently, and then enters the room. Evidently satisfied that it's unoccupied, Ellison strides to his desk and sits at it, his gun hand pointing towards the door.

Showtime.

'Are ye there, Ellison?' calls Charles hoarsely from diagonally across the corridor. He watches Ellison start and stand, but he remains behind the desk.

'Sands?' Ellison calls back.

Charles gasps for breath as if he were a drowning man, pausing between breaths for dramatic effect. If Ellison thinks he's seriously injured, he'll be less suspicious about a change in voice.

'Aye. Got ma money?'

'Where are you?' demands Ellison. 'Come out so I can see you.' Ellison takes a couple of steps round the desk towards the door.

'Stay put!' shouts Charles, coughing loudly. 'I can put … a hole right though you … from where I am,' he gasps.

Ellison comes to a halt, but he's looking hard at the door to Gwyneth's room; he knows now where Charles is hiding.

'Throw the money intae the corridor,' orders Charles.

'No. Not without the documents.'

'Documents?'

'Don't play silly buggers with me, Sands! I want Henrietta's photo and the sketch back.'

That should surely be enough, thinks Charles; he's admitted that he provided the murderer with Henrietta's details so as to carry out the killing. But it's still not as watertight as he wants…

'I've got them here ... dinnae fret yoursel'. But first, explain something ... I ken you think that Jew-boy stole your practice ... but why kill his wife? She was harmless.'

Ellison begins inching towards the door, speaking to distract and cover his movement. 'Harmless? The woman was a fucking landmine! It was only a matter of time before she went off, and it all went public. With my name splashed all over the papers!'

'Stay where ye are!' croaks Charles, but Ellison has almost reached the door of his room, and he doesn't stop. Charles backs away from the door shielding him, his pistol arm raised. His bluff is being called and he knows the only way to stop Ellison is to shoot, but he needs him to carry on talking.

'But the worst thing? She threw me over, and for Corbett! An arrogant oaf who treated her like a whore!'

The speech has covered Ellison all the way to the threshold and, as he utters the last word, he launches himself through Gwyneth's door and fires at the same time. The bullet smashes the window behind Charles. Charles stands, aims and pulls the trigger of his borrowed pistol at the advancing man. The trigger clicks and jams, leaving Charles unarmed and silhouetted against the window, a sitting duck.

Ellison pauses in his advance, his gun held in both hands, pointing directly at Charles's chest. 'Now,' he says conversationally. 'Where are the documents?' Only then does Ellison realise that something is wrong. 'Just a minute...' he says, and he reaches out with his left hand to feel for the light switch behind him. For a fraction of a second his gun arm wavers, and Charles launches himself at the desk standing on its end to Ellison's left, colliding heavily with it and causing it to topple over. Ellison's a big man, and although the weight of the desk knocks him off balance, he doesn't fall. The desk rolls off his shoulder and falls with a crash, knocking the door further closed. Ellison steps sideways and fires again, and Charles feels as if he's been struck in the left shoulder by a sprinting prop forward. He knows he's been hit, but also that if he backs away the next shot will finish him, so he rolls with the blow, allows it to spin him round and brings his right fist in an arc up to Ellison's head. He feels it connect with the other man's temple and both men go down in a tangle of limbs. At the same moment, the door swings violently open and connects with Charles's head. He sees stars, and then nothing.

CHAPTER TWENTY-FOUR

The first of Charles's senses to start operating again is his sense of smell, which registers antiseptic, washed linoleum and cabbage. This doesn't smell like the afterlife, he concludes, so that's a good start. He opens his eyes. He's in a darkened room but he appears still to have vision. Another hopeful sign. Then he tries to sit up and pain rages all down the right side of his body from his neck to his lower ribs, causing him to cry out involuntarily. He closes his eyes again and tries to stay still. He reopens them after a moment or two and sees an electrical cord trailing from a bedside table on his left. Gingerly, he tests the ability of his left arm to move and finds that, if he moves slowly enough, he can reach it without agony. His fingers inch towards it and, finally, he is able to press the red button at its end.

The door opens almost immediately, spilling bright light across Charles's bed from the corridor.

'Hi,' croaks Charles. 'Sorry to trouble you nurse, but can I have some water?'

The silhouetted shape at the door comes round to Charles's bedside. 'Charlie, it's me,' says Rachel's voice. 'I heard you cry out. Shall I call the nurse? There's a buzzer.'

'Where am I?'

'University College. Don't move. You've had surgery on your shoulder.'

Another shape briefly obscures the light from the corridor and a nurse enters. 'Good, Mr Holborne, you're awake. We were beginning to get a little worried.'

Rachel steps back and allows the nurse to stand beside Charles's bed from where she takes his pulse and blood pressure. 'Fine,' she concludes, rolling up the pressure cuff. 'Would you like to sit up?'

'Yes please.'

The nurse goes to the head of the bed and rotates a wheel, and the top third of the bed lifts up slowly. Even that movement hurts like hell, and Charles gasps.

'Pain?' asks the nurse.

'Yeah.'

'I'll have a word with doctor and see what we can do about that. Your friend can get you some water in the meantime. Small sips to start, please; you've had a general anaesthetic.'

She bustles out of the room and Rachel takes her place. Rachel pours Charles some water and holds the glass while he takes a few sips.

'Update, please?' says Charles when he finishes.

'You were shot in the shoulder.'

'Got that bit,' says Charles, wryly.

'As far as I can understand from the surgeon — he was a bit vague because I'm not a member of family — it more or less destroyed your clavicle and a bit of your scapula, in and out, so they've had to pin you. But it missed all the important arteries and nerves, so apparently you were lucky. Oh, and you were knocked out by the police officers when they charged into the room. So the medics were a bit worried about the anaesthetic on top of a concussion.'

'Clever chaps, those policemen.'

'Don't be too hard on them, Charlie. One of them took a bullet in the hand trying to disarm Ellison. He's in the room next door.'

'Oh,' says Charles, feeling bad. 'And Ellison?'

'In custody, charged with two murders and attempting to kill you. You had a policeman on the door for a few hours, but he's gone now, as you're apparently no longer a danger to the public.'

Charles smiles, but even that hurts. 'What's with my face?' he manages.

'You're very swollen all down the left side, as far as your jaw. Maybe where the door hit you?'

'Great. How long have you been here?'

'Since the early hours. The police called your parents, and they called me. We came together.'

'Where are they?'

Rachel takes his left hand gently and holds it in hers. It feels good. 'They went home to get some sleep when you went down for surgery. Your mum's been in a bad way since you went on the run. She's not slept for days. I said I'd wait and call them when you woke. I'll go and do it now.' She makes to leave, but Charles calls her back.

'Rachel.'

'Yes.'

Charles lifts his left hand and Rachel takes it again. 'You've been ... so kind ... so...'

'Stow it, Charlie —'

'No, I mean it. I'd never have managed without you. My guardian angel.'

'Oh, please! Let me go and make that call. Then I'll push off.'

'Why?'

'I don't want to be in the way when your parents arrive. I think you should be on your own with them, at least the first time. I'll be back at the end of visiting time.'

'I don't want to see them.'

'Oh, Charlie, surely now —'

'No. I'm not ready. Maybe I won't ever be.'

'But —' starts Rachel.

'No. I mean it. Maybe later, on my own terms, but not now. I haven't got the energy for it.'

Rachel stares hard at him, her eyes narrowed in the way that Charles now recognises as disappointment in him, and shakes her head. 'You took on an armed murderer and, according to the nice policeman next door, a Yardie boss,' she says quietly. 'Not to mention one of the Kray twins' gunmen. But you haven't got the courage to apologise to your own parents?'

'Courage? What are you talking about?'

'Just think about it, Charlie. I know how much they hurt you by cutting you out of their lives. But how do you suppose *they* felt when you changed your name and married Henrietta without a word to them?'

She turns on her heel and leaves.

CHAPTER TWENTY-FIVE

Charles shows his cards. 'Twenty-one,' he announces, and with his good hand collects the pennies on the table. DC Sean Sloane shakes his head and scowls good-naturedly. 'I played a lot as a kid,' explains Charles.

To prove it he places the discards on top of the pile and, with one hand, cuts the deck and shuffles it.

'So, you're a card sharp on top of everything else,' says Sloane good-humouredly. 'Is there no end to your criminal talents?'

Charles looks up at the police officer. He and Sloane have taken to having their afternoon teas in Charles's private room, and they while away the time by playing a few hands of cards as they chat. Charles was moved to a general ward after a couple of days, but the press attention had made the nursing staff's lives a misery and he'd been moved back, but with his name removed from the board on the door. The two men have become celebrities in the hospital, known by some of the younger staff as the "one-armed bandits." Their photographs are still on all the front pages.

Charles's recovery is proceeding rather better than that of his saviour. The policeman's had two operations on his right hand, but the blood supply to his index finger was destroyed by the bullet and, eventually, the finger was amputated.

'What time are you being collected?' asks Charles.

Sloane checks his watch. 'Any minute now.'

'And then what?'

'What do you mean?'

'Will they take you back, even missing a finger?'

Sloane laughs. 'Bricker seems to think so. They can't decorate me and fire me in the same week.'

There's a knock on the door and DS Bricker's head appears.

'Ready to go?' he asks. He addresses Sloane directly and doesn't make eye contact with Charles at all.

'For Christ's sake, Sarg, say hello to the man,' says Sloane as he stands. 'He's still sore you decked him at Fetter Lane,' he explains to Charles.

'Sucker punch,' mutters Bricker.

Charles holds out his good hand. 'Come on, Sergeant. No hard feelings, eh?'

Bricker pauses and takes Charles's hand with a reluctant grin. 'No, I guess not. I can't say I'd have done any different in your circumstances. I've got these for you.'

Bricker is carrying a large clear plastic bag in which are Charles's keys, his watch and some of his clothing. He puts it on the bed and hands Charles a pad of forms with the belongings listed on the top page. 'Do you want to go through all of it?' he asks.

'No, just give me a pen. Any news of Ellison?' asks Charles as he signs, with difficulty. 'Wasn't it his first remand this morning?'

'Yup. And he applied for bail.'

'He never had much judgment, in my professional opinion. And?'

'What do you think? One conspiracy to murder, one actual murder and two attempted murders in the space of a week. And an overheard confession? "Risk of further offences and of absconding."'

'Very right and proper, too,' says Charles.

Bricker turns to Sloane. 'I need to be back at the station.'

'Yes, sure.' Sloane holds out his left hand. 'Take care, Charles. See you at Ellison's trial.'

Charles takes Sloane's hand, grips it and locks eyes with the young officer. The two men regard one another silently for a moment with mutual respect. 'Thanks again, Sean,' says Charles. 'Obviously, for saving my life, but also for keeping an open mind.'

Sloane nods and smiles. 'Do you mind if I ask you a question?'

'Shoot.'

'What're *you* going to do now? You can't go back to those chambers, can you? We all know you didn't do it but … well, she *was* still the daughter of the ex-head of Chambers, wasn't she? Isn't it going to be…?'

'Embarrassing? Yes. I'm not sure, to be honest. Neville Fylde offered me a job, you know? He seems to think I'd make a decent career criminal.'

'Don't joke about that, sir,' says Bricker. 'I've always said it. Barristers think things through, work logically. They know how to assess evidence, and how to avoid the mistakes that get their clients caught. You proved me right.'

'Did you find my notebooks, with the details of the Sands and Plumber trial?' asks Charles.

'Yes,' answers Bricker. 'Ellison had them. But they're now an exhibit in the case against him, so you'll have to wait for them. But why do you want them back? If you want my opinion, sir, you shouldn't be allowed to keep those notebooks after a trial's over. They're an encyclopaedia of crime and criminals.'

'That's why I want them. They'd be useful if I pursue the other option.'

'Other option?' asks Sloane as he picks up his bag.

'Private detective.'

The two policemen stare at him, unable to decide if he's serious.

'Now, what sort of job is *that* for a nice Jewish boy?' asks Sloane with a smile.

'But as I've demonstrated, I'm definitely not nice. And as for Jewish, well, the jury's out on that one.'

The two police officers depart and Charles returns to sit on his bed. He realises that he's still holding Bricker's pen. *They'll have to add theft to the indictment*, he thinks. He gazes out of the window over the grey slate rooftops of Bloomsbury. There's still an hour until visiting time. He hopes Rachel will come. Somehow she's slipped into his life so completely that the thought of her not being there makes Charles uncomfortable.

The door opens behind him and for a second, lost in thought, Charles doesn't turn.

'Turn and face me!' says a familiar voice.

Charles whirls round, causing the pain in his shoulder to start again. Standing with his back to the closed door is Ivor Kellett-Brown. He holds a large bouquet of flowers in one hand and an old army revolver in the other. The second of these is unwelcome.

'I want to see the look on your face as I pull the trigger,' he says.

Charles is too surprised to reply. After all he's been through, all the narrow escapes, his mind refuses to accept that he is actually going to be killed by a crackpot ex-barrister wearing clothes that were out of fashion even in the 1930s.

He knows there's no chance of getting across the room fast enough to prevent Kellett-Brown from firing, so he leans back on his pillows, puts his feet up and smiles.

'What a lovely surprise, Ivor. Nice flowers; are they for me?'

'I'm quite serious about this, Holborne. If Ellison's not up to it then I certainly am. I'm going to shoot you. It's nothing less than you deserve. Get on your knees.'

Charles laughs heartily, as if the request were a joke. 'Fancy a cup of tea, old chap?' he offers, indicating the pot. 'There's plenty left. And biscuits. What news of the Temple?'

Kellett-Brown takes a step further into the room. 'Get on your knees!' he bellows, his cracked voice rising.

'Oh, come on Ivor. A joke's a joke, but you'll disturb the other patients.'

'This is no joke! I swear, I'm going to kill you. But first I shall humiliate you the way you did me!'

Kellett-Brown is shouting loudly now. Someone must have heard that, thinks Charles. And they have. The door bursts inwards and Kellett-Brown is sent flying. The flowers and gun fall from his grasp as he totters over, trying to catch the end of the bed. The gun skids halfway under the bed, and Charles hops off and kicks it into the corner of the room. DS Bricker grabs the falling Kellett-Brown in a rugby tackle, and Charles hears the air whoosh out of his would-be assassin's lungs. Bricker sits on his back and pulls his arms behind him.

'I'm arresting you on suspicion of attempted murder!' he shouts.

Sloane enters the room ahead of several members of nursing staff.

Charles goes to the corner of the room and, using Bricker's pen, lifts the revolver by its trigger guard. 'Got a bag?' he asks Sloane.

'Dear God, Charles, you don't half push your luck! If we'd left five minutes earlier, we'd never have seen him coming in.'

'How did you know who he was?'

'We didn't. But he was making a scene demanding your room number, and he looked a bit odd. He kept putting his hand into his jacket pocket and you could see the outline of that —' he points at the revolver. 'So we followed him up.'

Bricker has attached handcuffs to Kellett-Brown and is hauling him to his feet. 'Come on, you,' he says. He turns to Charles. 'Does he always smell this bad?'

''Fraid so.'

Bricker speaks to one of the nurses. 'Anywhere we can keep this bloke until the Met arrive? He's not really our concern.'

'Yes. Follow me. Shall we call 999?'

'Yes, please. I'll get one of the Met boys to take your statement, Charles.'

'Sure. I'm not going anywhere.'

Bricker drags Kellett-Brown out of the room. Sloane is about to follow, his hand on the door handle, but he stops again. 'Any more of your former colleagues want to kill you, do you suppose?'

'I hope not,' replies Charles, lightly. But then, with greater gravity: 'No. I don't think so.'

'You might want to think about that, Charles, when considering your career options. See you.' The door closes.

Charles resumes his place on the bed. He closes his eyes and waits until his thudding heartbeat slows to normal. He suddenly feels profoundly tired and wonders if he might be able to sleep, but he can't calm his seething mind. DC Sloane's final comment touches on something he's been turning over incessantly for several days. Every component of his life has been shattered, like the shards of a smashed mirror, and he has no idea how to put them back together again. Could he really go back to Chancery Court after two of his colleagues have tried to murder him? And then there are the tattered remnants

272

of his private life. He's no longer married, so where's he going to live? He knows he'll have to return to Putt Green, at the very least to sort out Henrietta's affairs. But to live there? No, what would be the point? It was never really his home. Henrietta chose it because it was close to her friends and her parents. It was she who lovingly restored it and created the garden. No, Charles doesn't want it. So it has to be cleared of Henrietta's belongings, which presumably should go to her parents, and then sold. But he can't face that, not yet at least. And then there's Rachel's parting shot, and the unresolved business with his family.

He opens his eyes and gingerly reaches over to the bedside table where a slip of paper protrudes from underneath the fruit bowl. Written on it in Rachel's firm angular hand is a telephone number, the number of his parents' home somewhere in north London.

Charles turns the scrap of paper over and over in his hands, contemplating the ever-shifting grey clouds as they scud past his bedroom window. Then he reaches for the telephone. *First things first.*

HISTORICAL NOTES

The Charles Holborne series follows the political and social events of the 1960s, a time of enormous societal change and violent lawlessness in London. The Krays, the Richardsons brothers and other gangs fought for control of the fortunes to be made from pornography, prostitution, illegal gambling and protection money, often assisted by corrupt Metropolitan Police officers. Operation Countryman, the operation to draft in officers from provincial forces to weed out the barrel-load of rotten apples in the Met, started the very year that I was called to the Bar in 1978, and some corrupt Metropolitan police officers were still being investigated until the mid-1980s. Governments have repeatedly refused to publish the findings of Operation Countryman.

The books also trace the start of the celebrity culture which we "enjoy" today. As you will see from the later books in the series, the rise of the Kray twins led to them being feted for their connections with the stars of sport and entertainment. There are photographs of them taken, for example, with Sonny Liston, Henry Cooper, George Raft and Liza Minnelli. It was an intoxicating mix of celebrity and gangster violence, which I explore further in the series as the Krays' star rose and then fell.

A NOTE TO THE READER

Dear Reader,

Thank you for taking the time to read the first Charles Holborne legal thriller. I hope you enjoyed it. I am following Charles's story through the 1960s and although each novel in the series may be read as a stand-alone, the next in the series, *An Honest Man*, follows on directly in time from *The Brief*.

Those of you have been to my one-man show, "My Life in Crime", will know that Charles and his history are based upon me and my own family. Mine was the first generation of Michaels to be born outside the sound of Bow Bells (as you will know, the test for being a "true Cockney") since 1492, when they arrived in the Port of London as refugees from the Spanish Inquisition. Much of the series is autobiographical. Thus, Charles's love of London and the Temple are mine; at the start of my career I experienced the class and religious prejudice faced by him; the plots are based to a greater or lesser extent on cases in which I was instructed as a criminal barrister; many of the strange and wonderful characters who populate the books are based upon witnesses, clients and barristers I have known, represented and admired respectively. I try to take no liberties at all with the operation of police procedure, the criminal justice system or the human heart; the books are as true to life as I can make them.

If you find any mistakes, I shall be delighted to hear from you. I always reply, and if you're right, I will make sure future editions are changed.

Nowadays, reviews by knowledgeable readers are essential to authors' success, so if you enjoyed the novel I shall be in your debt if you would spare the few seconds required to post a review on **Amazon** and **Goodreads**. I love hearing from readers, and you can connect with me through my **Facebook page** via **Twitter** or through my **website**.

I hope we'll meet again in the pages of the next Charles Holborne adventure.

Simon Michael

www.simonmichael.uk

Sapere Books is an exciting new publisher of brilliant fiction and popular history.

To find out more about our latest releases and our monthly bargain books visit our website:
saperebooks.com